WILDE RIDE

OTHER BOOKS BY
KELLY ELLIOTT

LOVE IS A COWBOY SERIES
Wilde Cowboy
Wilde Ride
Wilde Flame (tba)
Wilde Hearts (tba)
Wilde Night (tba)

MOOSE VILLAGE SERIES
This Moment
This Feeling
This Memory
This Heart

LOVE IN MONTANA (MEET ME IN MONTANA SPIN OFF)
Fearless Enough*
Cherished Enough
Brave Enough
Daring Enough
Loved Enough -
Forever Enough
Enchanted Enough
Perfect Enough
Devoted Enough
*Available on audiobook

BOSTON LOVE SERIES
Searching for Harmony*
Fighting for Love*

Falling for Her
Longing for You
*Available on audiobook

HOLIDAZE IN SALEM SERIES
A Bit of Hocus Pocus
A Bit of Holly Jolly
A Bit of Wee Luck
A Bit of Razzle Dazzle

THE SEASIDE CHRONICLES SERIES
Returning Home
Part of Me
Lost to You
Someone to Love
*Series available on audiobook

STANDALONES
*The Journey Home**
*Who We Were**
*The Playbook**
*Made for You**
*Available on audiobook

BOGGY CREEK VALLEY SERIES
*The Butterfly Effect**
*Playing with Words**
*She's the One**
*Surrender to Me**
*Hearts in Motion**
*Looking for You**
Surprise Novella TBD
*Available on audiobook

MEET ME IN MONTANA SERIES
Never Enough
Always Enough
Good Enough
Strong Enough
*Series available on audiobook

SOUTHERN BRIDE SERIES
Love at First Sight
Delicate Promises
Divided Interests
Lucky in Love
Feels Like Home
Take Me Away
Fool for You
Fated Hearts
*Series vailable on audiobook

COWBOYS AND ANGELS SERIES
Lost Love
Love Profound
Tempting Love
Love Again
Blind Love
This Love
Reckless Love
*Series available on audiobook

AUSTIN SINGLES SERIES
Seduce Me
Entice Me
Adore Me
*Series available on audiobook

WANTED SERIES
*Wanted**
*Saved**
*Faithful**
Believe
*Cherished**
*A Forever Love**
The Wanted Short Stories
All They Wanted
*Available on audiobook

LOVE WANTED IN TEXAS SERIES
Spin-off series to the WANTED Series
Without You
Saving You
Holding You
Finding You
Chasing You
Loving You
Entire series available on audiobook
*Please note *Loving You* combines the last book of the Broken and Love Wanted in Texas series.

BROKEN SERIES
*Broken**
*Broken Dreams**
*Broken Promises**
Broken Love
*Available on audiobook

THE JOURNEY OF LOVE SERIES
Unconditional Love
Undeniable Love
Unforgettable Love
*Entire series available on audiobook

WITH ME SERIES
Stay With Me
Only With Me
*Series available on audiobook

SPEED SERIES
Ignite
Adrenaline
*Series available on audiobook

SWEET ROMANCE/CLOSED DOOR

Kelly Elliott writing as Ellie Grace
Saved by Love
Amnesia

Wilde Ride Copyright 2026

Cover Design by: Jillian Liota, Blue Moon Creative Studio
Alternate Cover Design: Y'all That Graphic
Interior Design and Formatting by: Elaine York, Allusion Publishing, www.allusionpublishing.com
Developmental Editing: Kelli Collins
Copy Editor: Elaine York, Allusion Publishing, www.allusionpublishing.com
Proofing Editor: Julie Deaton
Proofing Editor: Joanne Thompson
Proofing Editor: Elaine York, Allusion Publishing, www.allusionpublishing.com

All Rights Reserved. No part of this book may be used, including but not limited to the training of or use by artificial intelligence, or reproduced in any manner whatsoever without written permission, except in the case of brief quotations embodied in critical articles and reviews.

This book is a work of fiction. Names, characters, places, and incidents are either products of the author's imagination or are used fictitiously. Any resemblance to actual persons, living or dead, events, or locales is entirely coincidental.

For a list of Kelly's backlist books, please visit her website at: https://kellyelliottauthor.com/library/

WILDE RIDE

NEW YORK TIMES & USA TODAY BESTSELLING AUTHOR
KELLY ELLIOTT

Wait! Before you begin *Wilde Ride,* have you read *Wilde Cowboy*? It's book one in the Love is a Cowboy series and is the origin story of the Wilde Family. My readers are always asking me for the parents' love story, so with this series, I've given you their story first! You, of course, do not have to read *Wilde Cowboy* before diving into *Wilde Ride*, but I highly suggest you do. Besides, Ladd Wilde is one cowboy you don't want to miss out on!

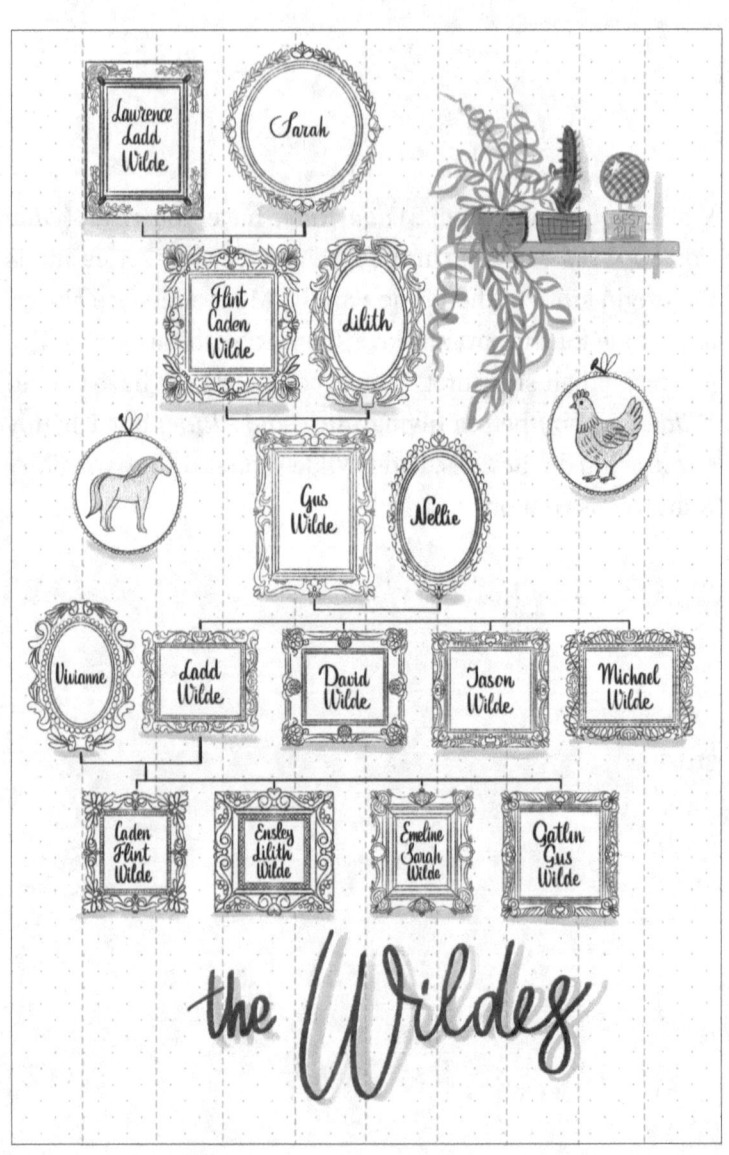

CHAPTER ONE

EMELINE

Graduation Night
2018

TWO WORDS.

Levi Tucker.

He was my brother Caden's best friend, and the moment I saw him walk into the backyard of my parents' house, I nearly died. His brown hair was covered by his favorite black cowboy hat, which he always wore. He was the most handsome man I'd ever laid eyes on. And that was saying something, since everyone I knew, including all my friends, constantly told me how good-looking my two older brothers were.

Levi was twenty-five and I was eighteen. But that wasn't the issue. The first issue was that he was my brother's best friend. If Caden had any idea of the naughty dreams I had about his BFF...well, he would send me away to become a nun.

The second issue? Levi didn't see me as anything *other* than Caden's baby sister.

The third reason was Caroline Larson.

Her father and my father were business partners and best friends. That meant she was always at our house and always trying to make a play for Caden, even though he'd been dating Rachel forever. When it finally became clear in their senior year that Caden had no interest in her, Caroline moved in on Levi.

I didn't like her at all. Of course, my best friends, Kate and Moreen, said it was because I was madly in love with Levi. And that *was* one of the reasons…but there was something about Caroline that made me think she was a snake. I didn't trust her one bit.

Speaking of my best friends, Kate and Moreen came rushing over to me. Kate with her beautiful copper skin and dark hair pulled up onto her head and her flowing white dress trailing behind her as she ran. Moreen's golden red hair was pulled back in a ponytail, and her beautiful face with its dusting of light freckles was bright with excitement. She was also attempting to get ahead of Kate. I loved them both like sisters. They knew everything about me. The good and the bad. Kate was hissing out my name as she drew closer. "Emeline, Emeline! Levi's here!"

"And she who shall not be named isn't with him!" Moreen added.

I smiled. I really loved these two. They were my ride-or-dies. If anyone was going to be there for me, it was Kate and Moreen. Well, besides my brothers, Caden and Gatlin. And okay, my older sister Ensley also ranked higher than Kate and Moreen, but only because she let me wear her clothes and told me to never pluck my own eyebrows. Plus, she had introduced me to Stevie Nicks.

Actually, that's not true. It was our mother. But Stevie wasn't cool in my eyes until I heard her music coming from my sister's car one day when she picked me up from school.

I grabbed their arms and started walking away from everyone. "You *guys*. Hush!"

Glancing over my shoulder, I saw that Levi was walking our way, holding a gift box. I quickly snapped my head straight. "Don't panic, but he's coming over this way."

"Deep breaths," Kate whispered.

Moreen calmly said, "Play it cool."

"As if I wouldn't." I bumped her arm and said, "Laugh like I just told you a joke."

Kate was in the theater, and I knew she'd make the laugh sound genuine. Moreen, not so much.

Hitting my arm, Kate said, "Oh my gosh, Emeline, you're too much."

I felt Levi behind me before he even said anything. "Emeline?"

Spinning around, I smiled. "Levi! Did you come with Caden?"

He glanced toward the house with a grin, then back to me. "No. Your mom invited me, though, and I didn't want to miss little Emeline's graduation party."

I felt my entire body sag instantly. "Little?"

His smile faded somewhat, and he rubbed at the back of his neck. He suddenly looked like he wanted to be anywhere but here, and that nearly destroyed me. He let out a nervous bubble of laughter. "I didn't mean it that way. You're not *little*. You're, uh...you're all grown up and beautiful."

That inflated me right back up. "You think I'm beautiful?"

Moreen hit me with her elbow as Kate cleared her throat, and I wanted to push them down the hill to give Levi and me privacy.

He glanced at them both, then back to me. "Um, well, yes. You are. But I shouldn't be saying that."

"Oh, you can say it all you want, Levi," Kate stated with a sugary smile.

Glancing at her, I said, "Kate, Moreen, didn't you need to go do that thing?"

"What thing?" Moreen asked, confusion written all over her face.

"That. Thing," I repeated.

Her brows shot up. "Oh yeah! That thing. Um, we'll just go do that thing that we're supposed to do."

"Yes. The thing. We're on it!" Kate added.

They both shot off like a rocket, leaving Levi to watch as they ran across the backyard in a fit of laughter. He turned back to me, two little wrinkles between his brows. "Are they always so..."

"Yes, they are."

He handed me the wrapped box. "I got you a gift."

My heart tripped over itself. "Oh wow! Thank you so much," I said as I took it from him. "Should I open it now?"

"Sure, if you want. I can't stay for long, so I'd love to see you open it."

"We can go over to the gazebo, and I'll open it there."

Levi smiled and motioned with his hand for me to lead the way. Once we were there, I stepped up and sat on one of the benches. Levi sat across from me on the other side of the gazebo.

I carefully removed the bow and set it aside before unwrapping the box. I opened it, moved the tissue paper out of the way...and stared. It was a shirt covered in pink and silver rhinestones. A *beautiful* shirt. I carefully lifted it out of the box, my mouth mostly hanging open as I took it in.

"Caden told me you were up for Miss Rodeo at the River Falls rodeo pageant. He said one of the nights you have to ride Ole Blue around with a flag, and I thought...well, I thought this would look nice on you."

My eyes lifted from the shirt to Levi. "This is stunning, Levi. I don't know what to say."

He grinned. "Ensley told me what size to get. I sent her a picture of it to make sure you'd like it. I know you love pink and silver, and when I saw it, I thought of you instantly."

I swallowed the lump that had formed in my throat. "You did?" I asked softly.

"Yeah. I was in Denver with Caroline, and she found a western wear store. We went in and looked around, and that's where I saw it."

The mention of his girlfriend felt like cold water being tossed on my head.

"Caroline thought it looked tacky, but she has a different style than you do."

That was an understatement. Caroline's father owned the local grain mill, a few buildings on Main Street, and was also a business partner of my father's. They co-owned the sporting goods store in town. She was the princess of River Falls. The girl had more money than she knew what to do with—and zero sense of style.

Deciding to keep my thoughts about Levi's girlfriend to myself, I simply smiled and said, "Total opposites."

He laughed. "Yes, you are."

I nodded, not sure if that was a good thing or a bad thing in his mind.

Clearing his throat, Levi stood. "Well, congratulations. I

hear you're following in the family footsteps and heading to Colorado State?"

I carefully set the shirt back in the box and stood as well. "Yep. Equine Science."

"I'm not surprised by that," he said with a soft smile. "You and your sister have always loved horses."

"Get that from our mother and grandmother."

"And the summer camps? Will you be coming home this summer to help with those?"

When I was thirteen, I presented my mother and father with a fully laid-out plan to start a summer camp on our ranch. I'd spent weeks going over every detail, and had even drawn out where some cabins could be built behind the horse barn. I also spoke with Uncle David and Uncle Mike, my father's younger brothers, to help with the start-up costs, after doing a ton of research to estimate a budget.

My mother and father were so impressed that they'd decided it was a great idea, and they presented it, along with me, to my grandparents, Gus and Nellie Wilde. They *also* loved the idea, and before I knew it, River Falls Cattle Company was the new home of Wonder in the Wilde Summer Camp. The camp was for underprivileged kids who weren't otherwise able to attend camps due to financial issues at home. My father had the idea of hosting a few events at the ranch to raise money, so the kids wouldn't have to pay anything at all.

By the time I was fifteen, the cabins had been built with donations from local businesses and private donors, and we hosted our very first summer camp. It's been a learning experience ever since, and with each passing year, we gain just as much as we give back. The camps are held for one week each, every June and July.

"I wouldn't miss summer camp if you paid me. It's my baby."

He grinned. "I always forget you were the one who came up with that idea at the ripe old age of...fifteen?"

I shook my head. "Thirteen. I was fifteen when we held our first camp."

Levi snapped his fingers. "That's right. Your mother always said you had the heart for philanthropy. I love that about you, Em. How you care for others like you do. Don't ever change that about yourself. Promise me that."

I felt my cheeks heat as I stared at the ground, then back to meet his light brown gaze. My gaze took in his handsome face. His jawline was strong, his cheekbones defined, his nose pure perfection. Don't even get me started on his eyelashes. Any woman would kill for them. He always wore a slight stubble on his face that made my fingers itch to touch him.

We stood there for a few moments before I turned and picked up the box. "I'll walk you back up to the house. I want to put this in my room so nothing happens to it."

Levi turned, and I took in his muscular build. He wasn't one of those guys who hit the gym all the time and had muscles that were too big. They were earned by hard work, and Lord, did it show in that T-shirt he was wearing. He got his exercise working on our ranch during the summers and on weekends.

"Sounds good; after you."

My heart pounded so hard, I could hardly hear a thing, it was so loud in my ears. For some reason I was becoming anxious, and I had no idea why.

"What are your plans for this summer?" I asked as we slowly made our way back up to the house.

He kicked at a rock. "I'm planning on taking Caroline to Belize and asking her to marry me."

I tripped and nearly dropped the box.

Levi quickly grabbed my arm to steady me. "Whoa, watch out there."

"Tree root," I quickly said as I started to walk once again. I looked at him, then focused ahead of me. "You're asking Caroline to marry you?"

He nodded.

"I thought you were starting vet school this year?"

"I still am, but there's been a change of plans."

Stopping, I turned to him. His voice sounded so unsure. I wasn't positive, but I swore I heard a slight sadness in his tone. "With school?"

He let out a humorless laugh. "No, life."

I frowned. "What do you mean?"

Levi glanced around as if making sure no one else was nearby. "Caroline is pregnant. She just found out. I'm going to do the right thing and marry her."

I sucked in a breath. And before I could think better of it, I asked, "Do you *want* to marry her?"

"I wouldn't be asking if I didn't want to marry her, Emeline," he retorted, his voice cold and distant. Then he closed his eyes. "I'm sorry. I didn't mean to snap. This wasn't something I was expecting, that's all."

"What about vet school?"

"I'm going to keep going. Caroline and I will be moving into a little house her parents found for us in Fort Collins."

Of course they did. Caroline's father would do anything for her.

"Well...that's good that you can finish out school and still work with your dad."

He rubbed at the back of his neck, and when his eyes met mine, I felt sick to my stomach.

"Why do I have a feeling you're not going to be coming back to River Falls?"

Levi kicked at the ground once again. "Caroline wants to move to Denver when I finish school. She thinks I'll make more money there rather than here."

My eyes went wide. "You're leaving River Falls completely? What about your dad and the practice? I thought the plan was for you to take over when he retires?"

He shrugged. "Plans change."

I blinked at him and slowly shook my head. "I guess they do. Is this what *you* want, Levi?"

"No. But sometimes you have to put your feelings aside for the people you love."

I narrowed my eyes. "That works both ways."

His eyes snapped up to meet mine. "You don't understand, Em."

It was my turn to shrug. "I guess not."

We started walking again, and when we arrived at the house, we faced each other. Levi flashed me that dazzling smile of his, and I returned the gesture. Holding up the box, I said, "Thank you so much for the shirt. It really is beautiful, and I can't wait to wear it."

"You're welcome. Maybe I'll see you around campus."

The chances of us seeing each other would be rare, but not impossible, since at least a few of our classes would be in the same area.

I wasn't sure whether I was happy or sad about that, now knowing that Levi was marrying Caroline. Before he'd dropped all his bombs on me, I was so excited for the chance of running into Levi at school. I'd even dared to hope we might get to hang out together.

"Maybe," I replied. Levi took a step closer and drew me in for a hug. It was an innocent gesture. He didn't linger or hold me too close. It was the kind you give a sibling. He stepped back, leaned down, and brushed a kiss to my forehead.

"See you around, Em."

My heart slammed against my chest. No one ever called me Em. Now Levi Tucker just went and ruined my first, and probably last, nickname.

He turned and started to walk around the side of the house. He glanced back, and I lifted my hand and waved.

"See you around, Levi."

Seven Years Later

A light knock on my door caused me to look up and Moose, my one-year-old chocolate lab, to let out a bark. I smiled when I saw it was my mother. I quickly stood and moved around the desk to hug her. Moose jumped up as well and nearly knocked me over. My little office was across the hall from *her* office, which was housed in the horse barn over on the east side of the ranch. It was close to my grandparents' house, and was the original barn built on the ranch when my great-great-grandfather settled this land. It had, of course, been changed over the years, but this barn felt more like home than my own house I'd grown up in. I was here all the time. The barn by my parents' house was for the cattle, so I hardly ever set foot inside unless I was helping out.

"I got your note that you wanted to talk to me."

"It's about the summer camp sessions."

She sat down in the spare chair in my office. "What about them?"

"I know we already have one week in June, one in July, but I was thinking we could add another one in August this year—but wait," I said when she went to speak what most likely was going to be an objection. "I was thinking this third week could be for kids with special needs."

Her brows lifted. "You've always talked about wanting to do that. Have you researched it? We would need the right staff at camp for that week."

"You know me, Mom. I've researched the hell out of it. I was thinking, what if it was for the whole family? That way, the parents—or at least one parent—could come with their child. After speaking with over two-dozen parents of children with special needs, every single one of them loved the idea of going to camp with their kids. Being there for them while watching them try new adventures. And you know that equine therapy was something I was fascinated with in college."

"I remember."

"Horses can calm riders with autism, allowing them to be able to focus on learning how to ride. There's a woman I met at a conference last December who uses therapeutic horsemanship to help campers concentrate on learning how to ride, communicate, and connect with the horses. It teaches them that they can live life as fully and independently as possible, taking into account each camper's situation. And imagine learning not only how to ride a horse, but how to care for one as well."

My mother smiled. "Would it only be for kids with autism?"

I shook my head. "I don't think we need to limit it to just that. We would, however, need to hire someone trained in therapeutic horsemanship to oversee the program. I've been trying to learn as much as I can for the last several months. We'll need to train our volunteers and camp counselors on how to interact with the campers—and by that, I mean, we'll need them to assist a bit more than they do with the other campers.

"We'll also need two volunteers, instead of one, to walk alongside the horses, to ensure the riders' safety. They'll need to know how to handle a host of different situations that might arise, both medically and emotionally. That's why I was thinking we could have the parents stay as well, because we could learn so much from them. They could volunteer, and help train our current volunteers. It would be a test run this summer, with a small number of campers, to see if this is even something we can offer in the future. Some kids would be day campers only, while maybe a few we can try out for overnight camping."

Another wide smile from my mother as she said, "Emeline, that's a wonderful idea."

I returned the gesture. "I think so too! Also, you know that new little perfumery that opened on Main Street a few months ago? Wonderland Whimsy, owned by Lilibeth Asher?"

"Yes. Lily and I stopped by there after they opened. The store's adorable, and she sells the cutest children's things!

And the candles—did you know she makes them all there? And does a class where you can make the candles *and* the perfume? It's *Alice in Wonderland* themed. And she also has an event space above the store. You remember her parents moved here first. Liam and Whitney. They're a lovely couple. Lily and I've gotten to know them while helping them get settled in."

Lily Waters was my mother's best friend, a recently retired teacher at River Falls Haven, an orphanage in town. They'd been friends for as long as I could remember. Together, they were such a huge part of the community, and I knew they'd welcomed Lilibeth's parents with wide-open arms.

"I know Lilibeth appreciates how welcome they've all felt."

Mom smiled and reached out to pet Moose, who was now sitting next to her. "Her name always makes me think of your great-grandmother, Lileth. I miss her something fierce."

"The few memories I have of her are all happy ones, and most of them have to do with horses."

We both laughed.

"She was a wonderful woman. You remind me so much of her, Emeline."

I leaned over and reached for my mother's hand, giving it a light squeeze.

"I'm sorry I got distracted with tangents for a moment. Why were you bringing up Lilibeth and the store?" Mom asked, clearly not wanting to remain on the subject of my great-grandmother. They were very close. My father said Lileth and my grandmother, Nellie, loved teaching my mom how to ride a horse. Lileth was still riding horses well into her 90s, and almost right up until the day she passed.

"She's a few years older than me, at twenty-nine, but Lilibeth and I have become good friends over the last few months. I'm sure you're aware already, since you know her parents, but when she got the idea for the perfumery and candle bar, she knew she wanted to open it in River Falls, so she could be close to her mother and father when they retired here."

My mother nodded.

"Right, sorry, now *I'm* getting off topic. I was telling her about our summer camps, the Christmas event we hold each year, and the annual fundraising rodeo. She wants to give back to the community, so she pitched me an idea. She'd like to volunteer to help with the camps, and even do a class to teach the kids how to make candles and perfume! I thought it was a wonderful idea, and something new and fun that we could add to the schedule."

My mother's face lit up. "I think it's a great idea! And she said she'd be willing to do this for free?"

I nodded. "She likes to volunteer. Said her father taught her early on that if she's able, she should find causes that are dear to her and give to them in any way she can. She also loves kids. Has a niece and nephew from her older brother Ron, who still lives in Denver—where she relocated from—and she misses them a lot. She's also *so* fun to be around. The campers will adore her."

Mom grinned. "She's definitely full of life. A bit of spit and fire in her, too, from the little I've been around her."

"Definitely. And I don't think I've ever *not* seen a flower tucked into her hair. She's also super friendly. I told her once that I swear she wakes up with a smile on her face and falls asleep with the same one."

"I think she'd be a lovely addition to the summer camps. Would she want to do all three sessions? That's asking a lot from her."

I nodded. "Yes, she wants to help not just with the classes she'll teach, but in any way she can."

"Won't her store be busier in the summer, though? How can she be here *and* there?"

"She wouldn't be at the camp every day, just the days she's scheduled to do the classes. Plus, she has an employee who can help at the store."

Mom thought for a moment. "And she is willing to volunteer her time? What about the supplies?"

"She said she'll cover it all. It's a way for her to give back."

My mother's brows rose slightly. "That's very generous of her."

"Lilibeth really wants to be part of the community, and like I mentioned, she loves kids. It's a win-win."

Clapping her hands, my mother beamed back at me. "I love both of these ideas. We'll need to meet with Jack to go over the legal aspects of the additional week of camp, so we know about liabilities and such, but I don't foresee any issues."

Jack Russell was a good friend of my father's, and the family lawyer.

Mom went on. "Mark and Berkeley volunteer for our camp sessions now, so I can ask them if they're willing to add a week."

Mark Johnson was one of only two doctors we had here in River Falls. His father owned a clinic in town, and Mark was his only son. His sister, Berkeley, was a nurse practitioner who also worked for the clinic. She and Mark each worked a week during the camps, staying on the property throughout the duration. That way, if any of the kids ever needed medical attention, we had someone here twenty-four hours a day.

"I already did, and they both said they'd have no issue adding another week."

"It seems you're on top of things then. You simply wanted my approval?"

I nodded. I never did anything with the camps without at least my mother's approval, even though I was basically in charge. My mom and grandmother still had complete control of the annual Wilde Christmas event, but of course, I helped. As for the ranch itself, my grandparents, Nellie and Gus, had retired and given control over to my two uncles and my oldest brother, Caden. They were the final say for anything that happened on the ranch.

"If you agree, I'll meet with Caden, Uncle David, and Uncle Mike to get the final approval for the additional week."

Mom stood and Moose jumped up, clearly ready to go wherever she was going. "That sounds like a plan. I'll warn you ahead of time, I think they're going to suggest doing a day camp first for the trial run...which might be a better idea, now that I think about it. Let's see how having a day camp with special-needs kids works first before we commit to overnight."

My mother was good at drawing me back in when I had an idea. I was usually the one to run at it a hundred miles per hour. I stood as well. "You're probably right. I was just so excited about adding this additional camp, but I can absolutely see your point. I'll pitch it to them as a day camp. We'll see how it goes and decide from there. Anything else you want to chat about?"

Following her lead, I walked around my desk and toward the door.

Mom paused as I spoke. "Aurora is looking like she's going to foal any day now, so I've asked Marshall to keep a closer eye on her. I'll check on her throughout the next few nights. I've also asked Marshall to start rotating the horses through the west pasture. I know Caden said they'd be harvesting hay in the south pasture soon. I did order a few new saddles for a couple of the ranch hands before they make the hike up the mountains to move the cattle."

"I checked on Aurora before I came in. She's ready to have that baby. Keep me updated, I'm going to be heading to town with your father. He has to stop in and do a few things at the store, then we're heading to Denver for a few days for that sporting goods conference. You're sure you've got everything under control? Our first camp is coming up in just a month."

I smiled. "Everything here is fine. Please go enjoy your weekend with Dad."

Smiling, she leaned in and kissed me on the cheek. "Thank you, Emeline. If you need anything—"

"I'll call Caden, Gatlin, or one of the ranch hands. Mom, the ranch is in good hands."

She laughed and nodded her head. "I'll see you later, sweetheart."

"Have fun—and don't get into trouble in Denver!" I called out as she walked down the aisle and toward the stalls, Moose hot on her heels. I was positive she would check on Aurora once more before she left.

"Moose!" I called out.

"He's fine!" Mom stated. "Don't be surprised if we bring him to Denver with us."

Laughing, I said, "Is he your dog or mine?"

When she didn't answer, I shook my head and turned to head back into my office—and froze.

Caden was walking toward me, in the direction my mother had just gone...and walking beside him was a person I certainly hadn't expected to see.

"Levi," I whispered as I forced my knees not to go weak.

CHAPTER TWO

LEVI

I PULLED UP AND parked outside the familiar barn I'd been to a thousand times. River Falls Cattle Company was a cattle and horse ranch that my best friend, Caden Wilde, managed alongside his brother, Gatlin, and his two uncles, David and Mike. A ranch that had been in his family for five generations, with Caden and his brother being the fifth. The equine side of the ranch was the newest addition, and was something that Caden's mother had started after her love of horses grew when she married, Ladd, Caden's father.

Drawing in a deep breath, I slowly let it out. I haven't been back to River Falls much in the last seven years. Now, I'd returned with my six-year-old son...and *without* my two-year-old daughter or my wife. I was back home trying to start a new life.

Caden, my best friend since elementary school, pulled up and parked next to me. He got out of the truck, a wide grin appearing on his face when he saw me. I opened the truck door and slipped out. As I made my way to him, he stuck out his hand.

"Fuck that," I said, pulling him in for a quick hug, hitting him on the back before taking a step away.

"Damn, it's good to see you in River Falls," Caden stated as he gave me a once-over. "Thanks for the last-minute notification that you moved back. What was *that* all about?"

I shrugged. "Didn't want to make a production out of it. We've been back for a few days. I wanted to get Rhett settled in before I made my presence known. Caroline's parents are happy, of course, to have Rhett so close. But with the divorce and all, it feels...strange."

He nodded. "I get that. How's Rhett adjusting to life here in River Falls?"

Smiling, I replied, "Rhett's in heaven knowing he can ride a horse anytime he wants. My mother's already spoiling him, and Dad...well, he's ready to announce that his son will be joining his veterinary practice. I've had to ask him to slow down a bit and let us get adjusted to being here."

Caden grinned. "I'm sure Rhett's going to be spoiled rotten by *both* your parents. That's something you're going to have to get used to. They have six years of spoiling to catch up on." Then his smile faded, and a concerned expression grew across his face. "How are *you* doing, Levi?"

It was a loaded question, with an answer that evoked a range of emotions.

Seven months ago, my two-year-old daughter, Brooke, was killed in a car accident. Caroline and I had gotten into yet another fight, and she'd threatened to take Brooke away from me. When I told her to try, she grabbed our daughter and took off. An hour later, I got a call that she'd been in an accident.

When I got to the hospital, a doctor gave me the news that my daughter had been killed instantly, and Caroline had broken her left leg and hand.

Nothing in my life was the same after that. The accident hadn't been Caroline's fault, but she'd blamed *me* for causing her to take Brooke and leave the house. She withdrew into herself, stayed in bed for days at a time, and essentially ignored our son.

Our marriage hadn't been on a solid foundation when the accident happened, and it crumbled completely not long afterward. In the end, it wasn't hard for me to decide to file for divorce and ask the court for full custody of Rhett. Caroline hadn't argued; she'd already moved out of the house and into an apartment. Sadly, Rhett not only lost his sister, but his mother as well.

"I'm doing the best I can. Trying to be there for Rhett and make life as normal as possible."

Caden nodded. "Is he still having nightmares?"

I nodded.

"Hopefully, the new surroundings will be good for him *and* for you."

"Yeah," I said, hearing the sadness in my own voice. We hadn't returned to River Falls very often over the years because Caroline couldn't stand the small town. When we visited, it was only for a weekend, and I hardly had time to see anyone. My mother and father visited Denver as much as they could, but with my dad being the only veterinarian in town, it was hard for him to take time off without feeling guilty if he couldn't find someone to cover for him. Caroline's parents had visited often, so at least that was good for Rhett.

Caden cleared his throat. "Have you heard from Caroline at all?"

Caroline had been served divorce papers three weeks ago, and I was still waiting for her to sign and return them.

"I can't remember the last time I spoke to her. Once she signed over custody to me, and the judge granted it, she stopped all communication. It was harder on Rhett than on me. He doesn't understand why Caroline left us. He overheard us arguing one night, and Caroline saying it was my fault that Brooke died. That was hard for Rhett to hear, and he came running into the room, calling her a liar. Yelling that it was *her* fault because she forced Brooke to go with her."

"Forced?"

I nodded. "Brooke didn't want to go with Caroline that night, and she was crying, and repeating my name over and over. Rhett watched the whole thing." I closed my eyes and drew in a breath before looking at Caden again. "She was screaming for me when Caroline walked out. The sound of her calling out 'daddy' haunts me every night. I should have taken her from Caroline. Better yet, I should have admitted the marriage had long since been over and left with the kids."

Caden shook his head as he put a hand on my shoulder and squeezed. "Levi, it wasn't your fault."

"A part of me knows that. But another part of me can't seem to let it go. I blame myself for letting Caroline take Brooke. I guess I figured she would blow off some steam, go for a drive, and calm down. I should've known better. Caroline wasn't the best mother, Caden. I hate saying that, but it's the truth. She cared more about herself than our kids. And the bad part is, now Rhett is old enough to understand that for himself. But still way too young to have to deal with this."

"Have you thought about therapy?" Caden asked.

"He's gone a few times, and I think it has helped him some. He misses his sister, I think, more than his mother. It's sad for me to even say that, but there it is."

Caden sighed. "We sure know how to pick 'em, don't we?"

I let out a humorless laugh. Caden had been dating his high school sweetheart, Rachel, since their freshman year. Caden and I were like brothers and spoke almost every day, so when they broke up, I was the first person he spoke to about it. When she eventually realized she wasn't going to have the wealthy lifestyle she thought she deserved, she broke things off—but didn't bother to do it until Caden was down on one knee, asking her to marry him. Ever since then, Caden had been withdrawn. He hardly ever went out, just stayed on the ranch. And as far as I knew, he hadn't dated since Rachel left him.

"Are you dating anyone?" I asked.

He'd motioned for us to start heading into the barn. He glanced at me with a blank look. "I have no interest in dating anyone."

"Caden, it's been almost what? Two years since she left you? When are you going to move on?"

He shrugged. "I have no desire to go through that again."

"Just because you and I have had bad experiences doesn't mean that all women are that way."

Caden stopped walking and turned to me. "Would you have married Caroline if she hadn't been pregnant?"

No one had ever asked me that question, but I knew plenty of people had wanted to over the years. My parents topping the list.

I pushed a hand through my hair and looked down the aisle of the barn. The smell of horse manure and hay filled my nostrils. I wanted to close my eyes and take it in. Instead, I focused on my best friend again. The guy I'd told everything to my entire life.

I let out a breath and shook my head. "No, I wouldn't have. Truth be told, we probably would have broken up eventually. We were just two different people who wanted two different things in life when it came down to it."

"You told me that night you got wasted, when you found out Caroline was pregnant, that you were positive she got pregnant on purpose. How did you know?"

My hand rubbed at the back of my neck as I looked into his eyes. "We were starting to grow apart, and she got paranoid that I was cheating on her at school. She later told me she panicked and stopped taking her birth control pills. Said it was the only way she could make sure we stayed together."

"She *told you* she got pregnant on purpose?"

I nodded. "Yeah, after Rhett was born. Claimed she wanted to come clean about it and start fresh. I did love her, don't get me wrong. Would I have asked her to marry without the pregnancy?" I shrugged. "I don't think so, Caden. I really don't, even though we had a lot of good times. And we weren't planning on having any more kids. Brooke was a happy accident. Then things changed between us, but I didn't think it was anything any other couple might experience. Until we started fighting all the time. I asked her for a divorce the day she got into the car accident. That's what we were fighting about."

"Jesus. I'm sorry, Levi."

With a half shrug, I attempted a smile. "It's not like it's your fault."

"Yeah, but I knew she liked me way back when, and I kind of pushed her in your direction to get her off my back."

Smiling for real now, I replied, "I wouldn't have Rhett or Brooke if you hadn't done that." A sudden pain pierced my heart. "Or at least, wouldn't have had Brooke for the short amount of time that I did."

Caden drew in a deep breath and let it out. We heard voices and turned to see Mrs. Wilde, Caden's mother, talking to his youngest sister, Emeline.

A strange sensation filled my chest at the sight of the latter.

"Just the person we were looking for!" Caden said, hitting me on the back and walking toward his sister.

Emeline called out to her mother, then turned and stilled when she saw us. Her smile slowly fell, replaced by a look of shock.

I hadn't ever come across Caden's sister on my trips back home to River Falls. She was either in college or off doing something whenever I was in town. Now, looking at her, I was stunned to see the young girl who used to chase us around the ranch, begging us to let her hang out, was now a grown woman. And a beautiful one at that.

"Look who I found!" Caden stated.

As we drew closer, I could see Emeline's beautiful blue eyes sparkle.

"Hey, Em."

Her cheeks turned a slight shade of pink as she watched us approach. "Levi! What are you doing here?" She closed her eyes and gave a brief shake of her head before focusing back on me and giving me a bright smile. "I mean, it's wonderful to see you."

She stepped forward and hugged me. A strong smell of vanilla with a hint of lemon penetrated my senses, and memories of a younger Emeline flooded my mind. She'd always had a smile on her face, and if she wasn't riding a horse, she was usually talking about them.

After giving me a slight squeeze, she stepped back. "I was so sorry to hear about Brooke. I hope you and Caroline got my card."

I nodded. "We did. And the flowers at the memorial were kind of you."

"It was the least I could do. Are you and Caroline in town visiting your folks?"

I shook my head. "I've moved back to River Falls."

Her brows shot up. "You have?" Turning to Caden, she said, "You didn't mention anything about Levi moving back."

Caden held up his hands in defense. "I just found out not that long ago myself."

She smiled at her brother, then turned back to me. "So, what made you guys decide to move back?"

Caden and I exchanged a quick look. "I just decided that Rhett and I needed a fresh start elsewhere, especially since he's been having a difficult time adjusting to the loss of Brooke."

"You and Rhett?" she asked quietly.

I nodded. "Caroline and I are divorcing."

She blinked a few times, opened her mouth to speak, then quickly shut it. When she didn't say anything, Caden cleared his throat. That seemed to snap her out of her shock.

"Wow, I...I'm so sorry to hear that."

Shrugging, I replied, "Don't be. It's harder on Rhett than it is on me. It's been a long time coming."

Emeline looked at her brother, then back to me. "I just can't imagine how difficult this is on poor Rhett. Will you share custody?"

"That conversation would require more time, plus I wanted to talk to you about camp for Rhett. Are you free for lunch?"

"Um," she glanced at her watch, "I've got a few things to do, but I could join you guys."

Caden quickly piped up. "It'll be just the two of you. I've got a meeting at one."

Her head snapped back to look at me, and for a moment, I thought for sure she was going to decline the lunch entirely. Instead, after a pause, she nodded. "Are you going to be around here for a bit longer, or should we meet somewhere in town?"

"Caden asked me to come and take a look at a horse; so how about if I give you thirty minutes? Is that enough time?"

"Which horse?" she asked her brother.

Caden laughed and held up his hands once again. "Just want him to take a look at Aurora." Before she could say anything else, he added, "Nothing's wrong. Just with it being her first foal, I wanted to make sure all was okay."

"Caden, you do realize I'm in charge of this area of the ranch?"

He grinned. "I do believe I'm *still* your boss."

Emeline rolled her eyes, and I had to look away before I laughed. Same stubborn Emeline...and Caden. They were two peas in a pod.

She finally looked back at me.

"Thirty minutes?" I asked again.

"Yes," she said with a smile. "Just come by and get me. This is my office."

She pointed to a room that used to be the tack room.

"You're not sharing your office space with the tack, are you?"

Emeline let out a laugh, and it made my chest flutter. What in the hell was *that* about?

"No, we moved the tack room. It's just an office now."

I nodded and replied, "Then I'll see you in a few."

"See you then."

Turning, she quickly headed into her office, shutting the door with a soft click.

I pulled my eyes from the door and turned to Caden, who motioned for me to follow him. We went through the barn and turned a corner, and I heard a horse nickering.

"That's our Aurora. She's the most vocal horse I've ever met."

I smiled. When we approached a stall, the horse looked up. One ear was forward, the other back, indicating her attention was divided at the moment.

"Who's in the next stall?" I asked.

Caden looked at me. "How'd you know there was a horse in there?"

"Well, there wasn't one in the stall we passed, and Aurora here has her attention divided between us and something else. I'm guessing another horse next to her."

"There's a mare in there with her three-day-old foal."

Pointing to the door, I asked, "May I?"

"Yep," Caden replied. "Please do."

Walking into the stall, I spoke in a soft voice. It didn't take long for Aurora to give me her full attention. She was a sweet horse, and she nickered a few more times.

"She *is* vocal."

"Told you."

"She's eaten today?"

"Yes."

I moved around her and took a good look from all sides. "She's dropped, and her sides are sinking in a bit." I moved to the back and attempted to lift her tail, to which she protested slightly. "Her tendons are getting looser, that's a good sign."

Glancing under the horse, I took a look at her udders. I glanced at Caden and asked, "Do you have cameras in the stalls?"

He frowned. "No, I honestly haven't thought about adding any. I'll have to talk to Emeline about it. She runs the equine part of the ranch, as she mentioned, so she knows the budget best, along with my mother."

"How many months have you known she's been pregnant?"

"Eleven months."

I nodded. "I know you know this, but once her water breaks, if she doesn't birth the foal within twenty minutes, you need to give me a call. First-time moms may not exhibit any signs of labor, so I highly recommend using a camera. Also, I suggest getting the horse and foal in the next stall out. If Aurora is agitated by the noise from next door, she'll hold off on her labor."

About two minutes later, Emeline walked up with Marshall. "Sorry to interrupt. We're going to take Kamaria and Lynx out to give Aurora some privacy. She's easily distracted, and I don't want their presence to hinder her labor."

Caden smirked. "There's a reason she's in charge over here."

I chuckled. "Who names these horses?"

Caden pointed in the direction of Emeline. "That would be my sister."

She glanced back and smiled. "Do you have an issue with Kamaria and Lynx's names?"

I held up my hands in surrender. "Not at all. They're... unique."

Emeline brought the foal out first and started in the opposite direction from Aurora's stall. "They're all named after stars or constellations," she stated, as she pointed up. "This is Kamaria."

"And Lynx?" I asked. "That's a star?"

"It's a constellation. Mom named her."

I looked at Caden, who shrugged. "I've learned not to question or argue with my mother and sisters. They have a strange way of doing things, but it always works."

Marshall walked out with Lynx. "I like her name," he said with a smile.

"I'm sure you do, Marshall!" Caden laughed. He turned to me. "The princess now has her privacy."

I turned back and ran my hands down the mare's neck. "There you go, girl. You have this whole side of the barn to yourself. Let that little one come out so you can get to feeling like your old self again."

Leaving the stall, I softly shut the door. Caden started walking in the direction Emeline had gone. "You've got to see this filly. She's nuts."

"Aren't they all?"

We walked out to the indoor arena, where Emeline was just letting the filly off her lead.

The young horse took off running around its mother with utter happiness. Lynx kept a close eye on Kamaria, and at one point, I swore she rolled her eyes. She was obviously a very protective mother, and she made it known to her foal that she wasn't happy with her carefree behavior.

I moved my gaze to Emeline, who smiled, watching the young one play and kick. I was struck by how beautiful Emeline was. Her brown hair was pulled back in a ponytail, and her body had definitely grown shapely over the years.

With a quick shake of my head, I focused back on the horses.

"She's amazing," Caden said.

Looking at him, I asked, "Who?"

He nodded in the direction of his sister. "Emeline. I always thought my mother and Ensley had the gift with horses, but after watching Emeline, it's clear she's more than just a horse lover. I swear she can read their minds. You should see her when one comes in from an abused or neglected situation, and no one else can even get near them. But Emeline, she just walks up to the horse and within no time at all, she's running her hands all over them, making them feel safe. I don't know how she does it."

"Natural horsemanship. Or as some call it, a horse whisperer."

Caden smiled. "Well, that's Emeline, for sure. She's got a gift."

I turned my attention away from his sister and asked, "How's the cattle side of the ranch? Any issues?"

He shook his head. "All good. We've started to push the last of the cattle up the mountainside for grazing. We've gotten one harvest of hay, and plan on doing another cut on the south pasture once we get the cattle off."

I glanced back at Emeline, only to find her laughing with a guy I hadn't ever seen before. "Who's that?"

"That's Jon. He's one of the new ranch hands we hired this year," Caden answered, looking in the same direction.

"He's young."

His shoulder lifted with a shrug. "He's twenty-eight, if I remember correctly. I think he has the hots for Emeline."

I looked back at Caden. "And you're okay with one of the ranch hands flirting with her?"

He burst out laughing. "I do *not* tell my sister what she can and cannot do. Either of them, actually. Besides, I trust our guys, and I know my sister. She makes sure the ranch hands know she keeps her business and her private lives separate."

We both turned to see Emeline laugh again and put a hand on Jon's arm. As if sensing us watching her, she turned and glanced our way, instantly dropping her hand. She tilted her head as if questioning why we were looking at her.

Turning, I started back for the barn. "If you don't need me to take a look at anyone else, I should give my mom a call and see how Rhett's doing."

"No, just Aurora. I'm sure I'll hear it from Emeline that I went around her to have you come out, but I wanted to play it safe. She's one of my favorite mares."

I smiled. "I get it."

"When will you start officially at the vet clinic?"

"I'd like to get settled in with Rhett first. It's going to be hard to find a place, so I need to get it into my head that I could possibly be with my folks for a while. I told my dad to give me about three weeks. That affords me some time to find someone to watch Rhett while I'm at work. I don't want to depend on my mother all the time. I'm hoping he can meet some kids before school starts in the fall, so he feels like he fits in more. That's why I want to talk to Emeline about camp. I know it's for underprivileged kids, but I was hoping I could get a pass."

Caden nodded. "Well, if he comes to one of the camps, I'm sure he'll meet a few kids his age. I'm not sure if they have any open spots, and I'll be the first to admit, I have no idea how Emeline runs the camps. But I know they have different age groups. The camps have actually gotten smaller over the last few years. The need isn't there as much as it was in the beginning, which is a good thing."

"Yeah, I figured they might be full. I know it's last minute, but I'm hoping I can pull the whole your-brother-is-my-best-friend card to see if she'll get me in."

He laughed. "I don't think you need that card. From what I remember, my baby sister always had a crush on you."

I stopped in my tracks and gaped at him. "What?"

He narrowed his eyes and gave me a look. "Come on, Levi. You can't tell me you never realized she liked you."

I glanced back at Emeline, who was now talking to Marshall, a serious expression on her face. "I had no idea she had a crush on me."

He frowned, looking bemused. "I thought that was why you always went out of your way to be nice to her."

"No. I just thought she was a sweet girl, and I liked her."

His brow raised.

"In a *brotherly way*, Caden." His brow went a little higher. "Okay, maybe not in a brotherly way toward the end. It was hard not to notice her once she got into high school."

He smirked. "Well, I highly doubt she's *still* crushing on you. But I'm glad I told you."

Confused, I asked, "Why?"

Laughing, he simply shook his head.

Before I could press the issue, Vivianne, Caden's mother, appeared at the other end of the barn entrance and smiled at us.

"Levi Turner, what in the world?"

I smiled. "Hello, Mrs. Wilde."

She waved me off. "Call me Vivianne; how many times do I have to tell you that? I practically raised you as one of my own!"

Laughing, I gave her a quick hug.

Caden spoke next. "Levi and Rhett have moved back to River Falls."

Vivianne smiled, but I could see the confusion in her eyes. "Caroline?"

"Divorced. Well, about to be, anyway. Just waiting for her to sign and send the papers to my lawyer."

She gently squeezed my arm. "I'm sorry to hear that, Levi. And I know I said it at the funeral, but I'm even more sorry about Brooke."

"Thank you, Mrs...er...Vivianne. And no need to be sorry about me and Caroline. It's been a long time coming."

"Will you share custody of Rhett?"

I shook my head. "No, I have full custody. Caroline gave up custody, but has visiting rights, of course."

A look of surprise washed over her face. "She gave up custody?"

"The accident impacted Caroline in a pretty big way. I told her if she ever changes her mind, we can open it up for discussion, but that once we moved to River Falls and Rhett started school, this is where she'd have to live."

"I'm sure it was an unbelievably terrible thing to lose a child like that, for both of you."

When I didn't say anything, she went on.

"What about Mitch? Has he seen Rhett since you've been back?"

Mitch was Caroline's father. I nodded. "He has. With him getting ready to retire early, he probably hasn't had a chance to let Ladd know we were back in town."

Vivianne smiled. "I'm sure that's it."

We both knew what I said was a lie. Mitch and Ladd were not only business partners, but best friends. Yes, Mitch was several years older than Ladd, but they still spoke every single day.

He didn't tell Ladd because he didn't want his friend asking about Caroline.

They had a strained relationship. After Caroline decided years ago that she wanted nothing to do with the family business, telling her father that we were moving to Denver instead, he had never really forgiven her.

"How's Rhett doing? Caden told me he was having nightmares since Brooke's passing."

"He doesn't have them as often. Some days are better than others, but with him losing his mother as well, he's struggling."

I didn't want to tell Vivianne that Rhett thinks Caroline doesn't love him, and that she left because of him. I would never be able to forgive her for that—*ever*. The way she'd hurt our son was something I couldn't understand. After all, she wasn't the only one who lost Brooke. We all did.

"We would love to have you both join us for Sunday dinner. I'd love to see Rhett and get to know him better. Ladd and I cannot wait to have grandchildren of our own." She shot a weary look at Caden, who took a step back.

"If you're waiting on me, you're going to be waiting a long time."

Vivianne rolled her eyes and laughed. "One day a woman's going to catch his eye and he'll be eating crow."

With a huff, Caden replied, "Don't hold your breath, Mom."

"Hold her breath for what?" Emeline asked as she walked over.

"Nothing," Caden said quickly before anyone could say anything. I hated that Rachel had broken my best friend so badly.

"Waiting for your brother to find a girl and settle down so I can have grandkids."

Emeline's eyes widened as she looked to Caden. "He's way too grumpy for any woman to put up with."

He smiled at his sister. "Thank you, Emeline."

She grinned at him before turning to me. "I'm actually free now. Ready for lunch?"

"I am if you are."

"Give me a second to grab my purse and sunglasses."

When Emeline slipped into her office, Vivianne raised a brow in my direction. "Going to lunch together, are we?"

Looking between her and Caden, who was attempting not to laugh, I replied, "I wanted to talk to Emeline about Rhett attending summer camp."

Vivianne's face broke out into a wide grin. "What a wonderful idea! You know, Levi, if you have some free time, we'd love it if you could pop by a few times during the camps, to talk to the kids about what it's like to be a veterinarian."

Now Caden did laugh. Then he cleared his throat when Vivianne shot him a warning look. What she was warning him about, I had no idea.

"I'd be honored to do that."

When Emeline walked out, Vivianne grinned at her. "Levi's volunteered to be part of the summer camps by talking to the kids about being a veterinarian. Plus, he'd like to have Rhett attend a camp."

Emeline glanced at me, eyes filled with excitement. "Really? The kids would *love* that! Your dad always said he'd try to come and do it, but he's always so busy, his schedule never works out with ours. Since you're just back in town, I bet we can work some days into your schedule before it gets too crazy."

"Um…" I looked around the small group, and noticed Caden had an amused smirk on his face. "I guess that's true enough. Right now, I'm not on the schedule at all."

Emeline gave an excited little jump. "This is going to be perfect! We needed another volunteer."

Concern set in. "Wait—you're just talking about me coming to talk about being a vet a couple times, right?"

With a wave of her hand, Emeline replied, "Among other things. Mom, we need to meet and discuss how to make this work. Oh—why haven't you left with Dad yet?"

"He needed to take a call before we left."

I looked to Caden, who simply held up his hands. "I tried to warn you."

Leaning in, I whispered, "You most certainly did *not* try to warn me."

He grinned. "You're going to have to learn to read the room. Or in this case, the barn."

I slowly shook my head and started to say something, but Emeline approached. She'd managed to disappear again. Apparently into her mother's office this time, coming back out with a calendar.

A *calendar*!

"I've got our camp calendar right here. We can do all the planning at lunch. And the best part, you'll be here while Rhett is at camp!" She hooked her arm in mine and started pulling me out of the barn. "Who's driving?"

"Um, I'll drive."

"Perfect! We can also head over to the campgrounds so you can see it."

Glancing over my shoulder at Caden, I saw him wave at me with his fingers while still grinning. I wasn't sure how I was going to get him back, but I'd find a way.

CHAPTER THREE

EMELINE

LEVI OPENED THE PASSENGER door of his silver Ford F-250 and held out his hand so I could use it to climb in. I tried to ignore the way his touch caused my entire body to flush with heat, not to mention my traitorous stomach, which felt as if it were doing an endless pirouette.

"Thank you," I said with a soft smile.

He shut the door and walked around the front of his truck to the driver's side.

Once he climbed in, I said, "If you'll just drive around the barn and head south, I can show you the camp. It's been a while since you've been there."

When he smiled, I swore it lit up the entire cab of the truck.

Turning my gaze away, I looked straight ahead. "Are you happy to be back in River Falls?"

Levi started the truck, and we were on our way down the gravel road. "I *am* happy, yes. Rhett loves it here. Or rather, he loves being on the farm with my mom and dad. His new favorite thing is to get up with Mom and help her feed the chickens. She's keeping him busy, which also keeps his mind busy."

Nodding, I replied, "He has the love for animals like his father and grandparents, I see."

Levi chuckled. "That he does. I had horses at our place in Denver, since we lived outside of the city and had a few acres, so I got him on a horse early on. He loves it."

I wanted to ask if Brooke had enjoyed animals but wasn't sure whether Levi wanted to talk about his daughter. "A boy after my own heart," I mused. "If I remember correctly, Caroline also liked to ride."

"English, not western. She won some events she competed in during high school, but that was about as far as her love for the sport went. She thought they smelled, and she despised having to take care of them. Brooke loved to ride as well. She was just starting to learn."

"I almost asked if she loved animals but I wasn't sure if you'd be willing to talk about her."

When he glanced over at me, his eyes were so sad. "I don't mind talking about her. I try to talk about her often around Rhett. It's painful, but I don't want her memory to fade."

"I'm so sorry that happened to you all, Levi. I can't even imagine how painful it is."

He let out a slow breath. "It is, but life goes on. Brooke wouldn't want us to sit around and cry all the time. She was so full of life, always had a smile on her face. I miss her energy."

"I wish I could have met her."

He looked at me again. More sadness. "Me too. Every time we came to town, you were never at the ranch. You would have adored Brooke, and she would have loved you and Ensley."

"I'm sure I would have," I said softly. "And I haven't seen Rhett since he was like three, maybe."

"He's growing up fast."

When the sadness in his voice became too much, I decided to change the subject. "We have one summer session in June and one in July. We're discussing the possibility of adding an additional week of camp in August, for children with special needs and their parents. It will be a different type of camp for the trial run. Only a day camp."

"Wow, that's exciting. So this will be your first year to offer that camp?"

I nodded. "It will, if we can make it happen. They'll get a fun week on the ranch, and we'll see if this is something we're going to be able to offer annually. We'll have to have properly trained staff on hand, and of course, all the legal stuff that goes along with something like this."

Levi laughed. "The legal stuff? That's one way of putting it."

Shrugging, I replied, "My mother takes care of all that. She's been doing this a lot longer than I have. I guess at some point I'll need to learn it all, but for now, she deals with the lawyers."

He pulled around the barn, and I pointed to a small parking area. "You can park there and we'll get out and walk around."

He pulled up and parked. "Wow, this place has changed since I was here last."

I smiled. "It *has* changed a lot. We're still on the small side as far as camps go, but that's how we like it, and our needs don't require anything on a larger scale."

"You know, when I was in Denver, I heard someone talking about the camps here at River Falls Ranch."

Surprised, I replied, "Really? Were they saying good things?"

Levi nodded. "They were basically saying they wished you would open it up to more campers, and since you catered to the local kids first and foremost, it's tough to get a spot."

"Yes, we do. But there are numerous camps available across the country, including in Denver. We began our work with kids by holding a Christmas Day event for the local orphanage, as you know. That's what first gave me the idea for the camps when I was thirteen. We've grown to what you see today, and I'm proud of the work we've done, but my mother and grandmother are really the ones who started it all with the Christmas event. I just added to it. Being able to help kids, give them a safe space on our ranch, has been a dream of my mother's for as long as I can remember."

"Not to mention what you've done."

I felt my cheeks heat. "Yes, it's been my dream as well. Come on, I'll show you around."

We got out and walked down the path. "That cabin over there, behind the trees? That's Ensley's place. She wanted to be closer to the barn since she's our farrier."

"Does she only work here on the ranch?"

"No, she works all over the River Falls area and beyond. It took some convincing for a few ranchers that a woman could do just as good a job as a man, but she won them over."

"I'm not surprised Ensley was up to the task. She's been out to prove herself since she was little, when she used to challenge me and Caden to races. She was always so sure she'd win, and I remember us laughing about it."

"Did she win?" I asked, giving him a smirk.

"She blew us out of the water. And I actually started slow the first time, thinking I'd be a gentleman and give her a head start. Big mistake *that* was."

I chuckled. "Yep, that was a mistake."

We walked a bit more. "Here are the cabins the kids stay in. There's a counselor assigned to each cabin, who stays with the kids at all times. They sleep in there with the kids as well, but in a separate little bedroom. We've had the same group of counselors come back for the last few years. They have to be at least sixteen and complete a training course, which we cover the cost of. They also learn CPR and basic first aid."

"Do they have any training for kids who might have... issues?"

I paused to face him. "Mental or physical?"

He shrugged. "Both."

"They're trained on what to look for if they suspect abuse, or if the camper might be in crisis, but they're kids themselves, keep in mind. We do have one certified counselor who volunteers for each camp. She's from Denver. We don't actually offer that type of counseling here at the camp, but we do find it helpful to have someone available in case we face an issue.

"Ninety-nine percent of the kids at the camps are local, and around eighty percent of *those* come from the orphanage. The rest are from low-income families. The kids from River Falls Haven are divided between the two camp sessions, to give them a chance to meet kids outside of the orphanage. They don't have to pay for camp, of course; it's offered free of charge to anyone living at River Falls Haven. We're able to do that through the rodeo fundraisers we do, as well as the charity dinner we host each year. We make most of our donations through those two events."

We started to walk again, and I stopped at the largest building.

"This is camp headquarters. The building is relatively new, having been constructed just three years ago. It's where the kitchen is, the dining hall, and the living room."

"Living room?"

I nodded as I opened the door. "Yep! It's exactly what it sounds like. A common place for the kids to hang out together. I wanted this to feel like a home as much as possible, not just like a rec center or anything like that. It was more for the kids from River Haven. The orphanage is actually pretty nice, but it doesn't exactly have a homey feel."

We walked past long rows of tables where the kids ate. I showed him the kitchen, which housed two industrial stoves, two huge sinks, two dishwashers, and a large industrial refrigerator. "Before we had this area, we mainly had food brought in each day for the campers. That got to be pretty pricey, and my father did the numbers and said we'd end up saving more money by having it all done onsite."

"Who does all the cooking?"

"My mother, grandmother, and several volunteers, some of whom are the mothers and fathers of the kids. They like giving back as much as they can."

He looked around and smiled. "This is impressive, Em."

Feeling a sense of pride and embarrassment at the compliment from him, I simply nodded and headed out of the kitchen. I wasn't sure why I felt embarrassed, though. Maybe it was because it was Levi. We walked into a huge open room with exposed log beams and walls, featuring a giant wood fireplace at the opposite end. Several sofas, chairs, and beanbags were scattered throughout the space.

"The loft up there," I said, pointing, "holds a pool table, a foosball table, a card table, and a Ping-Pong table."

"Wow! That sounds like fun."

Someone walked out of one of the three bathrooms to our right.

"Hi, Charlotte," I called out as I waved.

"Hey there, Emeline. We've pretty much cleaned up everything. I just need to stock the bathrooms, and when we get closer, narrow down the menus for each week."

"Charlotte, this is Levi Tucker. He's Caden's best friend and pretty much part of the family. His father is the local veterinarian."

Charlotte reached out her hand. "Charlotte Hastings. I'm the camp steward."

"Camp steward?" Levi asked.

"She's in charge of budgeting, shopping, and getting the daily menus in place. She also prepares all the snacks for the kids. Plus, she gets all the cabins ready and cleaned, as well as the main building."

Levi's eyes went wide. "Whoa. That's a lot."

Charlotte laughed. "Emeline's making it sound like I do it alone. Nellie and Vivianne have the last say on the budget, and I have a staff of three who help me do all the other work."

Glancing at me, Levi slowly shook his head. "My gosh, I never knew what a big operation this was—or *is*, I should say."

"Most of the others only work the weeks we hold camp in the summer, and if we have any other events here, but Charlotte works year-round, making sure everything stays okay with the cabins and we have no issues. We also rent out the cabins to companies that want to host work retreats, among other things. That's something we just started last year. They have access to the whole camp, but it's their responsibility to do all the cooking and cleaning. The income goes toward the summer camps and the Christmas event."

"What a great idea."

"That was Emeline's idea," Charlotte chimed in with a smile.

"Do you stay on the premises?" Levi asked her.

Charlotte shook her head. "No, no. I love it here, but after my long work hours, I enjoy heading home to my own little log cabin a few miles outside of River Falls. It's not far from here, though."

"Well, you do a great job of making the place look so good."

She smiled. "Thank you. Now, if you'll excuse me, I've got a ton of work to do."

"See ya around, Charlotte." Gesturing to Levi, I said, "Let me show you the cabins."

We walked a short distance. Like the main building, they were all log cabins, and each could hold up to ten kids. I'd had a hand in designing them when I was younger, and to this day, they're still one of the things I'm most proud of.

After we made our way through one of them, I turned to Levi. "If Rhett decides he'd like to join us, he'd stay in one of the four cabins over there."

"So it's co-ed then?"

"The camp, yes, but not the cabins. Boys stay with boys; girls stay with girls. We also hire a couple River Falls police officers to come and provide security at night. They watch to make sure we don't have anyone coming in or going out."

"Like, as in kids sneaking out?"

"Yes. We had a group of fourteen-year-old boys one year who decided it would be fun to meet down at the pier and do some night fishing. Unlucky for them, Caden found them. I don't think I have to tell you how *that* turned out."

His brows shot up. "I bet he scared the living shit out of them."

"Let's just say they won't ever try *that* again."

He chuckled and looked around. "Do you live on the ranch?"

I nodded. "I do. I live in my great-grandmother Lileth's cabin. It's back behind that row of trees. I kind of remember her, but only a few vague memories."

"I don't remember her, if I'm being honest." He looked around and said, "I think Rhett would love this."

I leaned against a tree. "And what does *Levi* think about volunteering to teach the kids all about the animals?"

He shook his head and stared off into the distance, a smile on his handsome face. "Well, when a pretty woman's asking, it's hard to say no."

"I'll be sure to let my mother know you said she was pretty."

Levi let out a bark of laughter. "She is, but I was talking about *you*, Em."

I felt my cheeks heat, and I pushed off the tree and started toward his truck. I turned and walked backward as I called out, "I hope that means you're paying for lunch!"

The drive into town was filled with easy conversation. Levi asked about the ranch, my parents, my uncles, and inquired further about the camp, as well as how I'd been doing over the last few years. And, finally, whether I was dating anyone.

"I've dated off and on. A couple of relationships, but they didn't last long."

"Why not?"

I shrugged and didn't say what I wanted to say. *Oh, because they weren't you, Levi.* So I went with the *second* reason they never lasted.

"Apparently, I work too much. Both of the guys I dated long term said that the ranch and the camps consumed all my time, and that I never made time for them. First of all, they knew that going in, and nothing will ever take me away from the ranch. I love that place, and I love my job. The horses are...well...they're everything to me.

"And the camp? Well, I *can* say they made me realize I was taking on too much. I'm the camp director now, but there are some tasks I should be delegating to others. I'm slowly getting better at that. So, I guess I can thank those guys for opening my eyes a bit. But no one is going to tell me how to live my life or spend my time."

He laughed. "You for sure have Wilde blood pumping through those veins."

Smiling, I turned to look at his handsome profile. "Wilde as in my last name, or W. I. L. D. kind of wild?"

"Both."

I grinned. "Fair enough."

When the conversation about me had nowhere else to go, I took the opportunity to ask Levi the one question I'd been dying to ask, but wasn't sure I should.

"So...you and Caroline?"

He glanced at me and shrugged before focusing back on the road. We were about to drive into town, so it was probably a question I should have saved for the drive back to the ranch. Or maybe he didn't want to talk about it. I was pretty sure it had everything to do with Brooke and the accident.

"Things between us hadn't been great for the last few years. Hell, our whole marriage, if I'm truly being honest. We fought a lot. Basically, if she wasn't sleeping, she was picking a fight with me. On the day of the accident, I told her I thought we should separate. She freaked out on me and said she'd never give me the kids. She went on about some other crazy things, then grabbed Brooke and said she was leaving."

He closed his eyes and drew in a slow breath.

"Brooke was crying; she didn't want to go with Caroline. I should have demanded that Caroline leave her with me. I don't know why I didn't."

I reached for his hand and gave it a squeeze. "There was no way you could have known what would happen, Levi."

He nodded. "I know. There are nights I wake up in a cold sweat, hearing Brooke cry out for me. Anyway, the accident wasn't Caroline's fault. A truck ran a red light. Brooke passed on impact, and for that, I guess I'm thankful. Caroline immediately blamed *me* for making her leave. She completely ignored Rhett for weeks, and when she finally managed to get out of bed, she started drinking. That's something I don't share with many people.

"I finally realized that my being there wasn't making things better. Rhett would overhear us fighting, hear Caroline blaming me. He unleashed on her one night, and told her that *she* was the reason Brooke died. That's when I realized I needed to get us both out of Denver. I asked for full custody, and she didn't argue, and had given written permission for me to move back to River Falls with Rhett. I served Caroline with divorce papers three weeks ago. I'm waiting on her to sign the papers so I can move on."

Stunned, I asked, "She gave up custody of Rhett, just like that?"

"Yeah. Pretty sad, isn't it? And Rhett, he lost his sister and best friend, *and* his mother. It's been tough on him."

"Where is she? Back in Denver?"

He drew in a breath and then quickly released it. "As far as I know. She moved out of our house and into an apartment right after the night Rhett unleashed on her. I told her about my plans to return to River Falls, and that if she ever wanted to share custody of Rhett, she'd have to move back. She just stared at me with a blank expression. The last thing I said to her was that she needed therapy...and I hope she gets it for Rhett's sake.

"Caroline's never going to win Mother of the Year, but she had a rare moment or two when she was a good mom. We had some good times, but it was pretty clear we weren't meant to be together. Brooke hadn't been planned. She was a happy surprise, but we hadn't planned on having any other kids."

Closing my eyes, I shook my head. "I'm so sorry, Levi. I'm sorry about Brooke, Rhett, *and* your marriage. It seems like a lot to lose in such a short amount of time."

"Thank you, Emeline. I appreciate it."

He pulled into a parking spot in front of Anna's Café. I stared at the building, then at Levi. "This is where you want to eat lunch?"

"Would you rather have pizza, or something else?"

Granted, River Falls was small, but over the last few years, we'd gotten more restaurants. The locals, however, still seemed to eat at the older places, like Anna's Café.

Nodding toward the door, I said, "It's just...Anna is Janet's sister. And Janet writes *The Daily Dirt* column."

He grinned. "Are you afraid we'll end up in the next edition?"

"Yes, I am. She doesn't have anything to write about. She actually wrote about Ms. Betty's chickens getting out, Levi."

"All of her chickens got out?"

I nodded.

"Did someone *let* them out?"

"Levi!"

"Sorry, you got me curious now about her chickens. I know how much she loves those birds, or at least she used to."

Rolling my eyes, I sighed. "All I'm saying is, don't be surprised if people talk when they see us together."

"About us eating together? Em, it's just lunch. Your brother is my best friend. I have a son whom I want to enroll in your summer camp, and I'm pretty sure I was volunteered to help at each session this summer, not just the one Rhett's attending. It's not like we don't have a *reason* to have lunch together."

"You're right. It's just a business lunch." I knew I sounded a bit childish, so I attempted to play it off. "You know how small-town gossip is. I just didn't want you to have to deal with it right off the bat, considering everything else you have going on in your life."

"Truth be told, Em, I don't give a shit what *anyone* says about me."

A small laugh slipped free. "Well, okay then. Let's go get some lunch."

CHAPTER FOUR

LEVI

THE MOMENT THE BELL above the door rang, I wished I'd listened to Emeline.

All heads turned and stared. And I don't mean a curious stare; I mean the kind where you just *know* the moment they get a chance, they're going to tell everyone who they saw together at the local café.

"That pizza sounds good right about now," I whispered as a young girl walked up to us.

"Too late," Emeline replied, an I-told-you-so expression on her face.

"Hey, Emeline. Table for two?" the young waitress asked.

"A booth, if you can, Lucy."

Grinning, she grabbed two menus and motioned for us to follow her. She tucked us into the back corner and set the menus down. "Thought you might like some privacy."

Emeline looked at me with one brow raised.

"It's fine, we don't need privacy...Lucy, is it?" I asked.

Her cheeks flushed. "Lucy Miller."

I didn't dare look at Emeline. "It's a business lunch. We're here to talk about my son attending a session at River Falls Summer Camp."

"And having Dr. Tucker here volunteer at the camp, as well," Emeline interjected.

Lucy's eyes lit up. "A doctor? Are you new in town? Will you be working at the new clinic that just opened?"

"No, I'm a vet."

Lucy nodded. "Thank you for your service. Were you a doctor in the military?"

I blinked at her a few times, until Emeline subtly nudged me. "Um." I shook my head, then replied, "A *veterinarian*. The other kind of vet. Not a vet like in the military... It doesn't matter."

Lucy looked confused.

Emeline smiled at the young girl. "An animal doctor, Lucy."

The light bulb went off. "Ohh! I'm so stupid. Daddy calls our local veterinarian a fleecer."

Emeline laughed, then quickly covered it up by coughing.

"He calls him a fleecer?" I asked, frowning.

She nodded. "Is that another name for a veterinarian?"

I looked over to Emeline, who was practically turning red from trying to hold her laughter in. She also gave up on a different table, and finally slid into the booth.

"No, it's not," I answered with a forced smile.

She shrugged, as if bored with the conversation. "What can I get you both to drink?"

"I'll have a water for now," Emeline stated.

"Same for me."

"Two waters, coming up!"

Turning on her heel, Lucy walked toward the counter. I took that moment to glance around. The café wasn't crowded, but there were still a good number of people here. All of whom were still watching us.

Anna's Café hadn't changed a bit. It still looked the same as when I was little, sitting at the counter when my father brought me in for a shake. I was pretty sure they hadn't remodeled it since it opened in 1955.

I focused back on Emeline, who was looking through the menu with a small smile on her face.

"I think I should let my father know what Mr. Miller thinks of him."

She giggled but didn't say anything.

Opening the menu, I asked, "Wait, who *is* her father?"

Emeline glanced over the menu. "That would be Jed Miller."

I groaned. "Janet's younger son?"

"That's the one. Anna's his aunt."

"Does Jed have just the one girl?"

Her eyes sparkled. "He has *four* girls."

I was positive my eyes went as wide as saucers.

"And three boys."

"Fucking hell," I mumbled. "Seven more Millers?"

She bit her lower lip and dropped her eyes back to the menu.

Leaning closer, I asked, "Do they all work here at the café?"

Dipping the menu so I could only see her eyes, I could tell she was smiling when the corners crinkled. "They've all worked here at one point, and at the newspaper."

Looking toward the kitchen, I sighed. "The cook?"

"That would be Monty, Jed's youngest son. Monty and Lucy are the only two left in town. The rest all left."

"Fled the town, huh?"

She looked up again, brow raised. "Fled the gossip."

"The gossip they caused, or were they subject to it?"

"Oh, family members aren't excluded when it comes to *The Daily Dirt*."

"Their own grandmother gossiped about them?"

"Yep."

When I didn't say anything, just gaped at her, she laughed and said, "They have an excellent BLT here."

"A BLT? Em, I can make that at home."

"Yeah, but is the bacon from your own farm, with an aioli sauce to die for?"

"Nope, it definitely is not."

I quickly reviewed the menu. When Lucy came back with our waters, we both told her we'd have the BLTs, and I added a Coke to my order. She took our menus, then slipped away.

"So, what would you need from me for this volunteering gig your mother signed me up for?"

Emeline set her water down. "Levi, if you don't want to do it, you really don't have to. Just because my mother guilted you, doesn't mean I'll hold you to it."

"I want to do it. I think it'll be a good way to re-enter the community and ease my way into my father's practice. He's been talking about retiring, and I'm not so sure I'm ready to do this all on my own."

"Was the vet practice you worked at very big?"

"Six vets, and two who were large animals only."

Her eyes went wide. "Wow. I take it you were one of the large-animal vets?"

"Not exclusively, but if the other two vets needed help, I'd step in."

"Are you looking forward to going to a smaller practice?"

I chuckled. "It may be smaller, but it's going to be a lot busier. Dad really should have brought in another vet years ago."

She smiled softly. "Maybe he's been waiting for you to come home."

Sitting back against the seat, I let out a small sigh. "Probably. I know he was upset with me when I decided not to come back to River Falls to work with him. It was what I'd intended, but..."

"Life happened."

"Yes, it did. Not exactly what I'd planned."

"What *were* your plans?"

"School, which I can't believe we never saw each other."

She smiled. "I know."

Sighing I said, "After school, the plan was to go back home to work with my dad. Then, of course, Caroline got pregnant and everything changed. She wanted out of River Falls and longed to live in a big city."

"Would you have gotten married, had she not been pregnant?"

"Your brother asked me the same thing earlier. Honestly, I'm not sure if we would have or not. I loved Caroline once. But we had different ideas about how we wanted our lives to go, and I shelved my dreams so she could have hers. I wouldn't go back and change anything though, simply because it got me Rhett and Brooke. Caroline never told me why she wanted out of River Falls so badly. I think she thought I was the only ticket out, though. And I suspect she was jealous." I shrugged.

"What do you mean, her only ticket out? Anyone can move if they want. And what or who would she be jealous of?" Emeline asked.

"Everything," I said with a frown. "My family, my friends. The fact that my parents were so supportive. You know her father well, so I'm sure you're aware that he was *really* upset when she wouldn't go into the family business. He refused to support her lifestyle if that was the case, so I think she saw me as a way to get out, and as someone else who'd take care of her. She stayed home and took care of Rhett after he was born, but then worked at a law firm as a paralegal."

Emeline leaned forward, her voice lowered. "Levi…are you saying she got pregnant on purpose? To trap you?"

I nodded slightly. "She did."

"That's terrible! And what a dishonest thing to do."

I sighed. "It is."

"I never did like or trust her."

My brows shot up. "Is that so?"

Emeline studied my face, then looked away and shook her head slightly, as if clearing her thoughts. "But…it's all in the past, and you're here now. That should be your primary focus. Helping Rhett and yourself heal from the loss of Brooke and focusing on starting a new life. I think Rhett will love it here."

Smiling, I replied, "You always were positive about everything, Em."

"I try," she replied with a shrug. "It doesn't do me any good to focus on the negative. Besides, I think everything happens for a reason. Maybe you needed to work in a larger clinic to prepare you for working for your dad's practice. And even though you didn't have Brooke for very long, I'm certain she brought immense happiness and joy to your family."

I nodded. "She did. I just hope Rhett adjusts to everything else. He's having fun right now, but he'll be going to a new school, trying to make new friends. He loved kindergarten, but first grade's going to be a whole new thing."

Emeline reached across the table and took my hand in hers. "Levi, everything's going to work out. Rhett will be able to meet kids at the summer camp. He can even go to more than one session if he likes it."

"That's nice of you, Em. I don't want to take up any spots meant for others."

"You won't be. Trust me. Plus, you're doing us a favor by volunteering for the camps. The *least* we can do is let Rhett go to more than one camp. If he doesn't like it, he doesn't have to, of course. He can always hang out with me or Mom. Hell, even Caden will put the little guy to work."

I swallowed the sudden lump in my throat. This was what I'd missed for the last seven years. Friends who would do anything for you, just to help you feel safe and happy. Now, Rhett was going to be able to experience that. If only Brooke had been able to as well.

The sudden feeling of guilt crept up on me, and I pushed it back.

It wasn't my fault she died. It was an accident. An accident.

"Thank you for that, Em. I'd always missed everyone, but I hadn't realized how much. It's good to be home."

Emeline smiled. It wasn't lost on me that she hadn't let go of my hand. When I glanced down, she quickly took it away and looked around the restaurant...probably to see if anyone else had noticed the small gesture of intimacy.

"So, I should get you the dates for the camps, and our current activities. The first one is next month, June. I always leave some open time in the schedule for things that pop up last minute, so it won't be hard to work in your visits with the kids. You can basically do whatever you want."

"It might be nice to just introduce myself and answer questions first, and then maybe throughout the week, I can bring in some animal bones and X-rays. The kids would probably really like that."

"That would be great! I'm assuming you mean of the animals?"

I laughed. "Yes, of animals."

"Why don't you bring Rhett to the ranch one of these days before camp starts, if you have the time. That way he can get the lay of the land and meet everyone, and it won't seem so new to him when camp starts. I know sleepaway camp for the first time can be a bit scary, so if he knows us, it might not be so bad."

"He's met Caden several times, so that's good."

"That *is* good. And I'm sure he'll love the ranch, especially if he loves animals."

"Thank you, Em."

"For?" she asked.

"For being you. For doing this for Rhett and already thinking of ways to make it more comfortable for him. He's had so many huge changes that it'll be nice to have him feel safe and happy again. It's been great seeing him with my mother, of course. They've been baking cookies and pies, and she reads to him every night. Which has been a nice break for me, if I'm being honest."

Frowning, she asked, "Did Caroline never read to the kids at night?"

My chest ached. I'd seen so many signs of Caroline pulling away from me and the kids, and if I'd only left before the accident, Brooke would still be here.

"Caroline wouldn't have won mother of the year, but she did have her moments. The last year or so, she'd been withdrawing. We'd grown apart, and unfortunately that extended to Rhett and Brooke, as well." I exhaled. "But like you said, that's in the past, and it's time to focus on the future."

"God, I'm so sorry again, Levi. That breaks my heart for poor little Rhett. I'm sure you did what you thought was right for your kids. I imagine it would be tremendously hard to take children away from their mother."

"I don't think I wanted to see what was happening. It would've meant admitting to myself that I'd made a big mistake. Brooke and Rhett weren't mistakes," I added quickly. "Don't take it that way."

"I would never. Now, how about we change the subject? I want this homecoming to be a positive experience for both you and Rhett."

Smiling, I said, "A change of subject, yes. Let's do that."

Before I could say anything else, a woman appeared at our table. Her darker blonde hair was plaited into two braids, with flowers woven into both. She wore a white sundress with a flower print, and a lightweight white sweater. She appeared to be in her mid- to upper-twenties and was quite lovely. Her smile lit up the whole café.

"Hey, Emeline."

Sliding out of the booth, Emeline hugged her. "Lilibeth! What are you doing here?"

"I'm here grabbing lunch really quick. Are we still on for our meeting tonight?"

"We certainly are. I spoke with my mother, and she's excited."

Both women looked at me, and I slid out of the booth.

"Lilibeth, this is Levi Tucker. He's a good friend of the family. Well, we all claim him, but technically, he's Caden's best friend. He just moved back to River Falls with his son Rhett, and he'll be working for his father."

"Wait, Oliver and Sam Tucker are your parents?" Lilibeth asked.

"They are."

She smiled even bigger. "I *adore* your parents. Your mother was so helpful when my parents moved to River Falls. Took them right under her wing. And your father got me in touch with Mitch Larson, who owns the building on Main Street where my business is located."

"That's how we met," Emeline added. "My dad told me about Lilibeth and her new perfumery and candle-making store, and I knew I had to meet her."

I smiled. "Mitch is my father-in-law."

Lilibeth let out a soft laugh. "Small-town living. I forget how everyone seems to know everyone else, or is somehow related. I haven't had the chance to meet your wife and kids yet, but when I first met Mitch, he showed me pictures of your kids."

This was the fucking part I hated. Before I had a chance to say anything, Emeline took Lilibeth's hand.

"You remember what I told you about Brooke."

Lilibeth's smile faded in an instant, and she closed her eyes for a brief moment. Looking back at me, she said, "I'm such an idiot. I'm incredibly sorry, Levi. I'm still trying to remember everyone. That was so insensitive of me."

"It's okay, Lilibeth."

A soft smile appeared on her pretty face. "Ignoring the fact that I put my foot in my mouth, I do apologize again."

"There's no need. Rhett and I have moved back to River Falls, and we're ready to start a new chapter."

She chewed on her lower lip, clearly unwilling to ask her next question.

"My wife and I are getting divorced."

"Mitch didn't mention it. I mean, I don't talk to him *that* often, and he did tell me that he has a strained relationship with his daughter."

I nodded. "Yes, they do. But the divorce is for the best, and I'm looking forward to the future."

She lit up again. "Well then, here's to a wonderful new chapter in your life."

Emeline smiled. "You'll figure out pretty fast that Lilibeth is one of the happiest people you'll ever meet. You think *I'm* positive? This woman gives new meaning to the words positive and upbeat."

Lilibeth waved off Emeline. "How old is your son?"

"Rhett is six, and I'm hoping he'll like small-town living better than life in Denver."

"I'm from Denver, too. After high school, I did a little tour of Europe, much to my parents' dismay, but it was a wonderful experience. I've been trying to talk Emeline here into going to Italy with me, but so far I've failed."

Before I could even reply, she went on.

"I'm actually from Castle Rock. Born and raised there, and so were my mother and father. Liam and Whitney Asher. Those are my parents."

I tried not to laugh. This girl was practically vibrating with energy. "We weren't that far apart, it seems. I lived in Highlands Ranch."

Bouncing on her feet, she replied, "I love it! Who knows, we might have crossed paths and not even realized."

I gave a slight shrug. "You never know."

Reaching for Emeline's hand, Lilibeth said, "I should let you get back to your lunch. I didn't mean to interrupt." She turned to face me. "It was a pleasure meeting you, Levi. I hope to see you around."

"Pleasure was all mine," I replied as I gave her a wave and watched her walk away. She wasn't that far off in age from me, and I couldn't help but wonder, when I was ready to jump back into the dating game, if she might be someone I'd want to date. Although, there wasn't the least bit of attraction there. And she wasn't nearly as beautiful as Emeline—

My heart felt like it stopped for a moment as my thoughts hit me like a brick wall.

I looked at Emeline, then back at Lilibeth.

"Talk later, Emeline!" the woman called over her shoulder as she practically skipped toward the counter.

Emeline and I slipped back into the booth.

"She's certainly friendly."

Emeline chuckled. "You have no idea. Lilibeth is a ball of energy who doesn't know how to slow down. She's the sweetest person I've ever met, with a heart of gold to boot. She's going to come to the camps and teach the kids how to make their own perfume and cologne. I think the kids will really love it. She's also going to do a candle-making class with them."

I glanced toward the register and watched as Lucy handed her a bag of food.

"Thank you, Lucy," Lilibeth said with a grin as she turned and headed out of the café, but not before waving once more in our direction. Emeline and I both waved back.

"What brought Lilibeth and her parents to River Falls?" I asked.

"Her mother and father retired here. They were tired of being in the city and wanted to live someplace quiet. Lilibeth wanted to be near them, so she moved here too. Her perfumery on Main Street is so cute. It's *Alice in Wonderland* themed."

"Nice. And good for her. I'm sure the kids will love having her at the camp. Rhett enjoys anything to do with science, so if making perfume and candles calls for mixing things, count him in."

"That's wonderful to hear."

"Is she married?"

The moment the words were out of my mouth, I regretted them.

Emeline's smile faded somewhat as she glanced down at the table and cleared her throat. "No. She's single."

Lucy brought our lunch over and set it down just at that moment. The bacon smelled heavenly. "Anything else I can get you?" she asked.

"I think we're good, thank you, Lucy," Emeline replied, her voice a bit more subdued.

"Her name...Lilibeth. That's kind of like the nickname for Queen Elizabeth. But her nickname was Lilibet, right?"

Emeline nodded. "I'm impressed. Yes, it is, and she was named after said queen. Her mother didn't like Lilibet, so she changed that part to Beth. And her middle name is actually Elizabeth. So, it's Lilibeth Elizabeth."

I screwed up my face. "Twists the tongue."

She grinned, but I could tell it was forced. "It does. But it's different."

We ate in silence for a few minutes before Emeline broke it.

"Are you going to start dating soon?"

Her question took me off guard. "What?"

"You asked whether Lilibeth was single. I just assumed that meant you're going to be jumping back into the dating pool."

I laughed awkwardly. "No, I was more curious than anything. Just trying to get to know all the people in town."

Emeline's mood had definitely changed. And now she suddenly went into business mode. "When did you want to discuss the schedule for your volunteering? We should also decide which camp you want to sign Rhett up for. That is, if he wants to attend."

After wiping my mouth, I set my napkin on the table. "I know you brought your calendar; we could do it now. Or I could stop by the ranch tomorrow and sit down to really take a look, unless you'll be busy. If we wait until tomorrow, I could bring Rhett with me."

She thought for a moment. "Is tomorrow at two okay?"

"Two works great for me."

She nodded as she pulled out her phone. "Then I'll add it to my calendar."

Lucy came by a few minutes later and took our plates.

"Let me get this, since I invited you."

Emeline winked. "Who am I to complain about a free lunch?" It seemed her friendly mood had returned.

"Did you need to get back to the ranch right away?" I asked.

She shook her head. "What did you have in mind?"

Leaning in and lowering my voice, I said, "I'm really intrigued to see Lilibeth's store."

Emeline sat back and cleared her throat. For a moment, I thought she was going to say she needed to get back to the ranch after all. But instead, she smiled. "Why, Levi Tucker, I do believe you've just painted a perfect way to end our lunch date."

I smiled. "Date?"

Her eyes widened and her cheeks turned pink. "I didn't mean it that way. I should have said business lunch."

She bit her lower lip, and my eyes instantly tracked the movement. A strange sensation of warmth filled my chest, and I almost had the urge to reach up and rub it. Instead, I jerked my gaze back up to hers...but it slowly returned to her mouth.

I had the most insane desire to kiss Emeline in that moment.

"We should go," she said, quickly sliding out of the booth, and I followed.

I glanced around the café as we left. A few people gave me curious looks, while others smiled. I sighed internally. *The Daily Dirt* was going to have a field day with this, and they certainly wouldn't call it a "business lunch," that much I knew.

Strangely enough, I wasn't the least bit bothered by that.

CHAPTER FIVE

EMELINE

MY HEART POUNDED IN my chest as I walked out of the café. I drew in a deep breath of fresh air and closed my eyes, willing it to settle down.

Had I imagined that Levi appeared to want to kiss me? In the middle of the freaking café?

Yes, you did imagine it, Emeline Wilde.

I opened my eyes and glanced behind me. Levi had stopped at a table, talking to whoever was sitting there. I hadn't even paid attention to who was in the café. I was too busy trying not to let my emotions show around Levi. The man I'd been crushing on since I'd first learned boys didn't have cooties had actually been sitting directly across from me eating lunch.

I started to pace back and forth in front of the café.

Why did I say *date*? What if someone heard me? Was that why Levi had been stopped? Were they asking him if we're...dating?

"Oh God, *The Daily Dirt*," I whispered.

I leaned against the building and looked up. "If only there was a time machine so I could take it back."

"What a curious thing to say!"

The sudden voice from beside me didn't make me feel any better.

Janet Miller. She owned Main Street Gifts...and was also the writer of *The Daily Dirt*, the gossip column in our local newspaper. The column's motto was, 'We dig up the dirt so you don't have to.' And Janet was good at digging up dirt. She pretended she wasn't the anonymous columnist, but everyone in town knew she was.

To give credit where credit was due, not all of the articles in *The Daily Dirt* were gossip...just the vast majority. I also had a sneaking suspicion that Janet's daughter, Grace, was behind some of the articles. Especially the ones geared toward my family. My mother said Grace had a thing for my father back in high school, and to this day she blames my mom for stealing him away from her. Even though Dad insisted he never once dated Grace—and he didn't meet Mom until they were juniors in college.

"Janet! Hi, how are you?" I asked with a sugary-sweet smile.

"I'm doing well, little Emeline."

I wanted to roll my eyes. The woman was forever calling me *little Emeline*. I was twenty-five years old, for goodness' sake.

"That's good to hear."

Trying not to let her see where my gaze went, I stole a glance into the café. Now would not be a good time for Levi to exit.

He glanced up at that exact moment and held up a finger, silently telling me he'd be right out.

No. No. No! Stay in there, Levi!

"What were you saying about a time machine?" Janet asked.

Acting as if I had no idea what she meant, I replied, "A time machine?"

"Yes, you said if only there was a time machine?"

I frowned. "Are you sure it was me?"

Janet looked around. Various locals were walking by, and she frowned. "I don't recall anyone being near you, but it could have been someone else, I suppose."

"I'd love to stay and chat, but I don't want to keep you."

Janet smiled. "I'm just heading into the café to grab lunch."

"Lunch..."

"Yes, have you eaten yet? You can join me if you'd like."

"In the café? You're going into the café? Right now?"

When her brows slowly drew down, I knew I'd made a fatal error by showering her with all my crazy talk.

Shit. Shit. Shit, Emeline. What is wrong with you?

The door to the café opened, and Levi stepped out. He placed his black cowboy hat on his head as he said, "Sorry about that. I got stopped by one of my father's friends, and let's just say he was lobbing questions about you and me left and right."

I shook my head, feeling slightly panicked. He clearly hadn't even noticed Janet.

"Levi Tucker? Is that you?"

Levi's head snapped to the left, and I watched as all the color drained from his face. "Mrs. Miller, how nice it is to see you!"

She gave him a quick hug, then looked between us—and boy, did she get right to the point. "Are you two a thing? Is your divorce final?"

"No!" we both said at the same time.

"It was a working lunch," I added. "Levi's going to be volunteering at the ranch for our summer camps, and we also discussed his son, Rhett, attending camp."

Janet completely ignored me as she focused solely on Levi. "I heard about you and Caroline. I'm so sorry."

How in the hell had she heard about the divorce?

He forced a smile. "No need to be sorry."

Janet leaned in. "I heard she gave up custody of your little boy. Is that true? Such a shame. I hope that isn't why you two are divorcing."

"The reasons are no one's business," Levi replied bluntly.

"No, of course not. My heart breaks for you three, and I say a prayer for you every night. I'm sure your little one is looking down on you all, though. I'm also sure your mother and father are so happy to have you home."

Clearing his throat, he said, "Yes, they are."

She reached out and placed a hand on his arm. "All the girls in town will be clambering to get your attention." Then she looked at me.

I held up my hands. "Not this girl."

Janet looked between us. "Well, of course not. Levi is so much older than you, little Emeline. There are plenty of single girls in town who'll be ready to go when you are, Levi."

I was two seconds from informing Janet Miller that I was a grown woman when she said, "My granddaughter, Logan, is the vet tech at your father's clinic. *She's* single, and I think she's close to your age. Have you met her yet?"

My mouth dropped open before I quickly shut it. Was she serious right now?

"No, I haven't been by the clinic yet, but it's on my list of things to do this week. I'm sure I'll meet her then."

"I think you're going to just adore her. She was crowned Miss Rodeo two years in a row."

Levi looked at me and smiled. "You still hold the record of four years winning, then?"

"Five. I won the year after I graduated." It was childish of me to correct him, but I was irritated and didn't care at this point.

Janet cleared her throat. "Yes, well, things changed so much after my Logan won. Made it easier for girls to win multiple times."

My arms folded over my chest. "She won *after* me," I corrected. "And isn't she twenty? That's not *close* to Levi's thirty-two, by any means. I'm closer in age to him than she is."

Janet waved me off. "Yes, but she acts older than her age, and I didn't realize you were in your thirties, Levi," she said as she playfully slapped his arm. "You don't look a day over twenty-five!"

Levi forced a smile. "Thank you for that, Mrs. Miller."

"We should probably get to that other meeting," I said to Levi, with another sugary smile in Janet's direction.

"Oh, you two are busy with the meetings, then." Janet winked.

Levi tipped his hat. "It was a pleasure seeing you, Mrs. Miller."

"Have a good day!"

I watched her enter the café. Levi motioned for me to lead the way, and as soon as we were out of view of the restaurant. I stopped and looked at him.

"She's going to write about this, you just watch and see! And she'll say something shitty about *me*, and how you're the perfect match for her precious little *Logan*."

Levi stared at me, his brows drawn together.

"Why are you frowning at me?"

"It's just gossip, Em. Everyone will know that. And do you not like Logan?"

I sighed and started walking again. "I'm sorry. I just get so jumpy around that woman. She's forever writing about my family, I swear. And as far as Logan goes, I don't know her that well. I'm just leery around Janet."

"It'll be fine."

Glancing at him, I said, "You've been gone a long time. You haven't had to deal with the gossip, so it's easy for you to say that. Lord knows what that woman's going to write."

"I think you're worried for nothing. She wouldn't write about me, not with the year I've had."

I raised a brow. "You say that now."

He rolled his eyes. "So, where's the perfume store?"

The other reason I was in a foul mood: Levi wanted to see Lilibeth again. Pointing to the sign, I replied, "Right there. Wonderland Whimsy."

We walked the few remaining yards to the store. I pushed open the door and smiled when I walked in. The place was adorable and full of Lilibeth's personality, so it was easy for my mood to lift.

"Wow, the smell really hits ya," Levi said as he shut the door behind me.

"Hi! Welcome to Wonderland Whimsy. Did you have an appointment for the perfumery?"

When I turned around, I drew in a sharp breath. "Moreen?"

My best friend from high school smiled back at me. "I didn't even see that it was you, Emeline!"

Confused, I asked, "What are you doing here?"

Moreen walked around the counter and gave me a quick hug. "Lilibeth hired me to help out at the shop. It's been a nice change, I've got to tell you that."

Moreen had been working for her mother's catering business, mainly as a waitress, but also helping with the cooking. She'd attended culinary school and hoped to open a bakery in town, but had yet to do so.

She looked past me and her eyes widened in surprise. "Levi?"

He reached out a hand. "Hey, Moreen, it's good to see you."

Absently taking his outstretched hand, she shook it. "Are you visiting?"

"No, I've moved back to River Falls with my son."

A shocked expression transformed her face. "Moved back for good?"

Nodding, he replied, "Yep, for good."

"I didn't think Caroline wanted to live in River Falls."

He gave her a soft smile. "We're getting divorced."

"Oh," Moreen said. "Gosh, I'm so sorry to hear that. I hope you got my family's card and flowers."

With a nod, he stated, "We did. It meant a lot to us, thank you."

When her eyes snapped back to me, I said, "My mother talked Levi into volunteering during the camps, talking to the kids about his job being a vet and taking care of animals."

"Did she? Wow, well, the kids will love that. I usually help Emeline out during the summer camps, but I'm going to be manning the shop here while Lilibeth also volunteers with classes for the kids."

"When were you going to tell me about the job change?" I asked.

She laughed. "Lilibeth hired me just a few days ago. I planned on telling you when we had our weekly lunch."

I knew Moreen had been terribly unhappy working for her mother, so I was glad to see she was able to find something else.

Moreen turned her attention back to Levi. "Let me offer you a tour."

He grinned. "Thanks."

Before she started the tour, she glanced at me and winked. I pushed her lightly and whispered, "Just go, will you!"

Moreen knew how I felt about Levi. How my heart was shattered when he told me he was marrying Caroline and having a baby with her. I assumed it was a simple crush, and not seeing him in so long had gotten me over said crush. Or at least, I thought it had. Seeing Levi again, it was clear those feelings were still there. And if anyone could see that without me saying a single word, it was my best friend.

"So, most of the storefront is the retail side of the business. We have a small section here for kids. The clothing is all made by someone right here in River Falls Valley. Lilibeth tries to obtain as many locally sourced goods as possible. You'll see *Alice in Wonderland* items sprinkled throughout the store, which gives the place that whimsical feel."

Levi reached down and picked up a teabag that had *Alice in Wonderland* on it. He turned it over in his hand, then set it back down before moving on. There were teapots, books, home good items, and more in the space. The store had a little bit of everything for everyone.

"Here are the candles that Lilibeth makes herself. She also has a room upstairs that you can rent out, and where you can make candles."

"It smells so good in here," I said as I picked up a candle for a whiff. "I can't wait for the kids to get to do this."

Levi smiled. "I think they'll have fun with it."

"Back here is the perfumery, where you can make your own fragrances."

Levi looked through the glass windows that separated the space, and said, "It's themed like a speakeasy."

Moreen laughed. "You're right, it is. I'd let you go in, but as you can see, Lilibeth is with someone right now. You two should sign up for this."

I turned my head so quickly to glare at my best friend that I almost got dizzy.

"It might be nice to see what it would be like for the kids, don't you think, Em?" Levi asked.

Moreen's mouth twitched before I turned to look at Levi. "Um, it would be, but I'm sure Lilibeth is booked solid."

"Actually, if you're both free on Friday, I can get you in around five."

I was positive I was shooting daggers at Moreen, who simply stood there with an innocent smile on her face.

Levi pulled out his phone. "I'll have to see if my mother can watch Rhett, but I'm down for a private lesson. Em?"

Trying not to freak out at the idea of spending even more time with Levi, and attempting to hide my feelings, I swallowed and replied, "Sure, that sounds like fun."

Moreen clapped. "Let me go write it down now. Feel free to head upstairs and check out the space up there."

Levi motioned for me to go first. As I climbed the steps, I plotted ways to get Moreen back for this. She was going to pay, that was certain.

"Wow, this is a great space!" Levi enthused as he walked into the large room. It held rows of tables and was decorated in the same speakeasy theme as the perfumery. "And she rents this space out?"

Clearing my throat, I nodded. "Yes, for private parties and such. I hosted a girls' night when Lilibeth first opened to introduce everyone to the place and help promote her business. It's been a hit since. Lilibeth said she even has people from surrounding towns book for birthday and bachelorette parties."

Levi smiled. "With the store below and this space above, I can see why she's doing good. She didn't limit it just to perfumery and candle-making. She made the store a home-goods type business with a little bit of something for everyone. Smart decision."

I smiled. "Did you go to vet school or business school?"

Laughing, he shook his head. "How did you and Lilibeth meet?"

"My mother knows her mom. She helped her get settled here in River Falls, along with your mom and our dads. My father told me about Lilibeth opening Wonderland Whimsy, and I was curious. We met and hit it off. She actually met Ensley first."

"Really?" Levi said as he walked over to the windows that looked out over Main Street. "This is a great spot for the store."

Nodding, I replied, "She's always busy."

"I'm not surprised," he said, leaning against the windowsill and folding his arms across his chest. "Brooke would have loved this, especially the *Alice in Wonderland* theme."

"She liked *Alice in Wonderland*?" I asked as I sat on one of the chairs.

"It was one of her favorites."

I didn't say anything, mostly because I didn't know *what* to say. I chewed on my lower lip and gazed around the room. When Levi finally spoke, I jumped a little.

"I should probably get you back to the ranch. I've taken up way too much of your time."

I stood, then pushed the chair back into place. "Yeah, I should check on Aurora. I'm sorry you didn't get to talk to Lilibeth."

Levi's brow furrowed before he said, "I just wanted to see the store, not talk to Lilibeth again."

"Oh, okay, well...did you want to walk around the store a little more before we leave?"

He shook his head before he motioned for me to go down the steps first, then followed.

Moreen walked up and smiled. "I'd say Lilibeth won't be long, but she's booked for an hour."

"It's okay, we saw her over at the café. Just let her know we stopped by so I could show Levi the store. I'll see her later tonight."

"Tonight? Do you guys have plans?" Moreen asked, a hint of surprise in her voice.

"It's mainly just a business meeting to talk about when she's going to come teach the classes for camp."

"Ah, that makes sense." The bell above the door rang, and Moreen quickly excused herself and greeted the customers.

"I see you two are still the bestest of friends," Levi mused.

"We are. Moreen is my ride-or-die."

"What about Kate? Is she still in River Falls?"

"No, she moved to New York. She's done a few Broadway shows there."

Levi's brows rose. "Wow! That is impressive."

I nodded. "Yeah. She's really happy."

"I thought Moreen wanted to open up a coffee shop or something like that."

"Bakery. I think it's still one of her dreams."

Levi stopped outside the shop and glanced up and down the street. He sighed. "It's good to be home." He met my gaze and held it for a heartbeat longer than he probably should have. "Ready to head back to the ranch?"

A part of me wanted to spend the rest of the day just hanging out with him, but I knew that would never happen. "Ready as ever."

With a smile, he motioned for us to head back to his truck.

CHAPTER SIX

LEVI

I WALKED INTO MY parents' house and set my keys down in the bowl I'd made for my mother when I was in second grade. It sat on an antique table in the foyer of our house. I loved that my mother had kept that bowl in the same spot all these years. It was simple things like that I'd missed most.

The sound of Rhett laughing was like music to my ears. He hadn't had much to laugh about the last few months. The thing I hated the most was the nightmares. He'd wake up crying out for his sister. I had to be thankful that Caroline wasn't fighting me on bringing Rhett back to River Falls. It had been a source of contention for most of our relationship. I'd stupidly thought that after a few years, she'd want to move back home. I was *very* wrong on that.

Being here was healing for Rhett, that much was evident to me. Even in just a few short days, I could see a difference.

The sound of more laughter pulled me from my thoughts. I walked into the kitchen, only to find my son covered in flour.

"What's going on here?" I asked as my eyes scanned the island that was filled with cookies.

"We're baking, Daddy!" Rhett stated before he shoved a cookie into his mouth.

"I see that. Are we expecting an army of soldiers for dinner, and we needed a dessert?"

My mother laughed. "We're going to take them to River Haven tomorrow. It was Rhett's idea to make the cookies to bring to the kids."

My heart swelled with pride and love that my son would think of something so kind. It wasn't a surprise; he was always trying to do kind things or say something nice to someone.

"How did we end up with an orphanage in River Falls?" I asked my mother as I reached for a cookie.

She glanced up at me. "They never taught you in school?"

I shook my head. "Not that I can remember."

A look of confusion appeared on her still beautiful face. There were a few more wrinkles than the last time we were here in town, but my mother said they were simply laugh lines, a sign that you were living a happy life. "You kids used to make ornaments for the trees for the Wilde Christmas event, and they never told you why?"

"I mean, yeah, they told us about the party for the orphanage, but how did it come about?"

She glanced briefly at Rhett, then back to me. "The origin isn't really a happy story."

"I can handle it, Grammy," Rhett said.

Smiling at him, she went back to cutting out cookies from the dough. "Well, a long time ago, religious organizations used to remove Indigenous children from their homes and put them in institutions, to help them learn how to live in our culture. They would go to boarding schools. There was one right here in River Falls. Eventually, over time, it ended up being an orphanage for children who didn't have parents."

"Why did they do that?" Rhett asked. "Take in-did-genrous kids from their mommies and daddies?"

"I wish I could explain it to you, Rhett," my mother said. She glanced at me again. "Maybe this was a subject best waited on for a few years."

I nodded.

"Do they still take them?" Rhett asked. "The kids?"

My hand reached for his head, and I gave his hair a quick ruffle. "No, buddy. They don't."

He nodded. "That's good."

The last thing I wanted was for *Rhett* to think he had to worry about being taken.

My mother gave me an apologetic smile and mouthed, "I'm sorry."

I returned the smile and changed the subject. "So, I went to see Uncle Caden today."

Rhett's eyes lit up. "You did?"

Rhett adored Caden, as had Brooke. He came to visit us often in Denver, which I was thankful for. Besides my parents, he was the only connection I had to River Falls.

"He has a horse that's about to have her first foal."

Rhett gasped. "Can I see it being born?"

"Maybe, if she doesn't have it in the middle of the night."

Bouncing on his toes, Rhett faced my mother. "Did you hear that, Grammy! I might be able to see a horse born."

The sound of my father walking into the kitchen caused us all to turn.

"What's this about a horse giving birth?" Dad asked before he walked up and kissed my mother on the cheek. "How are you, darling?"

She smiled as she replied, "I'm doing wonderful. How was your day?"

"Good. Long, but good."

He grinned at Rhett next and kissed him on the cheek, as well. "You've got some flour on you, bud."

Rhett laughed. "Granddad! I'm baking...of course I have flour on me!"

He held up his hands in mock apology, then turned to me. "Whose horse is in labor?"

"No one yet, but one of the horses over at the Wildes' place is pregnant with her first. It'll be any day now. Caden asked me to come over and take a look at her."

His brows rose. "Caden, huh? I bet that didn't sit well with Emeline. Those horses are her babies."

I chuckled. "She wasn't thrilled her brother went around her, but apparently this horse is Caden's favorite."

Dad grinned, then asked, "Was she close?"

"Yeah, I'd say in the next few days. Rhett wants to see it happen."

My father pointed to his grandson. "A boy after my own heart."

Rhett beamed. "I'm going to be a veterinarian one day and work with you and Daddy."

Dad tossed his head back and laughed. "I'm afraid by the time you get out of school, I'll be too old to still be working. I'll be sittin' back on a beach somewhere, drinking something cold and stiff."

"Stiff?" Rhett asked.

"We're going to let that one go," my mother said, giving Dad a look. "He's already had one conversation that was a bit too mature for his age this afternoon."

Rhett just looked at me, confused, and I winked.

"What's for dinner?" Dad asked as he eyed all the cookies.

"I've got a roast in the Crock-Pot. I'm surprised you didn't smell it."

Dad chuckled. "The only thing this nose smells is sugar and vanilla."

"Let me get this last batch in the oven, then we can eat. The roast is ready."

I walked over to Rhett. "Why don't you head on upstairs and wash up for dinner."

"But I've got to help Grammy clean up our mess," Rhett argued as he motioned to the flour all over the kitchen island.

My mother beamed with pride at my son. "You go on and do what your daddy says, he'll clean for you this time."

Rhett gave me a look that clearly said he was glad it was me, not him, doing the cleaning.

I helped him get the apron off and lifted him down from the chair he'd been standing on. "Wash your hands good, Rhett," I called out as he hightailed it out of the kitchen. Turning to the sink, I grabbed the dishcloth.

"Take off your cowboy hat," Mom said as she motioned with her head.

"Yes, ma'am," I replied, doing as she asked.

After I hung my hat up on the rack by the back door, I got to work cleaning the island while Mom slipped the last batch of cookies into the oven.

"I've got some bread over there we can heat up, Oliver, if you want to do that."

Dad took the bread out of the bag and set it on a small cookie sheet before placing it in the Breville oven I'd bought for them last Christmas.

"That little oven has come in handy more than once," she said with a wink in my direction.

"I'm glad you like it."

The three of us worked in comfortable silence. Once I'd cleaned the island and helped my mother put away all the ingredients she'd used for the cookies, I grabbed four bowls for the roast, along with silverware.

"Are we eating in here or the dining room?"

"Let's go to the dining room. I've been in this kitchen nearly all day. I'm afraid Rhett won't ever want to help me bake or cook again, but he was a good sport about it."

Shaking my head, I replied, "He's loving the time he's spending with you, Mom. Thank you for that."

"It's not a hardship on my part, I can tell you that right now. He's such a kind and well-mannered young man, Levi. You're doing great with him."

"I had good teachers."

Mom grinned. "Flattery will get you everywhere, son."

Rhett came bounding into the kitchen, all cleaned up. "Can I help?"

"Why don't you help me set the table." I motioned for him to head to the dining room. As I placed the bowls down, Rhett followed me with the silverware. "Did you have fun today with Grammy?"

He looked at me and smiled. "Yep! We sure made a lot of cookies today. I tried not to eat a whole lots, but it was hard."

I chuckled. "I bet it was. Rhett, I was talking to Emeline, who's Caden's sister. She takes care of all the horses on the ranch."

"Have I met her before?"

With a shake of my head, I answered, "No, you haven't met her yet. She's a good friend of mine, just like Caden. Anyway, she also runs a summer camp on the ranch. Would you be interested in going? They do all kinds of things, like horseback riding, hiking, archery, learning how to make things, and the campers even get to help around the ranch, so they can see what being a rancher is like."

He stopped and looked at me. "Like an overnight camp?"

Nodding, I replied, "Yes, it would be an overnight camp. But I thought it might be a good way to meet some of the kids you'll be going to school with. You'd be grouped in the cabins by age."

He narrowed his little blue eyes and asked, "Will girls be there?"

"I believe so, but not in your cabin. Is that a problem?"

I watched as the wheels turned in his head. "Nah, but will they be on their own side of the camp?"

Laughing, I said, "I'm not sure. We can ask Emeline more questions if you want. She said I could bring you to the ranch, and she'd give you a tour of the campgrounds. She gave one to me today. And I'll be at the camp as well, volunteering the week you'll be there. Actually, I think I roped myself into volunteering for each session."

"What's this about volunteering each session, where?" my mother asked as she walked into the dining room, followed by my father. They set the food down on the table and my stomach growled. Man, had I missed my mother's cooking.

"When I was at the Wildes' earlier this morning, Vivianne somehow managed to get me to agree to volunteer at the camp this summer."

My mother laughed. "Doing what?"

"Talking about being a vet. I was going to discuss it with you first, Dad. I know you're eager for me to start at the clinic."

My father wasn't wasting any time piling his bowl up with roast. "I haven't added any additional appointments, so I don't see a problem with you helping out. Just give me the dates you'll be there. I figured we would start you out part time, anyway. And once you feel comfortable, move you to full time. When you're feeling good about things, I'll cut back my hours. I think you volunteering at the camp is a good thing, though," he said, glancing over at me. "I wish I'd made it a higher priority to participate in more community activities. If I can offer one piece of advice, take the time to volunteer when you can."

"First of all, you *did* volunteer, Dad."

"When you were younger, yes. However, as time passed, and especially after you were gone, I focused increasingly on my work. River Falls may be small, but there are a plethora of animals to treat."

I nodded. "Second, I think your timeline sounds like a great plan."

"With the growth of the town, though, you might want to think about hiring a part-time vet once you get dug in."

"I can do it!" Rhett stated.

I winked at him. "I'll hold a spot for you until you graduate, buddy."

My parents laughed.

"I'm sure Caden was happy to see you and know you're home for good," Mom said, handing me the roast.

After fixing Rhett a bowl, I worked on my own. "He was. It'll be nice, being able to just drop by to see him."

"How's he doing? Vivianne told me he's never been the same after Rachel left him. He's more…" Her words trailed off.

"Moody?" my father added with a gruff sound.

I sighed. "Yeah, she really raked him over the coals."

"What does that mean?" Rhett asked.

"It means she didn't treat him very well," Mom replied.

"Every time he came to visit after the breakup, he wasn't in the best of moods, but he put on a good show for the kids. He seemed almost like his normal self when I saw him at the ranch today."

"Well, that's good. He needs to get back on the horse and get out there," my father said.

Rhett looked at me. "How come he isn't riding his horse? Doesn't he need it to work on the ranch?"

I grinned. "It's just a saying, Rhett." To my father, I added, "I think he's okay. They were together for a long time, and it's hard to walk away from someone whom you've given so much of your life to."

My mother's eyes turned sad as she looked at me.

Before she could say anything, I smirked. "I ran into Janet Miller today."

Her eyes turned from sad to bewildered. "At the ranch?"

"I can do you one better. Outside Anna's—after I finished having lunch with Emeline."

Dad groaned, while my mother shook her head.

"*The Daily Dirt* will have you featured this week," Mom said, giving me a look.

"Emeline said the same thing. She also told me that Janet, or her daughter Grace, seems to write a lot about the Wildes. Is that still happening?"

With a roll of her eyes, my mother nodded. "It is. I don't know what that family has against the Wildes, but they certainly seem to enjoy stirring up drama for them. Don't be surprised if you're connected to Emeline now."

"I just got back into town. I'm not even divorced yet."

"Do you like Emeline?"

The three of us turned and looked at Rhett. He didn't seem upset, but I knew my son. He could hold his emotions in like a champ, until the dam finally broke.

"Of course I do, as a friend."

He nodded and moved his fork around his bowl. "I wouldn't be mad if you liked her like a girlfriend. I want you happy, Daddy."

My breath caught in my throat, and I couldn't form words to speak. Thank goodness my mother came to my rescue.

Reaching for my son's hand, Mom smiled. "That is so sweet of you, Rhett. I'm sure when the time comes, your daddy will find someone who'll love both of you to the moon and back."

Rhett smiled. "And maybe I'll be able to have another little sister. Or a brother."

Just when I thought I could speak again, he drops *that* little bombshell.

My mother looked at me and softly replied, "Baby steps, Rhett. Baby steps."

CHAPTER SEVEN

EMELINE

MY PHONE BUZZED AND I picked it up to see it was Moreen, calling me again. I'd tried to avoid her calls because I knew she would have a million-and-one questions about Levi. I drew in a deep breath, let it out, then answered.

"Hey, girl, what's up?"

"What's. Up?" she replied. "Um, should we start with the fact that you've been ignoring me for the last twelve-plus hours? Let's start there, then move on to you having lunch with Levi Tucker. Why didn't you tell me he was back in town? He's getting divorced from she-who-shall-not-be-named! Why were you guys in the store? How are you feeling? Have those old feelings for him come back?"

"Oh my gosh, Moreen, slow down with the questions, will you?"

"I'm sorry, Emeline, this is HUGE. The one guy you've been crushing on since you were fourteen is back in town, single, and having lunch with you. Excuse me for freaking the fuck out!"

I sighed and closed my eyes. "Okay, I get the freak-out, but slow down anyway."

"Sorry, it's just...you've been avoiding me, then you had plans with Lilibeth last night and..."

Her voice trailed off, and I felt terrible for avoiding her. "You know you'll always be my very best friend, Moreen."

"I know that, but it's nice to hear it sometimes."

Now I could hear the smile in her voice. "It was a business meeting about the camp. Lilibeth is going to teach the kids how to make candles, perfume, and cologne. You know that. We were working out times and days she'd be able to make it work."

"I think the kids will love that. Now that we got that out of the way—*Levi?*"

Laughing, I leaned back in my chair and looked at my office door, which was closed. "I had no idea Levi was back in town until yesterday when he arrived at the ranch and met with Caden. He wanted him to check on one of the horses. Then the next thing I knew, he was asking me to lunch to talk about his son, Rhett, coming to camp. My mother may have also roped him into volunteering at the sessions before he gets too busy at the vet clinic."

"Go, Mrs. Wilde."

Sighing, I dropped my head back against the chair. "God, Moreen, I thought I'd gotten over this stupid crush on him."

"No such luck, huh?"

I stared up at the ceiling. "Nope. The moment I saw him, all those feelings came rushing back. I felt like I was in high school again. It's like my body woke up from a slumber I hadn't even realized it was taking for years. It was like... something supernatural. Like I could drag in a full breath for the first time in ages, just the strangest feeling. And it's all for naught because Levi Tucker will never see me as anything other than his best friend's little sister. And what kind of person lusts after a man who's going through a divorce and has lost a child? A monster! That's who."

"You are not a monster, Emeline. Don't be so dramatic. You're a girl who likes a boy who happens to be married."

"Ugh, Moreen. You can't say that anymore. He's definitely not a boy, and I'm not a girl. Plus, he's almost divorced."

"He's home for good, then?"

"Yes," I said on a sigh. "My heart breaks for him and Rhett. I can't even imagine. I tried so hard not to look at him as anything other than a friend, but those eyes. That mouth. His body! I had dreams last night, and let's just say they were R-rated. I woke up panting. *Panting*, Moreen. How am I going to be around him on a regular basis?"

"You'll be fine," she said. "You did it before, you'll do it again. Just remind yourself that he's off limits."

"Is he, though?"

She paused for a moment. "Okay, so he may be separated from his wife. But like you said, he isn't divorced yet, Emeline. He's had a traumatic loss, and if I had to guess, the last thing he's looking for is a relationship."

"Especially with his best friend's little sister, who's younger than him by seven years."

"What are you going to do?"

I thought about it for a moment. "There isn't anything I *can* do except be his friend. I need to push the idea of being with Levi Tucker out of my mind for good. Maybe now that he's back, I'll see how different our lives are. I mean, he's a father, and we have nothing in common. Right?"

"Um, I don't know about that," Moreen replied. "Okay, here's one! You're not ready to be a mother."

I bit my lip. That was something my best friend was wrong about. Why did she think I loved our summer camps so much? I adored kids, and I couldn't wait to have my own someday.

A light knock on my door had me sitting up. "Got to go, someone's here."

"Dinner tonight?" Moreen asked.

"Come in!" I called out. "Not sure yet, I'll text you later."

The door opened, and I expected to see my mother. Instead, the man I'd just vowed to move on from stood there with a brilliant smile on his face—and standing next to him, a mini version of Levi.

Yeah, there was no way I could push these feelings away.

"Okay, talk soon!" Moreen said as I hit the end button and stood.

"Levi, I wasn't expecting you until later this afternoon."

"Rhett was dying to come and see Aurora, and I thought I'd check in on her."

Rounding my desk, I smiled, then crouched to greet Rhett. I held out my hand. "Hi, Rhett. We haven't met yet. I'm Emeline Wilde."

Rhett's deep blue eyes sparkled as he smiled. "I'm Rhett Tucker, and it's a pleasure to meet you, ma'am. Are you dating anyone?"

Surprised, I jerked my head up to glance at Levi, who closed his eyes for a moment, clearly in exasperation. "I'm so sorry, Emeline. Rhett here knows better than to ask things like that."

"I wasn't asking for *you*, Dad. I was asking for me."

That time, I laughed. "For you, huh?"

He tipped his little black cowboy hat, and Levi let out a groan. This young man didn't act like a six-year-old. More like a sixteen-year-old.

"Well, Rhett. To answer your question, no, I'm not dating anyone. I'm afraid you're just a little too young for me, though."

"You could wait a few years."

I bit my lip so I wouldn't laugh again. Nodding, I gave him a thoughtful look, but before I could say anything else, Levi spoke.

"Rhett Tucker, I know you did *not* just say that."

Rhett shrugged his shoulders. "You always tell me it never hurts to ask. The worst that can happen is you're told no. So I took a chance."

I stood and covered my mouth with my hand and stared at Levi, who was also trying hard not to laugh.

"I *did* say that, but this is different. You're a little boy, and Ms. Emeline is a grown woman."

Why did it heat my body to hear Levi say those words?

Rhett kicked at nothing on the ground, then looked up at me and flashed a smile. "You don't have to wait for me, Ms. Emeline. But if you're not married in..." He closed his eyes and started counting on his fingers before looking at me and saying, "Twelve years, maybe we can talk then."

"Dear God," Levi said, scrubbing his hands down his face.

Smiling, I held out my hand again. As we shook, I said, "It's a deal."

Rhett grinned, then added, "And if you and my dad fall in love and get married, I'd be okay with that, too."

My eyes shot back to Levi. He simply shook his head and gave me a look that said, *Let it go*.

Clearing my throat, I said, "Shall we go see Aurora?"

Rhett fist pumped. "Yes!"

I motioned for Rhett to head back out of my office, where we ran into my mother.

"Mom!" I said, a little too eager. "Levi brought Rhett to see Aurora."

My mother bent down to say hi to Rhett. "My goodness, you've grown since the last time I saw you."

The little boy looked slightly concerned. "I don't remember you. I'm sorry."

Laughing, Mom said, "You were pretty young when your daddy brought you to visit, when your sister was just a baby, so I'm not surprised you don't remember."

I looked at Levi to see if my mother's mention of Brooke caused any pain, and it didn't appear that it did. As if he could feel my eyes on him, he returned my gaze.

I forced a casual smile, then looked back at my mother and asked, "Have you seen Aurora this morning?"

"I was here early enough to see you'd slept in her stall last night, Emeline Wilde."

I felt my cheeks heat.

"You slept in her stall?" Levi asked.

"I think she's close, and I wanted to make sure she was okay. Marshall took the first half of the night, and I came in around one in the morning to take over. He's back out there with her now."

Levi nodded. "Is she showing signs?"

I rolled my eyes. "She's a horse, and a stubborn one. She'll drop that baby while she's eating her oats, most likely."

We all laughed, and a second later, Rhett joined in, having no idea why we were laughing.

My mother took the boy's hand. "Come on, Rhett, let's go see how she's doing."

They started down the aisle of the barn. Levi took hold of *my* hand to keep me in place, and I ignored the flutter in my stomach at the contact.

"If we could hold back for just a moment," he said. His brown eyes were filled with worry.

"Sure, what's up?" I hoped my voice sounded void of any jitters, but if he didn't let go of my hand soon, I'd be swooning at any moment.

Seeming to realize he was still holding my hand, Levi dropped it like it was a hot potato. "I'm sorry about what Rhett said, about you and me."

I waved off his concern. "Don't even worry about it."

"I haven't talked to him at all about moving on with anyone, let alone you."

Don't let your feelings show on your face, Emeline.

"Of course not me. What a crazy idea," I managed to say, but even I could hear the hurt in my voice.

He frowned slightly, then went on. "I think he's in a weird place right now, with Caroline giving him up and us moving here. I think he feels like if we start over with a new family, everything will be better. I tried to tell him on the way over here that I wouldn't be dating anyone anytime soon, but my mother said he's worried about me and thinks I'm sad." He started walking, so I followed suit. With a soft laugh, he said, "I guess he thinks I need to be dating to be happy. I'd like to show him that I'm happy with it just being the two of us."

"So you're not going to date at all?" I asked before I could stop myself.

He shrugged. "I mean, I don't have any desire to date anyone right now. I've got a lot of emotional baggage I'm carrying around, and the last thing I'd want is to unload that on some poor woman. Not to mention, I'm a package deal. Not sure how many women in River Falls would want to become an instant mother. I'm not saying if the right person came along that couldn't change, though."

I nodded. "Have you thought about family therapy?"

"We did some back in Denver, after losing Brooke. But yeah. I think it would be a good idea to consider going again. Especially if my son is going to go around trying to solicit women for me."

Laughing, I replied, "Well, if I do say so myself, your son has good taste in women."

Levi glanced at me, his eyes landing on my mouth briefly. I tried not to overthink it.

With a devil-may-care smile, he replied, "He does."

I quickly turned my head and faced forward. "How great would it be if Aurora decided to have her foal while you guys were here?"

He chuckled. "That would be pretty—"

"Daddy!" Rhett cried out. "Daddy, come quick!"

Without hesitating, Levi raced toward his son. "What's wrong?"

We rounded the corner, and Marshall was standing in the aisle. "I was just about to call you, Emeline. She's in labor."

"What perfect timing, Aurora!" my mother gushed. "I'd better call Caden."

I rushed into the stall behind Levi. After a quick examination, he looked over at his son. "You're about to get your wish, Rhett."

The boy remained calm, but he gave me a little fist bump. He looked up at me and smiled. "This is the best day ever! I hope Brooke is watching down on us."

Reaching for his hand, I gave it a soft squeeze. "I know she is."

Levi let out a long sigh. "That mare is one hell of a good mother."

I smiled as I watched Aurora with her colt, who'd just gotten to his feet and was making his way around his mother. Rhett was sitting off to the side, taking it all in.

"What do you think, Rhett?" Caden asked. "Have any good names for the little guy?"

Surprised, I glanced at my brother. Aurora was his horse, so he had every right to let Rhett name the colt, but he also loved Aurora like no animal we'd had before.

Rhett beamed up at Caden, who'd clearly become the boy's BFF. Tapping his finger on his chin, he thought hard. "How about Whiskey?"

"Whiskey?" Levi and Caden said at the same time as I pressed my lips together hard to keep from laughing.

"Where in the world did you come up with that?" Levi asked.

Rhett shrugged. "That's the name of the brown cat in Grammy and Grandpa's barn. They have the same color."

Caden and Levi exchanged grins.

Levi stated, "It's not a star or constellation."

Caden's eyes sparkled, "I think Whiskey's a great name, and since you helped your father deliver him, and he's my horse," he looked at me and winked, "then Whiskey it is."

Rhett's eyes lit up with pure joy. "Do you mean it, Uncle Caden? We can really name him Whiskey?"

It was the first time I'd heard my brother laugh so genuinely, from the heart, since his breakup. I looked over to see my mother smiling.

Caden looked at Levi. "If your dad's okay with it."

Levi raised his hands. "Who am I to stand in the way of a perfect name?"

Rhett looked like he was about to jump in his excitement. But then looked at the mare and colt, and thought better of it. Instead, he wrapped his arms around Caden's legs. "Thank you, Uncle Caden! This really *is* the best day ever!"

"You ready to see where the camp is?" I asked.

He looked to his father who nodded.

"If Emeline is ready, we're ready."

Turning to Marshall, I asked, "You'll keep an eye on them for a bit?"

He nodded. "Don't worry, I've got it under control."

"And I'm not going anywhere," Caden said as he made his way over to Aurora and stroked her neck gently.

Turning to Levi and Rhett, I said, "We can all get into the Mule and drive over to the campsite."

Levi motioned for me to lead the way. "Sounds good."

With one more look at Aurora and her colt, I turned and headed out of the barn and toward the arena, where the Mule was parked. It seated four and would make the trip to the campgrounds fast and easy.

"When does the first camp start again? I meant to ask you or your mom yesterday."

"The second week of June."

"Is it almost June?" Rhett asked his father.

"A few more weeks, buddy."

Rhett asked his father a few questions about the colt, and his father patiently answered them all. It was so adorable listening to the two of them talk.

"When will Whiskey stop drinking from his mother?"

"Usually around seven to nine months he will stop nursing."

"Will he stay with her?"

"He'll stay close until he's weaned, then he won't need his mom anymore."

After that, Rhett remained quiet until we got to the campground and continued his silence as we toured the cabins and other areas of the camp. We ended the tour in the main building's living room.

"What do you think, Rhett?" I asked. "Would you like to attend camp here this summer?"

He smiled up at me. "Will you be here every day?"

"Yep. And your father will be in and out, as well."

Rhett looked around the large room before finally facing his father. "So not all kids need their mother?"

Levi's brows drew down. "What are you talking about, Rhett?"

"You said the colt won't need his mother after he's weaned. Does that mean I've been weaned from my mom? So I don't need a mother anymore?"

I could see the instant his son's words registered. The pain on Levi's face nearly caused me to cry. I slowly started to back out of the room, thinking this was a moment for father and son, but Levi caught my eye and shook his head.

"No, please stay."

Nodding, I sat down on a love seat and watched as Levi took his son's hand and walked him over to a larger sofa. They sat, and Levi drew in a deep breath before slowly letting it out.

"Rhett, no matter how old we get, our parents—both mothers and fathers—play a very important role in our lives. I still need my parents sometimes. Like when we decided to move here to River Falls. They said we could stay with them until we found a place of our own. I go to them for advice, or when I'm feeling sad. They're also some of the first people I want to share any happy news with."

Rhett looked down at the floor. "Then how come *my* mommy doesn't want me anymore?"

The saying "felt like my heart broke in two" had never been more real to me than in that moment. I wanted to walk over, sweep that child up into my arms, and hug him hard.

"Your mother does want you, Rhett. She's just in a really bad place right now."

"'Cause of Brooke?" he asked.

Levi nodded. "She's really sad still. She's kind of lost right now."

"I'm sad still. And I know *you're* sad still. I hear you talking to Brooke sometimes, and then I hear you cry."

Tears filled my eyes. *Oh gosh. Oh gosh. I shouldn't be here.*

I started to stand, but Levi shot me a look, and I sat back down. I quickly wiped my tears from my cheeks.

"I *am* sad still, and so are Grammy and Grandpa. Your

mom, though, well...she was in the car when the accident happened, and she's having a tough time with that."

"'Cause it was her fault?"

My eyes widened.

"It wasn't her fault, Rhett."

He stood and balled his little fists. "It *was* her fault! She made Brooke go with her, and I hate her for that! I never want to see her again!"

Rhett turned and ran. When Levi didn't make a move to follow him, I did. Rhett ran outside and across to one of the cabins and sat down on the steps, dropping his head onto his arms, which were folded around his knees. I quickly made my way over to him.

"May I sit down next to you?"

He looked up, and when I saw the tears, I nearly dropped to the ground. He nodded jerkily.

Sitting, I swallowed the lump in my throat and drew in a slow, deep breath before letting it out. "I never got to meet your sister Brooke. What was she like?"

His little mouth quivered with a slight smile. "She was loud."

I laughed, and he smiled.

"She really liked her Barbies and playing with all her horses. She had lots of toy horses."

"Did she like the horse?"

He nodded. "Yeah. Daddy teached us how to take care of her."

"It was a mare, huh?"

"Her name was Thunder. 'Cause when she ran, it sounded like thunder."

I smiled. "What did she look like?"

"Like Aurora. She liked Brooke a lot."

"Did you both ride her?"

He nodded, then wiped a tear away. "I miss my sister, Ms. Emeline."

Wrapping my arm around him, I said, "I know you do, bud. And I don't think you really meant to tell your daddy that you hate your mommy."

He looked up at me. "She doesn't want me."

"I think she's just sad right now."

He fiercely shook his head. "She doesn't want me."

My heart tore apart. "Why do you say that?"

Suddenly, he looked worried.

"Rhett...you can tell me."

"You won't tell my daddy?"

I chewed nervously on my lower lip. "I wish I could make you that promise. But I can't."

He sighed. "She told me so."

Drawing back just enough to look at him, I asked, "Wait, your mother told you she didn't want you? In those words?"

The poor little thing nodded.

"When?"

He shrugged.

"Was it before or after Brooke went to Heaven?"

Those deep blue eyes, which were the same as his mother's, looked up at me and filled with tears once again. "It was before. Brooke and I were playing, and I threw my soldier to make him fly, and he hit Brooke's eye. She started crying, and Mommy came into the room and yelled at me."

"Do you remember exactly what she said?"

He looked down at the ground and sniffled. "She told me not to ever tell Daddy, or anyone else, because she only said it 'cause she was mad."

I moved to crouch in front of him. Using my finger, I lifted his chin. "Rhett, no one—not even your mother or father—should say or do *anything* to hurt you, then tell you not to tell anyone else. That means *they've* done or said something bad, not you."

A tear slipped down his cheek—and that was when I made a vow to protect this child with everything I had.

"She...she said she never wanted me, and that she was glad me and Brooke didn't share the same father. I didn't know what that means, and I asked her. She got really, really mad, and told me to never tell Daddy what she said."

I nearly fell back onto my ass. Had Brooke *not* been Levi's daughter? Did he know?

I took both of his hands in mine. "She *did* want you, Rhett. Sometimes people who are unhappy say things to make *other* people unhappy. Even the people they love. It doesn't mean they actually mean it."

"But when Mommy fought with Daddy, she took Brooke and was gonna leave us. I wanted to stay with Daddy anyway, but I think she really didn't want me."

Lord help me, this is way over my head.

"You know what?"

"What?"

"None of that matters because you and your daddy are now in River Falls, and your sister is up in Heaven, watching all the adventures you're going to go on. She'll be with you the whole time."

He placed his hand on his heart. "Grammy says she's here, all the time."

I smiled. "Yes, she is. All the time."

Rhett suddenly lunged forward and wrapped his arms around my neck, squeezing me tightly. "Thank you, Ms. Emeline."

Hugging him back, I fought to keep my tears at bay. "Always, Rhett. I'll always be here for you."

CHAPTER EIGHT

LEVI

IT TOOK EVERYTHING I had not to go over to Rhett and Emeline. At first, they were sitting next to each other on the steps, then Emeline moved in front of Rhett. When I saw him wipe away a tear, I nearly walked over. Something inside of me told me to stay where I was.

Then Rhett threw his arms around Emeline and hugged her.

My knees about buckled out from under me as I stood there and watched my son show more emotion with Emeline than I'd ever seen him show to *anyone*. His therapist had said Rhett kept his feelings inside, and that was mostly okay because he at least talked to me about them sometimes. I just had to continue to be patient and let him know I was there anytime he needed me.

I thought back to a few minutes ago, when he'd declared that he hated his mother. Granted, Caroline wasn't the perfect mother, but she loved her children. I was sure of that.

Wasn't I?

Emeline stood, took Rhett's hand, and headed back to me. When I saw her face, I instantly knew something was wrong.

As she approached, she forced a smile. "I was thinking it might be kind of fun for Rhett to see the working side of our operation. Maybe Caden can show him what it's like to ride out on the ranch, if he's an experienced-enough rider."

Confused by the request, I replied, "He is. Is that something you'd like to do, Rhett?"

His eyes lit up. "Be like a real cowboy?"

Emeline chuckled. "Yep. But we need to go back inside and get your cowboy hat. Would you mind doing that while I call Caden?"

She wasn't giving me much of a choice in the matter. "Um, yeah, let's go get your hat, bud."

Emeline dropped Rhett's hand, pulled out her phone, and walked away.

As we walked back into the main building of the camp, I asked, "Everything okay?"

Rhett nodded. "I like Ms. Emeline a whole lot."

I smiled. "Yeah, she's one of a kind."

"Do you like her?" he asked as he placed his black cowboy hat onto his head.

"Sure, I like her."

"Will you date her?"

I let out a laugh. "I like Emeline as a friend. I've *always* liked her as a friend, but I don't feel that way toward her."

Except, suddenly, I felt like I was telling my son a lie.

He frowned.

"You're sure you're okay? Did you want to talk about what you said earlier?"

Rhett shook his head. "Not right now. I wanna go riding."

Giving him a nod, I said, "Well, let's go see if Uncle Caden is free."

As we walked back outside and toward the Mule, I saw a truck pulling up. It was the ranch truck, and sitting inside were Caden and his younger brother, Gatlin. You couldn't ask for more authentic cowboys than these two. Both got out, Gatlin basically identical to Caden in jeans, boots, a T-shirt that said River Falls Cattle, and a dark cowboy hat. His face exploded into a wide grin.

"If it isn't Levi Tucker!"

I walked toward him and reached my hand toward his outstretched one. We shook, then Gatlin pulled me into a quick hug, slapping the shit out of my back. He may have been younger than Caden by five years, but they might as well have been twins. The only difference in their physical appearance was that Caden's eyes were the color of the sky, and Gatlin's looked more gray.

"It's good to see you, Gatlin."

"I couldn't believe it when Caden told me you were back for good!" He glanced down and smiled at Rhett. Tapping his hat, he asked, "And who's this cowboy?"

"Rhett, this is Gatlin, Caden and Emeline's brother."

Reaching his hand out to shake Gatlin's, Rhett said, "Can I call you Uncle Gatlin?"

Gatlin glanced at me, then down to Rhett. "Hell yes, you can!"

Smacking her brother on the arm as she walked back up, Emeline said, "Gatlin! Language."

Looking sheepish, he replied, "Not used to littles."

"It's okay, it's not like he hasn't heard a curse word."

Rhett nodded. "My daddy says 'fuck' all the time."

"*Rhett*," I warned.

He covered his mouth with a hand and giggled.

"Little dude, how would you like to go riding with me and Caden? Maybe help us check on some cows?"

I watched as my son nearly exploded with excitement. "Can I, Daddy? Please?"

"He's a good rider, but you'll give him a calm horse? And no running. He's not there yet."

"I can run!" Rhett argued.

Caden grinned as he reached down and lifted Rhett effortlessly. "I promise we'll keep him safe, Levi."

I walked over and kissed Rhett on the cheek. He tried to squirm away as he pushed me and said, "Dad, not in front of Emeline!"

Holding up my hands in surrender, I took a few steps back. "Sorry. Listen to Uncle Caden and Gatlin, okay?"

Caden glanced at his sister.

"Thirty-minute ride?" she replied to the unspoken question. "We'll meet you at the barn."

"Sounds good," Caden said before they turned and headed to the truck.

Once they were driving off, I looked at Emeline. "So? Why did you send my son away?"

She swallowed hard. "There's something I need to tell you. Something that Rhett shared with me, and I thought it was best if he didn't see your reaction."

Panic instantly hit me square in the chest. "What is it?"

Wringing her hands, she motioned for us to go back into the building. She walked to the kitchen and retrieved a bottle of water from the fridge. "Do you want one?"

"What I want is for you to tell me what's going on, Emeline."

Sliding onto a barstool, Emeline closed her eyes, then opened them again. "I have to ask you a question first."

"Ask it," I said brusquely. I knew I was being rude, but I wanted to know what the hell was going on.

"Is Brooke..." She closed her eyes again and whispered *fuck*. Opening them, she met my gaze. "Is Brooke your biological daughter?"

Taking a step back, I let out a humorless laugh. "What the hell kind of question is that, Emeline?"

"Rhett was *really* upset."

I folded my arms over my chest and glared. "Yes, I witnessed that too."

She let out a breath. "He told me that his mother said she didn't want him."

I started to say something, but she held up her hand.

"Let me just get it all out. I asked him if she'd said that before or after Brooke had gone to Heaven. He said *before*. Then he said that Caroline had told him not to tell anyone... including you."

My arms dropped to my sides as I balled my fists. "Go on."

"Rhett said that one day when he was playing with his sister, he threw one of his soldiers into the air and it hit Brooke. She started crying, and Caroline came into the room and got mad at Rhett."

She paused, like she was second-guessing telling me this.

"Keep going."

Another exhale before she said, "Caroline told him that she'd never wanted him...and that she was glad Brooke and Rhett didn't have the same father. He didn't understand what she meant, of course. And when he asked, I think she must've realized what she let slip. She told him she didn't mean it, she was just upset, and that he wasn't to ever tell anyone, including you."

Confused, I leaned back against the counter. "She told Rhett she'd *never* wanted him?"

Emeline nodded, then frowned. "That was the part that stuck out the most?"

"You're referring to the part about not having the same father. Is that why you asked if I was Brooke's father? You think I'm not?"

With a shrug, Emeline replied, "What else am I supposed to think, Levi? A six-year-old wouldn't make up something like that. So I figured maybe she had an affair, and Brooke was a result. You said you were having problems in your marriage, so when Rhett told me that…"

Her voice trailed off.

Scrubbing my hands down my face, I drew in a deep breath and let it out. "How could she tell him she didn't want him?"

Emeline slowly shook her head. "I don't know. It broke my heart in two. I'll be honest with you, I wanted to choke Caroline. Then Rhett hugged me, and I nearly lost it. I knew I couldn't tell you any of this in front of him since he was already so worried about telling you."

Pushing off the counter, I started to pace. "I'm fighting between calling Caroline and bitching her out, and driving to Denver to personally confront her. Ask her what the hell she meant by them not sharing the same father."

"Don't be mad at me but…did Brooke look like you?"

"Yes! Even my mother used to comment on how much Brooke looked like me as a baby." I shook my head. "She was *my* child, Emeline. I know deep inside my soul that she was mine."

She stood and walked over to me, taking my hands in hers. "If you don't ask Caroline, you'll second-guess it for the rest of your life, Levi. But, in the end, it won't matter. Because you loved her and she loved you."

The feel of her hands in mine caused a strange sensation in my entire body that I quickly attempted to ignore. I didn't want to admit to myself how good it felt to have a woman touching me so tenderly.

As if reading my mind, she dropped my hands and took a step back. I reached into my back pocket and pulled out my phone. Hitting Caroline's number, I drew in a breath.

"I'll leave."

"No!" I said quickly. "Please stay."

Looking as if she wanted to be anywhere but here, she slid back onto the stool.

"What is it, Levi? I have a friend over."

"Hello to you, too, Caroline."

She let out a soft laugh. "Hello. If you're calling about the divorce papers, I'll sign them. I've been...busy."

"I'm calling because I want to know why you told Rhett that he and Brooke didn't have the same father. He has no idea what you meant. But I have a feeling *I* do."

The line went silent. Then she cleared her throat. "I was angry that day, Levi. You and I had been fighting, and I just vented."

"To our *son*? How old was he when you told him you never wanted him, Caroline?"

"It was before the accident. The day before."

"Fucking hell! How do you even say that to your own child?!"

"Because Rhett loved *you*, Levi! He worshiped the ground you walked on, and Brooke was following his lead. It was said out of anger, and I *told* him I didn't mean it. That I said it because I was upset with you and not him."

"Then you go and give him up. Do you know he said he hated you today?"

A sharp intake of breath came across the phone. She was silent again before she spoke. "Maybe it's better that he does. I'm not sure I can be a mother to him."

"What in the hell are you talking about?"

"I think he's better off without me in his life. He'll be happier, and you and I won't have to see one another."

"You hate me so much that you'd walk away from your own kid?" When she didn't say anything, I asked, "Was I Brooke's father?"

"Yes, of course you were."

"Why did you say that to Rhett?"

"I don't know."

I let out a humorless laugh. "You don't know?"

"She is...she *was* your daughter."

"Did you at any time think she might not be?" I asked, feeling a sickness roll through my entire body at the thought of Caroline cheating. When she didn't say anything yet again, I pressed, "Caroline?"

"It was a short affair, and I was lonely."

My knees almost buckled, and Emeline jumped up and reached for me.

"Are you okay?" she asked.

"Who is that?" Caroline barked.

Ignoring her question, I asked, "You cheated on me?"

"Levi, we were both so unhappy, and the marriage was clearly over. But I broke things off with him, and then I got pregnant with Brooke when we went on that trip to Italy to try to work things out with our marriage. Obviously, it didn't work. But I found out I was pregnant the next month, so I couldn't leave. There was no way I could raise two kids on my own, so I stayed."

"Fucking hell, Caroline. You stayed with me solely because you couldn't make it on your own? Are you *serious*? Why not just ask me for a divorce before you cheated? The whole damn marriage was started on a lie! What difference would it have made to end it before another one was started?"

Emeline stepped back and turned away from me. I knew she was debating whether she should leave.

"I could ask you the same thing? Who's the person with you? Moving on pretty fast, aren't you?"

I laughed. "Says the woman who *cheated*! Sign the divorce papers and stay the fuck away from me and Rhett, Caroline."

Instead of hanging up, I threw my phone across the room against the wall. Emeline jumped and covered a small yelp with her hands.

I dropped to the floor, back against the counter, put my arms on my knees, and buried my face in my hands. I could hear Emeline saying something, but I knew she wasn't talking to me.

How could Caroline cheat? How could she tell our son she didn't want him?

"Levi?"

When I finally looked up, it was to see Caden standing there. Glancing around the kitchen, I didn't see any signs of Emeline. "I thought you were riding with Rhett?"

"Emeline called me to come back. Gatlin's with Rhett, and Emeline left to catch up with them. What happened?"

My head dropped back against the counter. "Caroline cheated on me right before she got pregnant with Brooke."

Caden sat down next to me. "Oh damn. Were you Brooke's father?"

I nodded. "She said she broke it off a few months before she found out she was pregnant. She got pregnant in Italy, on the trip we took to try to mend our marriage." Glancing at Caden, I said, "She wanted to leave the marriage, but when she found out she was pregnant, she stayed because she knew she couldn't make it on her own," I said with a bitter laugh. "She only stayed because she couldn't afford to raise two kids."

Caden sighed. "We really know how to pick 'em, don't we?"

"At least you didn't get married to Rachel and have kids with her. Consider yourself lucky in that area."

The corner of his mouth twitched. "I asked. More than once."

"Should have been a clear red flag, my friend."

His smile grew wider, but I could see the pain in his eyes.

My head fell back again. "I don't love her, Caden. I did, a very long time ago. She used me to get out of River Falls, and I knew that, but I thought what we had was the real deal."

"You know what we need to do?"

"What?"

"Go out this Friday night. Get drunk and let off some steam."

I was about to agree when I closed my eyes. "Shit. Friday night, I'm going to this perfume-making thing with Emeline.

I doubt it will take that long, so maybe we can go out afterward."

His brows rose. "I'm sorry, did you say you're going to make perfume?"

"Her friend, Lilibeth, owns that shop on Main, and you can make perfume and candles. She's going to be teaching the kids at summer camp."

He rolled his eyes.

"You should come with us."

He gave me a puzzled look. "You want me to go to a perfume-making class?"

I laughed. "They make cologne, too. Just think, you can mix up your own scent and test it out when we go drinking."

"So you *do* want to go out?"

With a half-shrug, I replied, "I don't think we'll be at Wonderland Whimsy long."

Caden let out a groan. "Christ, we need to find your man card again."

I stood, and Caden followed. "My man card is fully intact."

"Says the guy going to make perfume at a place called Wonderland Whimsy."

"When was the last time you were out? Better yet, have you even been with anyone since Rachel?"

Caden grimaced. "I've had a few hookups. Nothing serious."

"I tell you what, you come with me and Emeline this Friday, and I'll go out afterward."

He closed his eyes and let out another tortured groan. When he opened them again, he nodded. "I'm only doing this because you need to get laid."

I laughed. "You actually think I'm going to find someone here in River Falls?"

"The number of people coming from Granby each weekend will help with that."

My brows raised. "You're hooking up with tourists?"

He shrugged. "Why not? I get what I want, the girl gets what she wants, and we go our separate ways."

I shook my head. "I'm not interested in one-night stands, Caden."

"You say that now."

Laughing, I rubbed at the ache in the back of my neck. "We should head over to the barn."

By the time we got back to the barn, Emeline, Gatlin, and Rhett were riding up.

"Dad!" Rhett called out as he approached.

"Did he just call me dad? One outing with your brother and sister, and my son grew ten years older."

Caden laughed.

I watched as Rhett got off the mare as if he'd done it a thousand times. Rushing over to me, he was practically hyperventilating.

"Take a deep breath, son," I said, as I knelt to get eye level with him. Damn if I didn't love this kid. He was the only good thing I had left in this world, and my only connection to Brooke. I could see her every time I looked into his eyes. It made me both happy and sad. There was no doubt in my mind, they were both my kids. I hated Caroline for what she'd put Rhett through, and now for causing even a single doubt that Brooke was my daughter.

"Daddy, guess what?"

My chest squeezed a little at the word daddy. I wasn't ready for Rhett to move to dad…or worse yet, father. I shuddered.

"What?" I asked with a smile.

"Uncle Gatlin roped a calf, and then guess who else did!"

"Tell me it wasn't you."

"It was Ms. Emeline! She did it better than Uncle Gatlin, and faster, too!"

"Hey!" Gatlin mock complained as he pulled the saddle off his horse for Marshall to grab. "Thank you, Marshall."

I glanced over at Emeline, who was removing her saddle and carrying it herself, following Marshall into the barn to the tack room.

"That doesn't surprise me. Did you know that their sister, Ensley, is a farrier?"

Rhett's eyes went wide. "She is?"

Gatlin chimed in. "If you don't meet her before camp, she'll be popping in and out helping, and she even demonstrates for the kids what she does."

Rhett looked back at me. "I want to meet her!"

"I'm sure you'll meet her before camp," Caden said, placing his hand on Rhett's head and ruffling his hair.

Jumping in excitement, Rhett threw himself into me, wrapped his arms around my neck, and said, "I'm so happy we moved to River Falls!"

I hugged him back. He drew away, a smile still on his face. "Brooke would have loved it here. But I know she's watching us, 'cause Grammy and Emeline said she was."

At that moment, Emeline walked out of the barn and looked our way. She smiled, and I returned the expression.

The feeling I experienced from earlier came back, but this time so hard it nearly knocked me back on my ass.

It was then that I realized why I didn't want to have a one-night stand with a stranger. And that reason was smiling at me, her blue eyes sparkling.

Holy shit.

"How about you help get this saddle off, and we'll get Dasher all wiped down and give her some oats," Emeline said to Rhett.

"Can I, Daddy?"

"Of course. You rode her, so you need to help get her all settled again."

Rhett ran off to help Emeline.

"She's a natural with kids," I said to her brothers, who stood on either side of me as we watched the two of them walk off with Dasher.

Gatlin smirked and slapped my back. "Watch out there, Levi. You might just find yourself charmed by Emeline, like everyone else. I can't even tell you how many guys have fought for her attention. But I swear if I didn't know any better, I'd say she was holding out for someone."

I glanced at Gatlin, who simply winked at me before he headed off in the same direction Emeline and Rhett had gone.

Focusing my attention on Caden, I saw him watching his sister and Rhett.

"Everything okay?" I asked.

He smiled. "Yeah. Everything is great."

CHAPTER NINE

EMELINE

"WHAT'S WRONG WITH YOU?" Lilibeth asked as she got everything set up for our perfume-making.

Letting out a soft laugh, I replied, "Nothing's wrong. Why do you ask?"

She gave me a look that silently said she wasn't buying my bullshit. "You're pacing back and forth. It's making me a nervous wreck."

I sighed and slid onto one of the stools at the beautiful mahogany counter located in the perfume bar, where Lilibeth did all the mixing. All the essential oils used to make the perfumes and candles were in dark bottles, sitting on glass shelves in front of a silver antique backing. Dark curtains hung down from the sides of the entrance into the perfumery. The rabbit light fixture on the counter, though, was a nod to the *Alice in Wonderland* theme of the shop. The perfumery section of the store was actually called "The Alice," which I adored.

Hoping to change the subject, I asked, "How many different notes do you have?"

Lilibeth looked behind her. "Twenty-five."

"How am I supposed to pick only five?"

She smiled.

"I love how you have cocktail-themed scents for the candles, and they come in barware. We'll have to change that for the camps, though."

With a wink in my direction, she replied, "I figured we would."

I tapped my finger on my chin. "Let's see, what are some cute ideas we can come up with?"

Lilibeth set out three small vessels. "You changed the subject. What's going on with you?"

I sighed. It was no use trying to hide it. "It's Levi."

She frowned. "Did he do something to you?"

A bark of laughter came out. "Did he do something to me? Uh, no, that's the problem."

Her brows came down in confusion. She looked adorable, as usual. Her dirty blonde hair was pulled up into a loose bun on top of her head, with small flowers tucked around the base. A few strands hung free, framing her face and neck. Her clothes were casual, with a flowy floral-print blouse and jeans. "I'm not following."

Moreen walked up and said, "She's had a crush on him since she was like fourteen, and now that he's back in town, she wants to jump his bones."

"You're horny, then?" Lilibeth asked, a broad smile on her face.

"I am not *horny*, thank you very much. And yes, I thought I'd moved on from my silly crush, but he had to go and move back home, then be all..." My voice faded.

Lilibeth leaned over the counter and waggled her brows. "Be all what?"

"Hot in a single-dad-slash-cowboy-slash-animal-lover sort of way. A man who loves his son, and his soon-to-be ex-wife cheated on him, and he was devastated to learn that and—oh shit. I said too much. You guys don't repeat that about his wife, okay?"

Lilibeth pretended she was locking it away with a key to her mouth and tossed said key over her shoulder.

Moreen's eyes were as wide as saucers. "Jesus, do you know how to bring the tea."

"Oh!" Lilibeth clapped. "What kind of tea should I serve?"

Moreen and I both looked at her in surprise.

"Babe, these aren't the type of men who want to drink tea," my friend answered.

"Or wine," I added.

Lilibeth looked thoughtful for a moment. "Whiskey?"

Moreen pointed to her. "Bingo." Turning back to me, she said, "Now what's this about Caroline cheating on Levi?"

I closed my eyes and internally bitch-slapped myself. Focusing back on Moreen, I said, "You cannot repeat that. Please, *please* don't repeat that. Not even to your mother."

She drew back like I'd offended her. "My mother? Do you honestly think I have that type of relationship with my mom?"

Tilting my head, I stared at her. "You have exactly that type of relationship with your mom. You told her when I lost my virginity."

Lilibeth laughed. "Oh my gosh, what?"

Moreen shrugged. "In Mom's defense, she *did* tell me that I don't have to share quite so much with her, after that."

Lilibeth looked at me and laughed. "Oh my God, I love this town."

I grabbed my friend's hands. "Moreen."

She gave me a reassuring smile. "I swear to you, I won't tell anyone."

The bell above the door rang, and we all turned. My jaw nearly dropped when I saw my brother Caden with Levi.

"Oh God, why does your hot brother have to be here?" Moreen whispered.

"Got a crush?" Lilibeth asked.

Moreen shook her head. "I'm not his type, but man, what I wouldn't give to fu—"

"Okay, Moreen!" I quickly said, cutting off where that sentence was going.

Lilibeth laughed, then lowered her voice. "I've never met him. He *is* cute, though."

"Warning, he's a grump," I said as I slid off the stool. "Caden, what did Levi do to talk you into this?"

My brother rolled his eyes. "Promised me we'd go out after this."

"We're going out after this, too," I said, leaning up and kissing my brother on the cheek. Stepping back, I smiled at Levi. "Glad you made it."

He grinned, and I ignored the way it made my heart speed up.

"Caden, you know Moreen, of course," I said, as I motioned to my friend.

"How's it going, Moreen?"

She smiled. "Going good. I'm just headed out. I'll lock up, Lilibeth. You kids have fun!" she called out as she headed toward the register.

"Thanks, Moreen," Lilibeth called out after her. Looking at me, she added, "I decided to close a little early tonight."

"Caden, this is Lilibeth Asher. She owns the store."

I watched as my brother took in Lilibeth. His gaze moved quickly over her body before landing back on her face. Before he could say anything, Lilibeth came around the counter and stuck out her hand, smiling from ear to ear.

"It's nice to meet you, Caden. Emeline has told me a lot about you."

He looked at her hand, then slowly reached out and shook it.

"I hope you're ready for a fun night of mixing and finding your special scent," she said with a wink.

Caden looked at Levi with an expression that could only mean one thing—he hated his best friend in that moment. Then his gaze moved to me, and I grinned.

Caden sighed, then focused on Lilibeth. "You can turn off the sales pitch, sweetheart. I'm already in the door."

Frowning, she slowly shook her head. "Sales pitch? And I'm sorry, but did you seriously just call me *sweetheart*?"

It was the first time I'd ever heard Lilibeth have a bit of an attitude, and I wasn't surprised it was Caden who'd brought it out in her.

"I did."

She plastered on a smile once again, this one with a sharp edge. "Like your sister said, it's Lilibeth, and I would appreciate it if you called me by my name. Not sweetheart."

The corners of my brother's mouth twitched with a hidden smile. His gaze moved past her to the bottle of whiskey she'd placed on the counter at some point. "Thank fuck. Whiskey."

"Please, help yourself," Lilibeth said before looking at Levi. "Thanks for coming, Levi."

"I'm looking forward to this."

She grinned. "Then let's get going! You can pick up to five notes."

"Notes?" Caden asked.

"The scents for the perfume."

I quickly made my way around the counter and started smelling different oils. "How in the world am I going to pick?"

Glancing to my right, I saw Levi totally getting into it.

He picked up a bottle. "Leather...okay. Fresh Dirt?" Taking a smell, he pulled back. "Very...earthy."

Lilibeth and I both laughed.

I pulled down the Jasmine, Lemon, and Rose. Then I grabbed the Magnolia, Cinnamon, and Cedarwood.

Lilibeth walked up and smiled. "These are great combinations, Emeline."

Peeking at my brother's picks, I saw he had White Musk, Amber, and Sandalwood. He'd also grouped Bergamot, Birch, and Oakmoss. Looking to my other side, Levi had pulled down Cedarwood, Sandalwood, Orange Blossom, Bergamot, Tonka Bean, and Patchouli.

Lilibeth stood in front of us with a wide smile. She placed small, thin round cotton pieces in front of us, along with a small jar of strips, as well as jars of coffee beans.

"You can do this two different ways. Dip the strips into your oil, then smell them as you build your scent. Or you can put one drop on the cotton pad, then smell *that*, as you add your additional scents. As you go, you can add more of something if you like. Play around with the different scents you have and the amounts you use. Be sure to write down what you do, though, using the notepads next to you. That way, you won't forget what combinations you used."

As we began, she observed, stepping in when we had questions.

"Levi, looks like you're more of a woodsy kind of guy," she observed. "And, Caden, you're clearly into musky smells."

"Musky?" he asked, a smirk on his face.

"Yes," she replied. "You picked deep, sultry blends that will give you intriguing, bold pairings."

My brother stared at Lilibeth for a long moment before he cleared his throat and got back to mixing his scents.

"What do my scents say?" I asked.

Lilibeth grinned. "You're a fan of sweet scents and florals that are romantic."

"Totally see that from her," Caden mumbled.

I glared at him. "Says the man who went with *deep and sultry*."

Caden shot me a dirty look.

"Levi," Lilibeth continued, "went with earthy, nature-loving choices. Very nice, rich scents you picked there."

Levi winked at Lilibeth, and a surge of jealousy ripped through my body. I snapped my head back to my little cotton circle. Of course, why *wouldn't* he be attracted to her. She was beautiful, close to his age, and her personality was infectious. Everyone loved being around Lilibeth.

I knew she wouldn't flirt with Levi, not after I'd shared my feelings for him. That didn't mean Levi wouldn't flirt with *her*.

I suddenly felt like a teenage girl, jealous of the head cheerleader who had the star quarterback's attention.

"I can't believe I'm doing this," my brother grumbled as he put two drops of the White Musk on his circle.

Okay, so not *everyone* loved being around Lilibeth.

As Levi and Lilibeth worked on his scents, I felt my mood grow sour. If I didn't watch out, I was going to become just as grumpy as Caden.

When I looked at him, he was smelling one of his circles and frowning. "Too much Amber."

"Let me smell," I said, sniffing the coffee beans, then his sample. My brows rose. "I like that."

He shook his head. "Smell this one," he said, practically shoving another sample up my nose.

I held up my hand. "Wait, Caden. Let me clear my nose!"

After taking a few deep breaths of the beans, I smelled the other sample. Smiling, I exclaimed, "That's *amazing*!"

He grinned. "I think so too. Almost smells like the cologne I currently wear."

"Your cologne is Musky Oakmoss, by Dossier."

My brother snapped his head around to look at Lilibeth. "How did you know that?"

It was her turn to wink, and I was glad it was at my brother, not Levi. "I know my scents, Mr. Wilde."

She glanced back to Levi, and I felt myself stiffen. "I'm sorry, Levi. I can't get a clear scent from you, other than the soap you use."

He laughed. "I don't normally wear cologne."

"What perfume do I like?" I asked her.

She waved me off. "That's so easy. You wear Marc Jacobs's Daisy."

My mouth fell open. "I can't believe you know that."

She giggled. "So many women wear it."

I frowned. "Well, that doesn't make me feel so good."

"That's why you're here, to make your own signature perfume," Levi said. When I looked at him, his smile nearly blinded me. For a moment, I forgot how to speak.

"Stop flirting with my sister," Caden warned as he lifted the cotton to his nose. He smiled widely, which was rare to see lately. "This is it."

Lilibeth smelled it and raised her brows. "Very nice. Did you write down the recipe?"

He scoffed. "Of course I did."

"While Emeline and Levi keep working on their notes, we'll get this mixed."

Caden asked, "Do you use a base of some sort?"

She nodded. "I do."

"What perfume do *you* wear?" Caden asked, surprising all of us.

"Just something I make here at the shop."

Caden leaned forward when Lilibeth leaned over the table. "You smell like...the sea and lilies."

Her eyes sparkled. "My perfume has notes of sea salt and lily. You have an excellent nose, cowboy."

If I knew my brother, he was about to make some sort of sexual joke. "Don't even, Caden!"

Levi laughed. Caden slammed his brows down, and Lilibeth looked confused.

"Damn, your sister knows you."

"For your information, I wasn't going to say anything."

With one brow raised, I stared at my brother.

The corner of his mouth rose into a smirk. "Fine. I was."

Lilibeth looked between the three of us. "What am I missing?"

I shot her a smile. "Nothing. Just ignore us."

"Um, okay, well, we're going to start by adding fractionated coconut oil, then the right proportions for the notes."

Caden got lost in the process of helping Lilibeth make his signature cologne.

"They make a cute couple," Levi whispered.

Focusing back on my brother and Lilibeth, I nearly snorted. "Beauty and the Beast."

Levi chuckled. "You hit that nail right on the head. But I think your brother needs someone like Lilibeth."

I didn't want to admit how relieved I was to hear him say that, but that stupid teenage girl came out before I could stop her.

I picked up my sample, which I finally thought had the best balance of notes. "What about you?" I asked without looking at him.

"What *about* me?"

"You don't think you and Lilibeth would make a nice couple?"

That time I *did* look at him. He glanced over to Lilibeth and studied her for a few moments. I was internally kicking myself.

Right before I looked away, he caught my eye. "Not at all."

Blinking a few times, I asked, "Why not?"

He gave a one-shoulder shrug. "I'm not interested in getting involved with anyone right now. I'm not even divorced yet. But...I mean, I guess if the right person came along, I could see myself dating again."

"I would imagine Caroline will be signing the divorce papers soon?"

He placed a few drops onto his cotton swatch. "I wish she'd just sign them and let us both get on with our lives. Honestly, though, right now I'm just focusing on helping Rhett heal."

"What about you? Don't you have to heal, as well?"

He looked at me, and our eyes met. I swore something passed between us, I just couldn't tell what it was. A soft smile appeared on his handsome face. "I guess I do. Life doesn't seem to be very…beautiful lately."

"That reminds me of that Bryan Adams song."

"What song is that?"

"I think it's called 'Life is Beautiful'. I like it, it's a good song."

He held up his swatch and smelled it before he said, "I'll have to listen to it. What do you think about this?"

I picked up the coffee beans and took a deep breath through my nose, then smelled his sample. I closed my eyes and sighed. "That smells like my kind of Heaven."

When I realized what I'd said, I snapped my eyes open to see him staring at my mouth.

His eyes lifted to mine. "Really?" he asked in a teasing tone.

"I just…I meant, it reminds me of riding. Horses! Riding *horses*."

He grinned.

"You know, the leather from the saddle, and the…just… that smell."

The way he was looking at me, with such an intensity, caused me to nearly sigh like a teenage schoolgirl. "It smells like something you would wear."

Levi's brows rose. "Does it?"

I swallowed and nodded. "Yeah, it does."

He reached over, lifted my sample to his nose, and took a deep breath. "Sweet-smelling with a hint of spice. Cinnamon?"

I was lost in his light brown eyes. Why was this man so damn handsome? He was making it very difficult not to want him.

"Perfectly describes the woman who will be wearing it."

My cheeks heated, and I tried like hell to look away, but I was mesmerized by him. I swore Levi leaned slightly toward me.

"You two look cozy," Caden crooned suddenly.

I jumped back, and my brother laughed.

"You okay there, Emeline?"

"Yes, you just scared me, that's all. Are you done?"

He held up his bottle. "Of all the people I thought would be finished first, I'm not him."

I giggled. "I've got my notes down, Lilibeth."

Levi held up his swatch. "I do as well."

After we mixed and bottled up our new scents, I pulled out my phone and frowned.

"What's wrong?" Lilibeth asked.

"I tried to get Ensley to go out with us, but she's declined. I asked where she was, and she told me."

Sadness filled his eyes. "What day is it?"

"It's the tenth," Lilibeth answered.

Caden and Levi exchanged equally concerned looks.

"What's with the tenth?" Lilibeth asked.

I drew in a breath and let it out. "Ensley's best friend from high school, Grady, passed away on this date ten years ago."

Lilibeth put her hands on her chest. "Oh my gosh, that's so sad. What happened?"

Caden walked away. He and Grady had also been close, even though they were a few years apart.

I cleared my throat. "He, um, he took his own life."

Now Lilibeth's hand covered her mouth. "I'm so sorry. I never should have asked."

"You didn't know," Levi said. "Everyone actually thought they'd end up together, even though they were just friends back then."

"Ensley didn't want them to ruin their friendship by dating. She's never really gotten over his death."

Lilibeth slowly shook her head, then looked toward Caden. "They were friends?"

"We all used to hang out together. Me, Caden, Ensley, and Grady. Ensley blames herself because she started dating someone, and Grady wasn't happy about it. But neither would ever cross that line. Of course, no one really knows *why* Grady did what he did. He was always the one in the group trying to make everyone laugh. It came as a complete shock."

"Again, I'm so sorry."

Levi glanced back at Caden. "I guess it's time to go." Levi bent and kissed me on the cheek, totally catching me off guard. All I could do was smile and nod. He looked at Lilibeth. "I had more fun than I thought I would. You two have a good evening."

Lilibeth walked toward the front door where Caden was standing, wearing a brooding expression. "I'm so glad you both came, and I hope you had fun, too, Caden."

"It was...different."

Laughing, Lilibeth unlocked the door. "God forbid you admit you had a good time, cowboy."

Caden smirked, then opened the door. "See you around, *sweetheart*."

Before Lilibeth could reply, Caden was out the door. She did however mumble asshole, which almost made me laugh.

Levi tipped his cowboy hat to both of us and called out, "See you around, Em. Thank you, Lilibeth."

"Sure thing. You guys behave tonight!"

I watched as Levi walked out the door, and Lilibeth shut it. I let out a breath and closed my eyes for a moment. I had to fight not to lift my hand and touch where he'd kissed.

Quickly turning, I started gathering the bottles of scents to put them back.

"Okay, the way you look at that cowboy makes even *me* get hot."

My mouth fell open. "I do not!"

Laughing, she replied, "The hell you don't. Even your brother told me you've had a crush on Levi since you were little."

"What?" I spun around and looked at her. "When did he tell you that?"

She tried not to smile. "When you were both smelling one another's scents and staring into each other's eyes."

"He did not!"

"Oh, yes, he did."

After taking a minute to gather my thoughts, I slowly shook my head. "My brother knew I liked Levi?"

She gave a small shrug. "Apparently."

"Was he mad?"

Frowning, she asked, "Why would he be mad?"

I threw my hands up in the air. "I don't know! I don't know *anything* anymore. Sometimes the way Levi looks at me, it makes me think he feels something between us. But then he'll go and say he's not ready to date. I'm so confused, Lilibeth."

Taking my hand in hers, she said, "Let's go out. We can dance with guys we don't know and just have some fun. Call your sister. Tell her she's going whether she likes it or not. Moreen's meeting us there."

"But Caden and Levi went out as well."

She laughed. "Are they the going-out police?"

I chuckled. "No, but what if we go to the same bar?"

Lilibeth tilted her head and regarded me for a moment. "I don't want to sound mean, but your brother doesn't really seem like the type who'd would go to Billy's Honky-Tonk. He seems more like the kind of guy who'd go to…what's the name of that bar outside of town? The one where all the old timers go and hang out."

I burst out laughing. "You mean the dive bar?"

"Yes, the one right on the edge of town."

"Billy's."

"No, not the honky-tonk."

"No, I know what you mean, it's Billy's. Billy *Junior* owns the honky-tonk."

Lilibeth frowned. "Why would he name his bar the same as his father's?"

"To be fair, he added honky-tonk after it."

She laughed. "Call your sister, tell her she's going out. I've got to change, so should I swing by the ranch to pick you both up?"

Taking my perfume bottle, I grabbed my purse. "Sure, that's perfect. See you in about an hour?"

"See you then."

I started to head toward the door, Lilibeth behind me. As I stepped out and headed to my car, she yelled out, "Wear something sexy!"

CHAPTER TEN

LEVI

"**NOTHING'S CHANGED, HAS IT?**" Gatlin asked as he slid a beer my way.

I chuckled. "Except you're bartending at the local honky-tonk."

He glanced around. "It's a nice change from being on the ranch all day. Gives me something to do instead of playing poker with the ranch hands every weekend."

"You don't enjoy ranching?"

His head pulled back. "Hell yes, I do. But why go home and sit alone when I can come and work here? I get to people watch, get all the gossip in town, and make some extra money."

When he lifted his bottle, I tapped it with mine. "And drink on the job."

Leaning forward so he could lower his voice, he said, "It's water. I have a few back here already filled, so when someone wants to buy me a drink, I'm not offending anyone. Kyle over there," he pointed to the other bartender, "he's only been working here two days. He's about two beers away from getting shit-faced. I told him my trick, but he insisted he could handle it."

I glanced down the bar, and the poor kid could barely stand up straight. "I think he's already hit the limit."

Gatlin followed my gaze. "Nah. He's still making drinks and pouring shots. Give him time."

Focusing back on Caden's younger brother, I laughed. "You're enjoying this?"

He nodded. "I sure as shit am. I told the little punk he wasn't going to be able to drink on the job, and he claimed he could handle his alcohol."

Taking another drink of my beer, I searched for Caden. It didn't take long to find him leaning his hand on a wall, a pretty girl staring up at him.

"How's your brother doing?"

Gatlin shrugged. "He doesn't really talk much about anything other than the ranch. This is the first time I've seen him here in a while. When he does come, he usually leaves with a Granby tourist who came to River Falls to Instagram her stop at a small-town honky-tonk. They're usually from New York City, Atlanta, or some other big city. We're the only honky-tonk around, so we get a lot of visitors."

I nodded. "Who's the girl he's talking to?"

Glancing in the same direction as me, Gatlin replied, "No clue. She's not from here. Like I said, those are the kind Caden goes for."

Taking a drink of my beer, I watched as the girl and Caden walked over to one of the three pool tables. He put some money down, then sat at the small table we'd gotten when we arrived.

"Is there a reason you're watching my brother?"

Turning, I smiled when I saw Ensley standing beside me. She was a sight for sore eyes. Her dark blonde hair was pulled into a ponytail and those Wilde blue eyes sparkled. I swore the woman never aged.

"Ensley Wilde. How in the hell have you been?" I asked, pulling her into a hug and lifting her off the ground for a quick second.

She hit my back. "Put me down, Levi!"

I did, and we both laughed.

"I'm doing good. My damn baby sister dragged me out tonight."

I leaned in and kissed her cheek. "How are you doing... today?"

With a one-shoulder shrug, she glanced around the bar. "I hate this day."

Taking her hand in mine, I gave it a little squeeze. "I know. So do I. I think I try to block it out as much as possible."

"Did Caden do something already?" she asked.

"Do something?"

"Yeah, you were watching him. I figured he's already told someone to go fuck off."

I shook my head. "No, nothing like that. I'm just worried about him."

Her eyes went back to her older brother. They were like two peas in a pod, or at least they used to be. Growing up, where one was, the other wasn't far away. I was hoping they still had that close relationship.

She let out a soft sigh. "Rachel did a real number on him, and I swear if she ever sets foot back in this town, I'm going to..."

I looked at her and smirked. "You're going to what?"

She flashed an evil smile. "I guess it's going to depend on my mood at the time."

Laughing, I shook my head.

Her smile slowly faded. "He hasn't dated anyone, and it's been two years."

"He thought she was the one. And Rachel painted a nice picture for him. Kids, growing old on the ranch. She knew what he wanted to hear, and she strung him along until she found something she thought was better."

Ensley nodded. "Bitch." Turning away from her brother, she said, "Speaking of. Are you divorced from *your* bitch yet?"

"Don't hold back, Ensley."

Rolling her eyes, she said, "I never liked her, Levi, and I never *hid* the fact that I didn't like her. I always thought she went out with you just to make Caden jealous. When that didn't work, she used you to get out of River Falls."

"Maybe," I replied, even though she was a hundred-percent right.

"There's no maybe about it. She got pregnant on purpose. You and I both know it."

"We had some good times, though. I did love her, once upon a time, and I think she loved me too."

She shook her head, and her attention went to the dance floor. There was never any love lost between Caroline and Ensley. Neither liked the other. Caroline had been jealous of my friendship with Ensley from the get-go, and Ensley never trusted Caroline. In the end, she was a better judge of character than I was.

Ensley smiled slightly, and I followed her gaze. Emeline was dancing with Lilibeth. They looked like they were having a good time. Two guys around their age approached and started dancing alongside them.

"They don't look familiar to me," I said.

Ensley turned to the bar and motioned for her brother to get her a beer. "They're tourists. That's the only bad thing about going out now. The tourists have discovered our little oasis."

"Holy shit, how did Emeline manage to get you out tonight?" Gatlin called over the music.

Ensley took the beer from him. "I owed her one."

Gatlin smiled softly. "I'm glad you came. Now don't sit here and pout, go enjoy yourself."

Looking as if she wanted to be anywhere but here, Ensley started for the dance floor. At the last minute, she turned and headed toward Caden, instead. I ordered another beer for myself and one for Caden, then turned to head the same way.

Two younger women stopped me, with one putting her hand on my arm.

"I'm sorry, haven't we met before?"

Glancing at her, I shook my head. "Don't think so."

I started to step around them when she stopped me again. Glancing pointedly at her hand, I snapped my eyes up to meet hers.

She quickly removed her hand. "You just look familiar. Did you grow up here in River Falls?"

I bounced my gaze back and forth, studying the two women. "I did. You?"

The handsy one grinned. "I did! Oh my gosh, I know who you are now!"

Amused, I raised one eyebrow.

"You're Levi Tucker! You look just like your dad," the young girl said.

Now I was confused. How in the hell did this girl know my father?

"I'm Logan Miller. I work for your father as a vet tech."

Oh shit. This was Janet's granddaughter, the one she wanted me to get to know. I could have sworn that Emeline said she was only twenty. I needed to get away from this girl, stat. "Are you even old enough to be in this bar?" I asked before I could stop myself.

Logan grinned, and her friend giggled. "We both turned twenty-one this past week."

Raising one of the beers in my hand, I replied, "Happy Birthday, ladies. If you'll excuse me, I've got to get back to my friends."

"I can't wait to work alongside you," Logan said with a sugary smile.

Forcing my own smile, I nodded. "Can't wait."

Quickly moving past the two girls, I zigzagged around people and finally got to the table.

"Where did all of these people suddenly come from?" I asked, handing the extra beer I'd gotten to Caden.

"It's that time of night when all the young ones come out," he called over the loud song playing.

I rolled my eyes as Ensley stood, took my beer, and put it on the table. "Come on, cowboy, we might as well dance since we're here."

"Who am I to turn down a pretty lady?"

Ensley laughed. "Still know how to flatter, I see."

Once we got to the dance floor, we took off two-stepping.

"Heard you're going to be volunteering at the camp this summer."

I smirked. "One conversation with your mother and I somehow managed to *volunteer*."

She smiled. "You'll have fun. The kids are great. I love doing little demonstrations for them. And my sister runs those camps like a well-oiled machine, let me tell you."

Speaking of... I glanced around the dance floor and spotted Emeline dancing with another guy who seemed to be about her age. She was laughing at something he said...and I found myself wanting to be the one who made her laugh like that.

He pulled her closer and whispered something into her ear.

An instant rush of anger swept over me. Feeling caught off guard by the reaction, I quickly turned away.

Focusing back on Ensley, I saw she was looking at me with a smirk. "Why, Mr. Tucker, you look like you're ready to tear someone's head off."

"What?" I asked. "I do *not* have that look on my face."

Ensley glanced over her shoulder. "That's Luke. He's one of the ranch hands on our place. He's had a thing for Emeline since his first day of work."

"What's he do on the ranch?" I asked, looking back to see him dipping Emeline, and she was once again laughing. No, that wasn't anger I was feeling. It was jealousy.

"He's on the cattle side."

"So he doesn't work directly for Emeline?"

When Ensley didn't answer, I looked at her. A single brow was raised. "Why so many questions about Luke and Emeline?"

"Well, I mean, if she were his boss, I don't think it'd be appropriate for him to be dancing with her like he is."

Ensley busted out laughing. "Oh my God! When did you become such a prude?"

"I'm not a prude," I said right before I spun her.

"If you're not a prude, then why are you worried about—"

Her voice cut off when I spun her again, in a sad attempt to get her to forget where her train of thought was going.

"Do you like Emeline?" she asked as soon as I reeled her back in.

A bark of laughter slipped free. "Of course not! I just don't want to see some jerk trying to take advantage of her, that's all. Besides, getting involved with anyone isn't something I'm interested in right now."

She gave me an assessing look, those blue eyes of hers playful. "You know, Emeline's had a crush on you since she was like fourteen. Maybe even before that."

I rolled my eyes. "Your brother already told me, and I highly doubt she still does."

She shrugged one shoulder. "Maybe not. But then, you don't see the way she looks at you."

"Ensley," I warned. "We're friends."

A wicked smile appeared on her face. "There's such a thing as friends with benefits, Levi."

I groaned. "Stop it."

The song ended, and as we headed back to the table, someone tapped me on the shoulder. It was Logan Miller.

"Dance?"

Right at that moment, Emeline and Lilibeth were making their way toward our table. I quickly grabbed Emeline's hand.

"Emeline, I think we're up next."

Confused, she started to say something, but I quickly herded us back toward the dance floor. "I'm sorry, Logan. Promised this one to Emeline."

Once we got to the dance floor, the next song started. I cursed when I realized it was a slow song.

I drew Emeline closer and tried to ignore the scent of her damn perfume. It was fucking intoxicating.

"Um, what was that about?" she asked as we shuffled together slowly.

"Logan Miller wanted me to dance with her."

Something passed across Emeline's face...and for a moment it looked like disappointment. But why she would be disappointed was beyond me. We danced for a few moments in silence.

"So who was the guy you were dancing with earlier? The one who liked to dip you?"

"Luke?" she asked with a laugh. "He works on the ranch. He's been asking me out, I swear, since the first day he started working for us."

I frowned. "Have you told him no?"

Her head drew back some at my tone. "Yes."

"Maybe he needs to learn that no means no and to stop harassing you."

Her brows flew up. "He's hardly *harassing* me, Levi. He's a nice guy, and if he didn't work for my brother, I might go out with him."

That admission bothered me more than I thought it should. All I could do was nod.

"Why didn't you want to dance with Logan?"

I looked down into those blue eyes and realized if I stared long enough, I could get lost. Closing my eyes to break the connection, I turned my head before opening them again, glancing around the dance floor before looking back at Emeline. "For one, she's way too young for me. Second, she works for my father, and will soon be working for me. That's a line I do *not* intend to cross. Plus, I'm not the least bit interested in getting involved with anyone."

Emeline smiled slightly, but it didn't reach her eyes. "Yes, you keep saying that."

We danced in silence until the song was over, then stepped apart.

"You can't avoid her forever, you know."

"If I can get back to the table to sit, it'll be easier to let her down."

With a confused expression, she asked, "Why is that?"

"You stepped on my foot and made me twist my ankle. I can't possibly dance now."

Her mouth dropped open. "I have never in my life stepped on a dance partner's foot!"

Winking, I replied, "First time for everything."

Once we got back to the table, we found Caden and Lilibeth in a heated discussion. Sitting, I glanced between the two.

"How would you even know, Caden? Have you ever done the swing?"

Emeline was about to say something when Caden shot her a warning look, then focused back on Lilibeth. "What makes you think I haven't?"

Lilibeth looked him up and down, then smiled. "I'm sorry, you just don't seem like the type of guy who'd swing dance."

Caden leaned forward. "Are you suggesting that just because I'm a man, obviously I can't dance?"

She motioned toward him with her hands. "Of course not, but you're so..."

He raised his brow. "So what?"

She shrugged. "Not a very...cheerful kind of guy, and the swing is a cheerful kind of dance."

Caden's brow rose. "Are you saying I'm too grumpy to dance to a country swing?"

Lilibeth's eyes sparkled. "That's *exactly* what I'm saying."

Tipping his hat, he replied, "At least you're honest."

She stood. "Okay, cowboy. Give me two minutes."

The three of us watched as Lilibeth walked over to the DJ, then made her way back to the table. She held out her hand to Caden, who I was pretty sure had drunk just enough beers to actually do this.

The woman sitting beside him, the same one he'd been talking to earlier, shot Lilibeth a scathing look.

Still holding out her hand patiently, Lilibeth said, "Let's go, cowboy. Show me what you've got."

Emeline grinned widely. Meanwhile, I felt bad for Lilibeth. She had no idea what she was getting into.

As they walked to the dance floor, the DJ told everyone to make a bit of room in the middle of the space.

"She has no idea Caden can dance, I take it?" I asked Emeline.

"No," she said on a laugh. "And *he* has no idea Lilibeth took almost twenty years of dance lessons!"

I tossed my head back and laughed. "This is gonna be good."

Shania Twain's "That Don't Impress Me Much" started, and we both laughed again.

I couldn't tell who was more shocked, Caden or Lilibeth, when they started to dance. They instantly fell into a rousing country swing.

"Oh my gosh! Look at her spinning!" Emeline shouted as she clapped, and Ensley whistled.

I watched, thoroughly entertained, as Caden and Lilibeth moved across the dance floor with so much ease, it seemed as if they'd been dancing together for years.

"How are they doing those dips and turns like that? They're so in sync," Emeline said, smiling from ear to ear as she watched the two dance.

"I have no clue."

As the song ended, Caden pushed Lilibeth out into a spin that seemed as if it would never end. The last note ended with him dipping her, and her leg coming up. The crowd went wild, including everyone at our little table. Even the woman Caden had been talking to all night.

Another song instantly started, and Caden and Lilibeth both stood there for a moment. She took a step toward him and said something. He closed his eyes briefly and drew her closer. They started to dance as other couples moved around them in a slow two-step.

I watched my best friend as he seemed to let go of something when Lilibeth lifted her gaze and met Caden's. She smiled, then rested her head against his chest.

Turning, I looked at Emeline, who was also watching her brother and Lilibeth. She smiled softly, then glanced down. I would have given anything to ask her what she was thinking in that moment.

She must have felt my gaze on her because she lifted her head and looked directly at me. "If I ever see Rachel in this town again, I'm going to kick her ass for hurting my brother like she did."

I let out a soft laugh. "I do believe you'd do exactly that."

Her eyes searched my face before she asked, "Dance again?"

Suddenly aware of the crackle in the air between us, I replied, "I think I'll sit this one out."

The look of hurt passed so quickly over her face, I would have missed it if I hadn't been staring at her so intently.

"Emeline?"

The sound of another man's voice caused us both to turn to see Luke standing there.

"Would you like to dance?"

She stood. "I'd love to."

I watched them walk out to the dance floor. When he drew her close, and she wrapped her arms around his neck, I had to fight the urge to go cut in. Instead, I grabbed my beer and drank the rest of it as I tried to ignore the way my chest ached to see Emeline in another man's arms.

When I glanced at Ensley, she raised her brows. "What was that you were saying earlier?"

I turned away and looked back to the dance floor, trying not to seek out Emiline and Luke. When the song ended and Caden returned to the table, I stood.

"Ready to leave?"

He looked flustered for a moment, but he nodded and said, "Let's get the hell out of here."

CHAPTER ELEVEN

EMELINE

I SAT BACK IN my chair, pulled out a Swedish Fish, and popped it into my mouth. My mind drifted back to last weekend and the moment that passed between me and Levi. Had I imagined the way he'd looked at me?

"Don't be stupid, Emeline. Of course you did. He declined your request to dance, remember?" I exhaled and shook my head. "He's not interested in you, so you need to just move on."

The sound of the knock on my open door caused me to let out a small yelp, then look to see my brother standing there with a grin on his face.

"Taking to talking to yourself now, little sister?"

"No. I was working something out in my head."

"Something? Or *someone*?"

My head tilted as I regarded my brother. "No idea what you mean."

He sat down in the seat across from my desk. "Levi."

"What *about* Levi?"

"Really? Are we going to do this?"

I folded my arms over my chest, stubborn to the end.

"Apparently, we are, because I have no idea what you're talking about, Caden."

"You like him. I've always known you do."

For some silly reason, tears stung the back of my eyes.

As if my brother could sense I was about to lose it, he reached across the desk and held out a hand.

Placing mine in his, I sighed. "It would never work."

Frowning, he asked, "Why not?"

"Oh, let's see. For one, he thinks I'm too young. Second, he told me he has no interest in dating. And three, I'm your sister."

"Why does you being my sister matter?"

I shrugged. "I don't know. Isn't there some kind of code? Like sisters are off limits or something?"

Caden laughed. "If there is, I don't know about it. Emeline, the only thing I want is for you to be happy. As long as the guy treats you like you deserve, I'm not going to sit here and tell you who you can and cannot date."

I smiled, but it faded slowly. "I appreciate that, but it doesn't change the fact that Levi isn't interested in dating anyone, least of all *me*."

He gave a one-shoulder shrug. "You didn't see the way he was glaring at Luke when we left the bar Friday night."

A little bubble of hope welled up inside me. "He was not."

"Even Gatlin and Ensley noticed. She said Levi was asking about Luke."

I frowned. "Really?"

He nodded. "Listen, I don't know if Levi is ready to start dating, but I *do* know for a fact that he's not heartbroken over Caroline. I think his healing has more to do with Brooke and starting over in River Falls with Rhett. I know I don't have a great track record, but would you care for some advice from me anyway?"

"Yes, please," I said, as I leaned forward in anticipation.

"Give him time, be his friend, and don't try to hide what you're feeling."

My eyes went wide. "You want me to tell him I have feelings for him?"

"No, that's not what I'm saying. But don't be afraid to show them."

I felt my face screw up in confusion. "That doesn't make any sense. You're saying...flirt with him?"

"No. I mean, a little flirting wouldn't hurt. I'm just saying, don't be afraid to show your feelings, Emeline."

I sighed. "I don't know if I can do that. What if he only looks at me as a friend?"

Caden stood. "Like I said, I'm not the best when it comes to stuff like this."

Standing as well, I replied, "I saw how you treated Rachel. You *are* good at stuff like this. You were just with the wrong person, that's all. Speaking of—what in the world was that with you and Lilibeth on the dance floor? I haven't seen you dance like that in so long!"

He rolled his eyes. "The only reason I danced with her was to shut her up. My God, that girl is so...*peppy*. Is she always like that?"

"Happy? Positive? Caring? Yes, she is. And she'll be helping me with the summer camps."

"As long as she stays away from my side of the ranch."

With a frown, I asked, "What do you have against Lilibeth?"

He gave me a look that said my question wasn't even worth answering. "She's annoying as hell. Just keep her on *your* side of the ranch."

Before I could say anything else, he turned and walked out of my office just as my mother appeared.

"Morning, Mom," Caden said, bending down to kiss her on the cheek.

"Well, good morning, Caden darling." Her eyes bounced from Caden to me. "Is everything okay?"

"Everything's peachy," he replied, glancing back at me before he walked away.

My mother shook her head and walked into my office. She reached down and took one of my Swedish Fish. "How do you eat these things and stay so thin?"

I shrugged. "Good genes?"

She chuckled, motioned for me to sit back down, and she took a seat as well.

"Is everything okay?"

"Yes, why wouldn't it be?"

Studying her face, I replied, "Because you seem like something is wrong."

"Fine. There are two things we need to talk about. One—*The Daily Dirt*."

Leaning forward, I scowled. "What did they say this time?"

"They mentioned the annual pie contest."

"This early?"

She nodded. "You know why, don't you?"

Now I had to fight to keep the smile off my face. My mother and Grace Miller always went toe-to-toe in the annual pie contest. My mother's cherry pie had won more than

Grace's caramel apple pie, which, honestly, was heavenly. But Mom's cherry pie was to die for.

"Can't say I do," I answered.

Mom's mouth fell open slightly, as if I'd offended her by not knowing the reason. "It's obvious. She's trying to hype up her stupid caramel apple pie by writing about it!"

Pressing my lips together, I nodded gravely. "Did she write about her pie?"

Sighing in frustration, my mother nodded. "*Yes*, Emeline, she did! She mentioned how many times she's won, and then, at the end of the article, she said this year's cherry crop isn't looking so good! What in the hell? She doesn't even grow cherries."

My hand flew up to cover my smile.

"This isn't funny, Emeline Wilde. The woman is raising doubts about the cherries. People are going to have it in their heads my cherries are no good."

"Mom," I started in a calming voice, "no one is going to think your cherries...aren't good." I had to press my lips together to keep from giggling. After a stern look from my mother, I got myself in check. "Everyone loves your cherry pie, and no matter what Grace or Janet writes, people will know your cherries are as delicious as ever the second they taste them."

She leaned back in her chair. "I need to fight fire with fire. I've gone too many years letting that woman take digs at me in her little subtle ways. No more!"

I jumped when she shouted the last two words. "What do you mean, fight fire with fire?"

Mom stood, placed her hands on her hips, and smiled. "I'm going to have an article written in my *own* newspaper!"

"What?" I asked, nearly knocking over my chair as I stood. "You don't own a newspaper."

She chewed on her lip and nodded. "Can't talk right now, Emeline. I need to do some research."

Blinking, I rushed to follow her to her office across the hall. "Mom, you can't just start a newspaper."

She sat down behind her desk, pulled the old-fashioned Rolodex toward her—which I *still* didn't understand why she used—pulled out a card, and held it up.

"Ha! Here we go." When she saw my confused expression, she smiled. "I'm going to call a friend of mine in Denver."

Shaking my head, I asked, "And?"

"She owns *The Colorado Post*. I'm going to ask her to do an article about River Falls and our annual pie contest, and mention me and my *famous* cherry pie."

I was pretty sure my mouth was hanging open in stunned silence.

"Don't you see?" When I didn't say anything, she went on. "Not only will it bring even more people to River Falls, which will be great for the economy, but they'll come just for my pie! It'll drive Grace mad!"

I held up my hands and closed my eyes. "Okay, wait, Mom. Where is this *really* coming from? You don't have to prove anything to Grace Miller."

"I know I don't, but she crossed a line when she went after my cherries. And my hen!"

Blinking at her, I asked, "She insulted Mildred?"

Mildred was my mother's pride and joy. We often teased her that she loved Mildred more than her own kids.

"Yes! In the same article, she said Mildred wasn't really an Orpington! She crossed *two* lines."

"What about all the times she went after the family? Like when she claimed it was really Gatlin working as a farrier, and not Ensley?"

She waved me off. "*Everyone* knew those were made-up lies."

"What about when she said I didn't deserve to win the state championship in barrel racing?"

Snapping her head up, she pointed at me. "I went down to the gift shop and demanded she retract that!"

I bit my lip. I'd forgotten she'd done that.

"Are you trying to say I care more about my cherries and chickens than I do my own kids?"

"No. But *do* I need to remind you about the time when the new pediatrician asked you my birthdate, and you gave him *Mildred's* birthday, instead."

Her cheeks turned pink. "That was one time, Emeline. Are you ever going to let that go?"

"You got my birthday mixed up with a chicken's, Mom."

She stared at me...then sat back in her chair with a sigh. "Oh my God...what is wrong with me?"

"It's okay," I said, kicking at nothing on the floor. "It hurt at the time, but I'm over it."

When she didn't say anything, I glanced up to find her scowling at me. "I'm not talking about that, Emeline. I'm talking about letting Grace get to me. I lost my head for a moment."

"Good. I'm glad you see that."

She smiled softly. "Thank you, sweetheart."

"Sure thing. I'd better get back to work."

Turning, I started to leave...then stopped and glanced back at her. "But I'd still call your friend in Denver. That *was* a genius idea."

She winked. "Oh, I intend to."

I headed back to her office when I remembered she'd had *two* things to talk about. She was already on the phone with her friend. Smiling, I turned around and walked away. Whatever the second thing was, it could wait.

I pulled up and parked behind Ensley's Ford F-250. I was the only one in the family who drove a pickup truck solely when needed. Otherwise, I was in my Subaru Outback, which I loved.

Opening the back, I let Moose jump out, and he headed straight to the front door of my mother and father's house.

The door opened, and he flew past my father and, most likely, straight for the kitchen. Dad laughed as he shook his head.

"I'm beginning to think he likes you and Mom more than me."

He drew me in for a quick hug. "Nonsense. It's just that Grandma and Grandpa's house is more fun."

"I guess so," I replied.

"He'll be happy to see Rhett here."

I nearly tripped over my own two feet. "Rhett?"

Dad glanced back at me. "Levi and Rhett are here."

"For Sunday dinner?"

He stopped and turned to me, a surprised look on his face at my incredulous tone. "Emeline, Levi's like a son to us, and if there was ever a time he and Rhett needed family, it's now."

I blinked a few times. "I didn't mean it like that, Dad. I was just surprised, I guess."

The look of disappointment on his face was brief, but I never wanted to see that again. "I didn't think you meant anything by it. Now, let's go see my granddog."

He headed toward the kitchen, and I drew in a few deep breaths. I hadn't seen Levi since the honky-tonk—over a week ago. The memory of being in his arms was still seared in my brain. But regardless of what Caden said, I needed to remind myself that he wasn't interested. He'd made that clear, and I needed to respect it.

I headed in the direction my father had gone. My parents' house wasn't like modern homes. When they built it, the open-floor concept wasn't a thing, or at least, it wasn't as popular. Stepping into the ample kitchen, I glanced around quickly but only found my mother and father, Moose begging at Mom's feet.

"Where is everyone?" I asked.

Mom looked up and smiled. "Hi, sweetheart. They're all in the backyard playing games."

"Did you need any help with dinner?" I hoped she'd say yes and not send me outside. I wasn't ready to face Levi just yet. I wasn't sure why I was being such a coward. I was going to have to see him a lot over the summer.

"Everything's taken care of. Your father and I are making a salad, and dinner will be ready soon. Head on out back with the rest of the kids. Take Moose with you; he'll love playing with everyone."

Whelp, looked like I was heading out back. I forced a smile and made my way through the kitchen. I stepped out onto the back porch that stretched the length of the house, and Moose shot right by me. Six steps led you off the covered porch and into a large backyard with lush grass. A volleyball net was set up on the right. Caden, Gatlin, Ensley, and Levi were playing. The latter two were partnered up against my brothers.

My eyes landed on Levi, and I had to grab the porch rail to keep my legs from going out from under me. He had his shirt off and was covered in sweat. Six-pack abs led to a massive chest, and his arms were... Well, they were pure perfection.

Looking at the sky, I whispered, "Why do you hate me?"

A whistle blew, causing me to jump. Rhett was standing right between the two sides, and he pointed toward Ensley and Levi. "That's another point for Team Daddy— A dog!" he shouted, dropping to his knees. And Moose, who lived up to his name—all eighty-five pounds of him—ran right to Rhett, knocking him over and covering him with kisses. The sound of Rhett laughing made my chest tighten slightly.

"You cheated!" Caden shouted.

Laughing, Ensley retorted, "How did I cheat?"

Caden glanced at Gatlin. "Tell me you didn't see her hit that two times in a row?"

Gatlin shrugged. "Honestly, I was watching the way this motherfucker's abs flexed when he jumped."

"Language Gatlin!" Emeline said.

Levi laughed as he flexed, and I nearly let out a whimper. One more look above. "Really? *Why?*"

"Christ on a cracker, Levi, are you taking steroids?" Ensley asked, squeezing his biceps. I had never envied *or* hated my sister until that moment.

"It's called working out." He winked. Then, as if he could sense my stare, he looked over to me. I quickly started down the steps, my eyes focused on the grass in front of me.

"Emeline!" Gatlin cried out. "Thank fuck!"

"Gatlin!" Ensley cried out. "Rhett is *right* here!"

My brother slapped a hand over his mouth. "I'm sorry, little dude, I keep forgetting!"

Rhett shrugged and went back to playing tug with Moose. He'd somehow found a tug toy in the backyard. I couldn't help but chuckle.

"Get in here and play with us. We need you!"

I looked around at everyone except Levi. I did everything I could to avoid him, in fact. "As fun as that sounds, Mom said dinner's almost finished."

"No!" Caden and Gatlin shouted at the same time.

"They're up by one!" Gatlin added.

I put my hands up, a silent way of saying *don't shoot the messenger*. "Sorry, but I didn't come here to play; I came to eat."

Turning to Rhett, I held out my hand. "Want to sit next to me? We can talk about camp, which starts soon."

Rhett quickly took me up on my offer, leaving poor Moose standing there with his tug toy.

"Can your dog sit by us too?" Rhett asked.

"Moose usually sits by my father, but I bet if you sneak him a cucumber from your salad, he'll be your very best friend."

Rhett jumped in excitement. "Come on, Moose! I'll give you a cucumber!"

Moose barreled by us and straight to the back door. I glanced in Levi's direction and saw he was putting on his T-shirt. He looked up, and our eyes caught. He smiled, and I returned the gesture before he could see my cheeks heat for getting busted ogling his body. I dashed up the steps and into the house, Rhett in tow.

Once inside, Rhett let go of my hand and rushed over to my mother. "Is there anything you need me to do?"

My mother and father both smiled down at him, with Dad ruffling Rhett's hair. "You are such a great kid. Go wash your hands is all you need to do."

Rhett rushed off to the half bathroom, Moose running behind him. My mother and father both looked at me with quizzical expressions.

"What?"

Neither said anything, and before I could ask why they were looking at me that way, everyone else walked in and chatter quickly filled the kitchen.

"Wash up!" my mother shouted, and people splintered off in different directions.

Rhett reappeared in the kitchen first and was tasked with bringing the breadbasket into the dining room. I helped bring out the lasagna, while Dad put the salad and four different bottles of dressing on the table.

"Where do you sit, Ms. Emeline?" Rhett asked.

I pointed to my usual spot. "Right there."

"Is that someone else's spot?" he asked, pointing to the chair at the end, next to mine.

The warmth that spread through my chest was foreign to me, but it made me smile. If I wasn't careful, I was going to fall in love with another Tucker. "Nope, no one sits there, so you're more than welcome to."

Levi was the first to enter the dining room. He drew in a deep breath through his nose and smiled at my mother. "I've missed your lasagna."

"Rhett, did you want your dad to make your plate, or may I?" I asked.

"You can, Ms. Emeline," he answered. Taking his father's hand, he led him to the seat next to mine. "Dad, you sit here."

Without even questioning his son, Levi sat down. I was positive my mouth was hanging open as I stared at the little matchmaker in training. Looking at Mom and Dad, I saw they both attempted to hide their smiles—and failed.

"Where may I sit?" Rhett asked my father.

Dad cleared his throat and schooled his face as he pointed to his own chair at the head of the table, next to Levi. "You can sit at the head of the table."

Rhett's eyes went wide. "I can?"

I took a plate and cut a small piece of lasagna. I held it up for Levi to see.

He nodded. "Perfect amount. Salad, Rhett?" Levi asked.

"Yes, please! Ranch dressing on my salad, Daddy. And make sure there's a tomato in there!"

I placed the plate in front of Rhett and nearly melted when he looked up at me and smiled. "Thank you, Ms. Emeline."

Sitting down, I tried to ignore the fact that Levi was so close to me. My mind wandered to the days when he would come over and eat dinner with us regularly. He always sat across from me, and I would dream he'd glance up and blow me a kiss. Or he'd finally ask if I wanted to see a movie or go to dinner. Of course, that never happened.

"Em?"

Levi's voice caused me to jerk, and I looked over at him. "Yes?"

He chuckled. "You were a million miles away. I said your name like three times."

"Oh, sorry. I've got a lot on my mind with the camp starting soon."

He smiled, and I had to tear my eyes away from his mouth. When my gaze met his, I cleared my throat and focused back on my food.

"Are you excited about helping out, or is it more of a hardship?" I asked before taking a bite of my lasagna.

"It's not a hardship at all. I'm actually looking forward to camp. Rhett is, as well."

I glanced at Rhett, who was engaged in a very animated conversation with Gatlin.

Laughing, I motioned to them. "He really likes Gatlin."

Levi grinned. "He loves all of you guys."

"I thought he was going to sit next to me. He asked if anyone was sitting there."

"Really?" Levi asked, glancing at his son, then back to me. "I have a sneaky feeling he wants us to be more than friends."

Coughing, I quickly grabbed my water.

Levi laughed softly. "Don't worry. I think it's just a phase he's going through. The therapist, back in Denver, said that Rhett's worried about my happiness."

Studying Rhett, I ached for the little guy. He had such a tender heart. "That's got to be hard on a kid who's only six. To worry about his parents, I mean."

Levi nodded but didn't say anything.

The rest of the meal was filled with different conversations between smaller groups. Levi and Gatlin started talking about the cattle ranch, while my grandfather Gus, Caden, and my father discussed buying a new tractor. My mother, grandmother Nellie, and Ensley were chatting about one of the horses Ensley had recently shoed, and how she needed to be rehomed.

When I looked over at Rhett, he smiled at me before shoving a forkful of salad into his mouth. I returned the gesture and sat back in my chair, quietly observing everyone.

"What about you, Em?" Levi asked.

Setting my glass of wine back on the table, I glanced at him. "I'm sorry, I wasn't listening to what you were talking about."

Gatlin replied first. "Levi was saying he thinks we should do a clinic at the ranch."

"A clinic?" My gaze bounced between Gatlin and Levi. "What kind of clinic?"

Levi wiped his mouth and set his napkin on the table. "Something that focuses on the production side of cattle ranching. Topics could be about bovine reproduction, artificial insemination, health, and nutrition. You could have them throughout the year as well since guests wouldn't be at the mercy of a school schedule."

Gatlin nodded his head and pointed his fork at me. "We could do it for the equine side of the ranch, as well. A riding and horsemanship clinic. We could teach about breeding and raising horses skilled in working cattle. Ensley can even teach a farrier clinic."

Levi added, "For people who are interested in hoof care. She could talk about how to become a farrier, what her day is like, advanced shoeing techniques."

"What are we talking about?" Ensley asked from down the table.

"Levi has some great ideas about teaching clinics," Caden stated, obviously already aware of Levi's thoughts.

My father leaned back in his seat. "That sounds interesting."

"Caden and I were talking about it. It would be another way to bring income to the ranch," Levi said, looking from my father to me. "I was wanting to get your input as well, Emeline, since some classes might be a few days, and people would be staying in the cabins."

"I think it's a great idea," my mother put in before I could reply.

Panic was suddenly setting in...panic that these clinics could push out the summer camps since those would be for profit and my camps obviously aren't.

Gatlin looked at our father. "Dad, you talked about possibly starting clinics before, remember that?"

He nodded. "It was something that your uncle Mike pushed for years ago."

"That's right," Caden said. "I remember him talking about it."

"What about the camps? I wanted to do a camp in August for kids with special needs."

All eyes shot to me.

My mother smiled. "We would never stop the camps, Emeline. But you have to admit, they *are* getting smaller and they're only two weeks out of the year. The rest of the time the cabins sit empty unless rented out. And if we can use the cabins to generate more income, that would benefit not only the ranch, but the camps and the Christmas event as well. I've also been meaning to talk to you about the camp for kids with special needs. The idea is amazing, and one I don't want to push aside, but I think it's going to take a bit more research than we thought. At least, according to the lawyers.

We have to make sure we have everything covered. It's a very high-liability situation, and one that I don't want to rush into too quickly."

"Was that the second thing you wanted to talk to me about today, before you got sidetracked with the cherry pie?"

My mother's brows rose. I knew my voice sounded condescending, but why hadn't she spoken to me about something so important before springing it on me in front of everyone else?

"Yes. It was."

"I agree about the clinics," Grandpa Gus stated as he circled the conversation back to the clinics. "They'd be a good source of income for the ranch."

My grandmother glanced at me. "Don't worry, Emeline. The camps have become a rich part of our history on the ranch. They're not going anywhere."

I smiled at her slightly, even though my stomach was reeling. "Who would be in charge of these clinics?" I asked in a tone that sounded angry.

Caden frowned slightly. "Gatlin and I can handle the cattle clinics. I know Mom is taking a step back, but we can speak with Marshall and see if he's onboard with taking on that task, since you manage the camps and have your work here on the ranch."

"You mean put Marshall in charge of the equine clinics and not me? You don't think I can handle it? The camps are only two weeks out of the summer, I'm pretty confident I can add more to my plate," I stated as I glared at my older brother.

His frown deepened. "No, I don't think anything of the sort. But I can't read your mind, Emeline. And honestly, you seem like you're against the idea of the clinics."

"I'm not *against* them, Caden. I literally just found out about them, after all. Can you at least give me time to process the fact that my camps are likely going to be downsized and replaced?"

The entire room fell silent.

Clearing his throat, Levi turned to me. "I don't think anyone is talking about replacing the camps, Em. It was just a suggestion, since the cabins sit empty most of the year, unless they're rented for retreats and such. I thought it would be a good place to look for additional income. It might even help with the camps, if you have any deficit in the fundraising."

I felt like a complete idiot now. Here I was, throwing a tantrum...and for what reason? I didn't have one.

I forced a smile. "No, you're right. I'm sorry I overreacted. It's a good idea. I just need a moment to process it all."

My eyes caught Ensley's. She smiled softly and motioned for me to join her in the kitchen. "If we're done, I'm going to clear the table."

I stood quickly. "I'll help."

Mom stood as well, but Ensley told her and Grams to sit back down. "Emeline and I have it. You two relax."

Picking up my plate, I forced another smile. "Anyone else finished?"

Levi went to stand. I put my hand on his shoulder. "You're a guest. Please, keep chatting. Ensley and I will take care of this."

"Thank you, girls," Mom said with a slightly concerned smile.

After grabbing a few plates, I followed my sister to the kitchen. Ensley put her dishes on the counter, turned to me, and sighed.

"Emeline, what was that all about?"

Setting the dishes in the sink, I leaned against the counter. Tears pricked at the back of my eyes. Looking into my sister's gaze, I whispered the words I'd tried to deny for so many years.

"I think I'm in love with Levi. No, I *know* I am—and I don't know what to do about it. Now I feel like everything I've worked for is slowly slipping from my hands."

Her eyes widened. "Oh shit. I need Mom for this one."

CHAPTER TWELVE

LEVI

ONCE EMELINE AND ENSLEY headed to the kitchen, I said, "I didn't mean to make Emeline upset, or make her think I don't care about the camps."

Vivianne waved off my concern. "Emeline lives, eats, and breathes those camps. She has since she was young, and I think for a moment she thought we were going to phase them out."

"I didn't mean to suggest that at all."

Ladd shook his head. "You didn't. Emeline has always dreamed big, and I love that about her. But the truth of the matter is, it's getting more expensive to run the camps since we don't charge the campers. Her idea for a camp for kids with special needs is amazing, but would cost even *more* to run."

"Have you ever thought of opening them up to paid campers?" I asked.

Nellie shook her head. "That isn't why we started the camps. It was never about making a profit off of them. The need is diminishing; therefore, the camps are shrinking. That, in itself, is a good thing. That means fewer kids are growing up in poverty in River Falls, and there are fewer kids at River Haven, which is a community goal we're very proud of. The clinics are a great idea, Levi."

"I agree," Ladd said. "Gatlin, Caden…get with your uncles Mike and David. Put your heads together and come up with a business plan. Then we can all meet. Levi, I'd love to have your input as well. I think it would be advantageous to have a vet on hand for some of these clinics."

I nodded. "I agree, and I'm here to help in any way I can."

Ensley entered the room and went straight to her mother. She bent down, whispering something into her ear.

Vivianne stood. "Excuse me a moment."

Turning to Caden, I said, "If I upset your sister in any way, I won't forgive myself."

"You didn't."

"Maybe I should go talk to her."

"I think something else is bothering her. My mother and sister can handle it."

Gatlin and Ladd started to clear the rest of the table. I stood and offered to help.

"Nonsense," Nellie said. "Let's head into the living room."

Gus helped his wife up, and they motioned for Rhett to follow. Moose was stuck to Rhett's side like glue, and I knew my son was loving it.

Once it was just me and Caden in the dining room, I raised a brow. "What was that *really* about, man?"

He shrugged. "I don't even pretend to understand women anymore."

I laughed, but it didn't sound authentic, even to me. I followed Caden into the living room with an uneasy feeling

I couldn't shake. I glanced back and could see through the large opening to the kitchen. Vivianne was hugging Emeline...and my heart felt like it dropped straight to my stomach.

~

"Daddy."

The feel of someone gently pushing on my shoulder caused me to stir.

"Daddy! Daddy, are you awake?"

I opened one eye and found my son standing over me, a wide smile on his face.

"I'm awake now, Rhett."

He tugged on my arm. "Get up! Get up! Today is camp day!"

Laughing, I let Rhett pull me into a seated position. He crawled onto my bed and started to bounce on his knees.

I dragged my hands down my face. "Son, what time is it?"

"It's six!"

Frowning, I slowly shook my head. "Why in the world are you up so early? We don't even drop you off until ten this morning."

He shrugged. "I'm happy, that's all."

I swung my legs over the side of the bed. "I'm glad you're excited about it, bud."

"You'll be there today, right, Daddy?"

"All day. I've volunteered to help get everyone to their cabins and settled in."

He smiled. "Can we make French toast for breakfast?"

I let out a breath. "We've got everything packed up and ready to go, so I don't see why we can't make some French toast."

Rhett stood on my bed, jumped a couple of times, then jumped off.

"Do you think Moose will be with Emeline?" he asked right before he got to the bedroom door.

"I'm not sure, buddy."

I hadn't seen or spoken to Emeline since we'd had dinner with her family. She'd texted me information about camp—what Rhett would need, how I would be helping out, things like that.

I stumbled to the bathroom. After splashing water on my face, I got the day started. Breakfast was filled with Rhett going on and on about how excited he was for camp. I was hoping he'd be able to make some friends before the start of school this fall. He was going into first grade, and I was pretty sure most of the kids, if not all, had gone to kindergarten together, and so they would already know each other.

"Dad, did you pack my toothbrush?"

"Dad?" I asked, placing his bag into the back seat of my truck. "When did I lose the title 'Daddy'?"

Rhett rolled his eyes. "I have to practice so I don't say it in front of my new friends."

I lifted my chin. "Ahh, got it. We're playing it cool."

He nodded. "Let's go!"

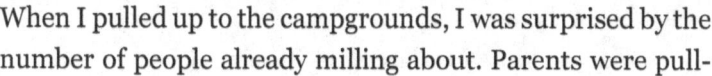

When I pulled up to the campgrounds, I was surprised by the number of people already milling about. Parents were pulling sleeping bags and suitcases out of trucks and cars, as volunteers helped them find the right cabins. Larger vans were parked to the side, each emblazoned with the name River Haven. My heart broke for the kids from the orphanage. I knew they tried their best to give the kids good memories, but I couldn't imagine what life was like without parents.

I glanced at Rhett, who wore an excited expression.

"I hope I meet my new best friend!" he said with a smile as he scanned the crowd of adults and younger kids.

Feeling a tug in my chest, I ruffled the hair on the top of his head, only to have him push my arm away.

"*Dad*! You're treating me like a baby."

I held up my hands in defense. "Habits are hard to break, kiddo."

As I surveyed the crowd and smiled, I watched all the kids filled with excitement. Mine included. I had insisted they let me pay for Rhett to attend. Of course, that was only after Vivianne and I had argued about it for thirty minutes straight. We had the means, and Rhett wasn't going to attend unless they allowed me to pay. We haggled over a number, and she eventually agreed.

But...once some of these people found out Rhett was the son of the new veterinarian in town, they might start to question why he was attending.

"Shit," I mumbled.

"What's wrong?"

The sound of Emeline's voice behind me made my stomach feel like I'd just tipped over the peak of a roller coaster and started the freefall.

What in the hell is that about?

I quickly told myself she'd simply scared me. Turning—my breath got caught in my throat.

Her hair was pulled back into a low ponytail, and she wore jeans that hugged her curvy body in all the right places. Her white T-shirt had River Falls Summer Camp on the front, and she was wearing a baseball cap. Fuck, if she didn't look adorable.

"Em."

The way I said her name softly caused her to look a bit surprised. My cheeks heated, and I started talking too fast. "I just got to thinking. What if people think Rhett isn't paying for the camp, since none of the other kids have to? We're not from an underprivileged family. I don't know why I didn't think of this sooner."

Emeline smiled as she put her hand on my arm and gave it a slight squeeze. A bolt of heat raced through my body.

"It's okay." She chuckled. "We have kids at camp who are part of our family all the time. My uncles' grandkids all attended. And even though my mother argued about it, you *insisted* on paying. We won't share that, of course, but it'll be okay."

"I just don't want him..." I glanced down at Rhett, who was talking to a young girl around his age as they both pet Moose, who'd made an appearance after all. "To be treated differently by the staff or the kids. I don't want them to think he's..."

"Privileged? He is, if we're being honest. And don't worry, I plan to have Rhett do a lot of helping out, so it doesn't seem like he's being treated any differently. It would really only be the older kids who'll likely figure out who he is."

"I see you've already thought about this."

She shrugged. "When my uncles' grandkids come to camp, we do the same for them. The kids who've been coming to camp the longest know that the Wilde kids attend, as well, but that they're required to help out a bit more. Pull their weight, if you will."

It felt so damn nice to know that Rhett was being treated as if he were a Wilde. "That means a lot to me, Em, that you think of Rhett as part of the family."

A wide smile broke out across her beautiful face. Christ, when did this girl become such a beautiful woman? A flash of desire swept over me, and I fought the urge to pull her into my arms. I quickly turned away to see the young girl and another boy, also around the same age as Rhett, skipping away hand in hand.

Moose and Rhett watched after them, the dog not moving from my son's side.

"Moose is trained well."

Emeline nodded. "He's a good boy."

"Who was that?" I asked Rhett.

"That's my two new friends! Katie and Jimmy. They're twins and they live in a place called River Haven. They don't have a mommy or daddy."

Crouching to get to his eye level, I nodded. "I know, bud."

"They said none of the kids from there have a mom or a dad. How come?"

I glanced up to Emeline in a silent plea for help in explaining this to my six-year-old.

She squatted next to me. "River Haven is an orphanage. I think your grammy talked about it with you and your daddy."

How in the hell had she known that?

"It's a place where kids who've lost their mother and father can stay when no one else can take care of them."

"Where did their mom and dad go?" asked Rhett.

"Well," Emeline started, "some have gone to Heaven. Some were too young to be able to care for babies. And some went to live at River Haven because their mother or father didn't take very good care of them. *But*, they have us. And we're like a family to them. This is why we have the camp, Rhett. So that the kids from River Haven, and other kids who can't afford to do fun things like go to camp and ride horses and such, can come here and feel safe and loved. And do lots of fun things."

Rhett frowned. "Can we not afford to do fun things anymore, Daddy?"

Before I could answer, Emeline replied, "You're my special guest at camp. Since you're basically family, you'll be asked to help out a bit more. Don't worry, though, you'll still get to do all the fun things with the other campers."

I watched as my son's eyes lit up. "So, I'm like your helper?"

Emeline nodded. "Yep!"

"I can help with anything, Ms. Emeline!"

"Of course! That's why I'm so thankful you're here. But first, let's get your stuff to your cabin, and then you can start helping me."

Rhett hugged Emeline, then stepped back. "I'll be the best helper ever!"

Moose barked, and we all laughed.

"Moose and I both know you will be."

Before I could reach for his stuff, Rhett tossed the sleeping bag over his shoulder, reached for his bag, and said, "Let's go, Dad! I need to help Ms. Emeline."

As we put Rhett's things away, a few more kids came into the cabin. Jimmy was one of the kids, and he lit up when he saw Rhett.

"You're in my cabin!"

The two boys exchanged excited bouts of running around before they were seated on Rhett's bed, and he was telling my son all about horses.

An older woman, maybe in her late fifties, walked up to me. "Jimmy and his sister Katie love horses. They haven't been with us long at River Haven."

"What happened to their parents?" I asked, keeping my eyes on the boys.

"They passed away in a boating accident. No living relatives on either side."

Turning to look at her, I asked, "Were they from River Falls?"

She nodded, then faced me. Holding out her hand, she smiled. "I'm so sorry, I'm Leanne Rogers. I'm the director at River Haven."

"Levi Tucker, that's my son, Rhett. I've known the Wildes pretty much my entire life. Caden Wilde and I are best friends."

Leanne grinned as she shook my hand. "I know your father. He donates to River Haven often, and we appreciate it very much."

"Sounds like my father. I'll be taking over his practice, and I can assure you, that means carrying on with his dedication to helping the community."

She gave me a nod. "That's appreciated."

I looked back at Jimmy. "Do you mind if I ask who his parents were?"

"Jim and Lori Mills."

The ground felt like it shifted under my feet. I'd known them both in high school. Played football with Jim, and had even taken Lori out a few times.

"But...Jim and Lori both had parents here in River Falls."

Leanne sighed. "All deceased. Jimmy and Katie were living with their maternal grandparents after their parents' accident, but both ended up getting very sick and passed within a few months of one another."

Caden walked into the cabin, smiling when he saw Rhett sitting with Jimmy and another little boy, who must have come in when I wasn't paying attention.

"Looks like Rhett and Jimmy are hitting it off."

Frowning at Caden, I asked, "Why didn't you tell me Jim and Lori Mills passed away?"

His smile faded. "It happened almost the same time as Brooke. I didn't want to bring you more bad news. I thought I *did* tell you, though. I'm sorry about that."

I shook my head. "No, it's okay." More senseless death.

"Brooke?" Leanne asked.

Caden gave me an apologetic look.

"My daughter. She passed away in a car accident earlier this year."

Leanne's face went from curious to stunned to sympathetic all within a few seconds. "I'm so sorry for your loss."

"Thank you."

Clearing her throat, Leanne said, "I'd better go see who else I can get settled. It was nice to meet you, Mr. Tucker."

Tipping my hat at her, I replied, "The pleasure was all mine."

Two teen boys entered the cabin, introduced themselves, and said they were camp counselors assigned to this cabin and the one next door. They were both high school seniors and had been volunteering at the camp for the past five years.

The cabins were all named after constellations, which paired with the fact that all the horses were named after stars and constellations. Rhett was in Orion. I'd heard Jimmy tell Rhett that his sister, Katie, was in Aquarius.

Caden and I slipped out so the counselors could get things going with the kids. I waved goodbye to Rhett, who waved back. He looked so happy. I had a strong feeling this camp was going to be better for him than I'd even initially thought.

The rest of the day was filled with what some might call organized chaos. The kids spent time with their cabinmates, getting to know each other. Then, after lunch, they all gathered in the camp's central area and started playing games. The older kids helped the younger ones when needed. The laughter alone was enough to make anyone's bad day better.

Even Caden, who was a grump to the highest level, got in on the action. It was nice to see him laughing and enjoying himself. The only time he seemed unhappy was when Lilibeth was around. She was also volunteering today, and I swore I saw her everywhere. Her long blonde hair was in a single braid with flowers woven through the length. She practically beamed happiness, which was the opposite of Caden.

They ended up having to partner in the three-legged race, and you would have thought Caden had been paired up with the devil himself, given how he acted.

Once dinner was done, the kids all went to the living room to watch a movie and settle down. It would be an early night, since tomorrow was filled with endless activities.

Rhett had proved to be a good helper, and I was so proud of him. I could see him volunteering at this camp when he got older. It was clear he enjoyed being involved.

Caden and I walked back to the barn to make sure everything was set up for tomorrow. The younger kids, ages ten and under, would be going horseback riding. The older kids will either do archery or head to the lake to fish and swim.

"You take part in the camps more than I thought," I said as we entered the barn.

He shrugged. "I always try to help the first few days, since things are a bit crazy. Then I go back to my side of the farm and avoid this like the plague."

I laughed. "It's a lot of work. I was stunned when I pulled up and saw all the people."

"Yeah, it's a lot to manage, and my mother and sister do a great job with it. Emeline gets the volunteers and counselors lined up each year. I don't know how she keeps up with it all, but she does. There are only two camp sessions, but it's a hell of a lot of work on top of what she already does on the ranch."

Marshall and a few other hands were setting out saddles in the aisle of the barn.

"Getting ready for tomorrow?" Caden asked, hitting him on the back.

"Yes, sir."

"How did you guys afford to buy all these saddles for the kids?" I asked.

"Fundraisers. The rodeo fundraiser brings in the most, and then Emeline hosts a charity dinner every winter, which is our second-biggest fundraiser. Some of them were donated by community members, as well."

Emeline walked around the corner, leading a beautiful white and brown paint mare. It was saddled up, and she was wearing riding gear.

"Taking your ride?" Caden asked.

"I am."

"Your ride?" I asked.

"She always checks the trails before they take the campers out," Caden replied before his sister could.

"Do you mind if I ride out with you?"

That seemed to surprise Emeline. She glanced at her brother, almost as if asking for his permission, before turning her attention back to me. "No, I don't mind. You can ride Leo. He's been itching to get out and stretch his legs."

"Stallion?" I asked wearily.

Caden smirked. "No, he's a gelding."

I followed Caden, got the gelding saddled up, and met Emeline in front of the barn.

"Ready?" she asked with a smile that lit up her entire face. It was clear that being on horseback was her happy place. I couldn't blame her for that. It was mine, too.

"Lead the way."

We walked side by side away from the barn and toward a trail that I'd ridden a dozen times in my youth with Caden and Ensley.

"I haven't been on this trail in forever," I said, as Emeline took the lead.

"I used to hate that I couldn't ever go with you guys when you went riding. Mom always told me I was too young."

I chuckled. "Trust me, you weren't missing out on anything. Caden and Ensley would spend most of the time fighting with one another. Each one thought they knew the best way up to the lookout point."

"We've added a few trails that you haven't been on."

My horse followed hers as she turned to the right. It was indeed a trail I'd never taken before. "Is this heading toward the lake?" I asked.

"Sure is."

The trail widened, and I moved up alongside her.

"Today seemed to go good, from what I saw."

She smiled. "It did. The first day is always a little overwhelming, but once the kids get settled, everything falls into place."

When we arrived at the top of the trail, it opened into a large meadow. The sun was hanging lower in the sky, but we still had at least another hour before sunset.

Emeline got off her horse, tossed the reins over the saddle, and let her roam. "You can leave them, they won't go anywhere."

"Where are *we* going?"

Glancing back over her shoulder, she winked. "It's a surprise."

I couldn't ignore the way my heart felt like it kicked into overdrive as I watched Emeline walking in front of me. My eyes drifted to her perfect ass, and I nearly moaned. My dick came to attention, too, and I had to admit this was the first time in ages that I'd desired anyone sexually.

Christ, this was *Emeline* I was gawking at. Caden would kick my ass.

As if she'd read my mind, she called out, "Enjoying the view back there, or did you want to join me?"

Picking up the pace, I quickly made my way to her side. "The view *was* pretty damn nice, I have to say."

She smiled as her cheeks turned a bright shade of pink. "How do you think Rhett did today?" she asked.

"Great. He met a little boy named Jimmy, and they hit it off."

"Jimmy Mills?"

I looked at her, noticing her intense focus as we climbed an incline.

"Yes. His parents died in a boating accident, I was told. I went to high school with them both."

She nodded. "Yeah, it was really sad. They went to live with Lori's parents, and within months, they'd both passed from pneumonia. They couldn't find any other living relatives, so the kids had to go to River Haven. Breaks my heart. I heard a young couple from Estes Park wanted to adopt Katie, but not Jimmy. I think that it's so incredibly cruel to separate siblings, especially *twins*. They have a special bond."

I nodded. "Yeah, I agree."

We made it to the top of the trail—and I froze. The scene before me looked like a picture. Damn, I missed these views. The ragged edges of the mountains rose over the valley, lit by the evening sun. Dots of snow scattered across the mountaintops seemed to glow a light pink. I couldn't imagine what it would be like once the sun started to set.

"Oh wow! This is beautiful, Em."

"I know. It's one of my favorite places on the ranch. I found it one day while following the wildlife path. Then I showed it to Uncle David, and the next thing I knew, there was a riding path. I used to come up here to think."

"Do you bring the kids up here?"

"No. The pasture we rode up in is where we bring them. They collect wildflowers, bring them back to camp, and the kids can press them to take home. It's a bit too dangerous to bring them up here, what with the drop-off right there."

"I bet it's beautiful at sunset."

She walked over to a large boulder and sat on it. "It is. You should see it in the winter. The way the sun hits the snow on the sides of the mountains, it looks like Heaven opened and diamonds spilled out. It sparkles."

I joined her on the boulder and stared out at the view. I could get lost in my own thoughts easily, sitting here.

"Em, I wanted to talk to you about the clinics."

Drawing her legs up closer to her chest, she rested her chin on her knee. When she didn't say anything, I went on.

"I didn't mean for you to think the guys should replace the camps. I didn't mean that at all. Caden and I were talking about profits and such, and I thought the clinics would be a good addition to the ranch. Please know I wasn't trying to push you out."

Keeping her head on her knee, she turned her head and smiled softly. "The camps are growing smaller each year. I know it's a good thing that our need for them is lessening, which hopefully means more families are doing well. Or the kids at the orphanage are getting adopted. It's just...I've worked so hard on these camps to grow them to what they are today. I know we could open them to paying campers, but that isn't why we started the place. And my idea of doing a camp for kids with special needs is something I really wanted to try."

"Why can't you?"

She sighed. "I had a meeting with Caden, Uncle David, and Uncle Mike, as well as my mother. The insurance cost alone would be more than we could afford right now. Then you have to hire the right staff, who are certified to work with kids with disabilities." She drew in a deep breath and slowly let it out. "We do great with the fundraising, but it wouldn't be enough to cover the current camps, plus one that would require so much additional cost."

"If the other camps are growing smaller, could you combine the free sessions into one per summer, to help with the cost? Maybe do a few paid camps as well? You've got it all down pat, and I know people would pay."

"But again, it goes against why we started the camps."

"There's nothing wrong with making a profit, Emeline."

She shook her head. "It would be so much more work." She looked at me, and her eyes were filled with sadness. "I think this is a dream that's slowly going to fade away, sooner than later. Holding the clinics makes more sense for the ranch. We might even be able to do more fun things with the cabins."

"What about doing a dude ranch?"

"A dude ranch?"

"Yeah, why not? People would love to do that."

She chewed on her lower lip, then looked back out over the view. "Can you imagine people coming onto the ranch and Caden having to deal with them?"

We both laughed.

"He would lose his ever-loving mind."

"He would." She exhaled. "Maybe it's time I concentrated on growing the equine side of the ranch. I really do love my job, and the camps are so much work. I know my mother was glad to step back from the major planning and handling of them. Now I see why. I can't imagine doing a camp every single week for three months. No, thank you."

"Em, you've been doing these camps for several years. Do you think maybe you're simply longing for something different?"

She shrugged. "Possibly. Something just hit me that night that you brought up the clinics. It's almost like something shifted in me. I want more. The only problem is, some of what I want is..."

"Is?" I asked.

She looked like she was struggling to say what she wanted to say. "Unattainable...that's the only word I can think to describe it."

"What is it that's so unattainable?"

I studied her profile while she remained silent. The desire to pull her into my arms and tell her I'd do literally *anything* if she would simply smile was almost overwhelming. I never had a connection this strong to Caroline.

I'd *always* had a connection to Emeline, though, even when we were younger. She just had something about her that I was drawn to.

She looked at me, and our eyes locked. The air between us seemed to heat, and my body came to life as her eyes darkened, and when she licked her lips, I dropped my gaze to watch the motion. We both leaned closer to one another.

I was about to bridge the remaining distance between us when Emeline scrambled back.

I frowned. "I'm sorry, I thought you—"

She quickly stood. "That's the problem, Levi."

Confused, I also stood. "What's the problem?"

Emeline motioned between us. "This! You've repeatedly said you aren't interested in a relationship, yet the more time I spend with you, the more confused I get. I want..."

I took a step closer. "You want what?"

Her mouth opened, then quickly shut.

"Em, please tell me what's going on in your head."

"I can't."

"Why not?"

She slowly shook her head before dropping it with a sigh. "It's *you*, Levi. You're the one I want. I have for years, and I thought..."

Her head lifted, and our eyes met.

"I thought it was a crush I was over, but I'm not. If anything, my feelings for you are stronger than ever, and everything in my life feels like it's changing, and all I want is..." She closed her eyes and whispered, "You."

"Em—"

Her eyes snapped open, and she took a step away from me. "You don't have to say anything. I know the last thing you want is a relationship. *I know*. And I also know you think I'm too young for you. And then there's Caden, even though he told me he's fine with it, and Rhett, and just stupid *life*!"

Walking up to her, I did the only thing I knew was right in this very moment. I cupped her face in my hands, and kissed her.

She opened to me almost instantly, and the kiss immediately grew deeper.

Emeline melted against my body as she wound her arms

around my neck. I dropped my hands from her face and gripped her hips, drawing her body closer to mine. This kiss was unlike anything I had ever experienced before in my life. My fucking knees felt weak, and my heart pounded so hard in my chest, I was sure Emeline could feel it.

After what felt like an eternity, we slowly drew back. I leaned my forehead against hers and drew in a deep breath.

"You're not too young, Em. And Caden isn't a problem. And I *wasn't* wanting a relationship...but then you came back into my life and everything changed."

She moved her head back. "What do you mean?"

I smiled as I tucked a loose strand of hair behind her ear. "My marriage with Caroline wasn't a happy one. We had happy *times*, and I'm grateful for my kids, but something was always missing, and I could never put my finger on it. Maybe it was because we were forced into marriage so young, I don't know. Together, we were like wind and fire. She was always angry, discontent, and no matter how hard I tried to make her happy, I just fanned those flames instead. It was a dangerous combination. We didn't *match*.

"I wish Caroline all the best, but she wasn't the person who caught my soul on fire. Since I've been home, spending time with you has made it crystal clear that *you're* that person, Em. Every time I'm near you, something inside me comes to life. I've been trying to ignore it, because a part of me keeps saying I need time for myself and for Rhett. But he's thriving here beyond all my expectations...and I'm tired of fighting whatever this is between us."

She swallowed hard. "Levi, I have to be honest with you about something."

"Please do," I begged.

Her eyes closed, and she seemed to be debating before she snapped her eyes open again, and she just let it all out.

"I feel something so profound that I can't explain it, and I don't want to hide it anymore. My mother told me that I needed to tell you how I felt, and so did Caden, but I didn't want to lose our friendship. But then I think about Ensley and Grady, and I don't want to go the rest of my life regretting that I wasn't honest with you about how I feel."

"How do you feel, Em?"

Her eyes fell to the ground.

I placed my finger under her chin and lifted so her eyes met mine once again. "How do you feel, Emeline?"

Pressing her lips together, her eyes filled with tears.

"Please," I whispered.

"I'm in love with you, Levi. I know you don't feel the same way about me, and that's okay. I don't want it to come between us, or for you to feel awkward around me." Her eyes closed. "Oh God, I should have kept my mouth shut."

I drew her to me and held her tight as she buried her face against my chest. "I'm glad you told me, Em. I can't say I'm in love with you—"

She tried to pull away, but I wouldn't let her go.

"But I *can* say what I feel for you is so much more than friendship. Truth be told, Em, I've always been drawn to you. Even when we were younger, there was something about you that made me want to spend time with you."

She lifted her head slightly and peeked at me. It was so fucking adorable, I wanted to kiss her again.

"I've got a crazy idea," I said with a wink.

"What's that?" she asked, her eyes lighting up.

"What would you say to going out on a date with me?"

A smile erupted across her beautiful face. "I'd say I like that idea." Then she glanced over my shoulder. "Look at the sky."

When I turned, I was captivated by a reddish-pink sky. It somehow felt like the most perfect place on Earth for us to express how we felt about one another.

"We should get going before we lose daylight," she said.

When I looked back at Emeline, she was gazing out over the valley. It was clear she loved this place with her whole heart.

I took her hand in mine and brought it to my lips. Kissing the back of her hand, I smiled at her.

"We could count this as our first date," she said softly, her eyes drifting to my mouth as she spoke.

Nodding, I quickly pulled her to me, causing her to laugh. "In that case, I think we should probably kiss once or twice more, don't you think?"

Wrapping her arms around my neck, she nodded, lifting up to her toes. Her mouth met mine in another explosive kiss.

If just kissing this woman was driving my body insane, I didn't even want to think about what it would be like to make love to her.

My hands slipped under her shirt, and when I found her nipples hard under her bra, I rubbed my thumbs against them, causing her to moan. The sound traveled straight to my cock, which throbbed in my jeans. I hadn't even taken myself into my own hand for the last few months, and if this kept up, I'd come in my pants.

Emeline's hands found their way under *my* shirt, and the feel of her skin on mine was enough to make my mind go blank. For a moment, I considered pulling her to the ground and taking her right there. Luckily, I regained power over my dick, and my mind started to work again. I wasn't about to have sex with Emeline on the ground, out in the open. Not for our first time.

She drew back eventually, panting as if she'd just run a marathon. "We should stop."

"Agreed," I said, my own breath sounding heavy. "I'm going to guess you're not gonna be able to break away this week for that date?"

Looking sad, she slowly shook her head. "I don't think so. Starting tomorrow, it's going to be very busy days."

"Then we're going to have to get creative."

Her brows lifted. "Creative?"

"If you think I can see you every day and not at least kiss you again, you're crazy."

She giggled as she took my hand. "I'm sure we can figure something out. We need to get going."

We headed down the path, walking hand in hand until we got to the pasture. Both horses were still there, only a few feet from one another.

Emeline whistled, and her mare lifted her head, then happily trotted over to us. The gelding followed. We mounted up and rode back down the trail in silence. It was a comfortable silence, though. Giving me time to think about how I'd let Rhett know that Emeline and I would be going on a date.

I didn't think he would have a problem with it, but how would everyone else feel?

CHAPTER THIRTEEN

EMELINE

I WAS POSITIVE THAT once we got back to the barn, everyone would know Levi and I had kissed. Hell, my lips still tingled, and my heart rate hadn't returned to normal.

As we rode up, Levi looked my way and winked. I couldn't help but smile back at him.

Marshall approached us, along with Caden and Lilibeth. When my eyes met hers, she attempted not to grin but lost the battle.

"Trail okay?" Caden asked as Levi dismounted.

Levi nodded to Marshall as he took the horse's reins. "Thank you, Marshall."

"Everything was fine," I replied, sliding off and quickly walking my horse toward the wash station.

"We can take care of the horses, Emeline," Marshall said with a smile. "I've got Tommy here to help out."

"Are you sure you don't mind?" I asked.

Marshall chuckled. "It *is* my job."

I squeezed his arm. "Thank you, Marshall." Turning to face everyone, I couldn't help but notice how Caden was glaring at Lilibeth. "Is everything okay?"

Lilibeth grinned. "It is. We had a bit of a situation earlier, but everything's fine now."

Caden made a grunting sound.

I took in my brother...and noticed he was soaking wet. "Caden, why are you wet?"

He shot a look toward Lilibeth, who covered her mouth with a hand to hide her smile, and that seemed to make Caden even angrier.

"*She*," he dramatically pointed toward Lilibeth, "made me look like an utter fool."

"You did that all on your own, cowboy," Lilibeth retorted, hands now on her hips.

Levi glanced between the two of them. "What happened?"

Caden shot Lilibeth yet another dirty look.

She motioned for him to tell the story. "Please, do tell them what happened. I don't think I could do it justice."

Caden rolled his eyes, then sighed. "One of the kids got stuck."

"Stuck?" I asked. I knew it wasn't anything bad because Lilibeth's shoulders were bouncing in her sad attempt to keep from laughing. "Stuck in what?"

Now the corners of Caden's mouth twitched as he fought not to smile. "A flowerpot."

Levi and I both said at the same time, "A flowerpot?"

Lilibeth burst into laughter and turned her back on us, walking away some.

Caden cleared his throat. "He thought it would be fun to try to sit inside that big terracotta pot that Grams has had for years."

"He?" Levi asked. "Please tell me it wasn't Rhett."

This time, *Caden* covered his mouth...and turned away slightly.

"For fuck's sake," Levi muttered. "Did my kid get stuck in a damn pot?"

Caden nodded. "He did. But I got him out."

Lilibeth was bent over, crossing her legs. "I'm going to pee!" she cried out as she fell into another fit of laughter. I couldn't help but giggle, and I wasn't even sure why. Although the picture of little Rhett stuck in the flowerpot *was* kind of funny.

Caden lost the battle to stay mad and finally chuckled.

"All right, so if he got out and he's okay, what's so funny? And, Caden, that doesn't explain why you're wet and why you seem pissed at Lilibeth?" I asked.

As if remembering he was supposed to be angry, Caden stopped laughing and glared at Lilibeth again. "Because I had it all under control, and *she* was trying to micromanage the situation."

"The situation of my son being stuck in a pot?" Levi clarified.

"Yes. I knew how to get him out."

It was Levi's turn to smile. "Because you have experience with being stuck in pots?"

Lilibeth positively screamed in laughter. "I said the same thing!"

"No, I just knew how to get him out, and this one started to argue with me in front of Rhett's entire cabin, and then... well...it doesn't matter. I got Rhett out."

"He tried pulling Rhett out. But he lost his grip, stumbled backward, and landed in the water trough!"

My hand flew to my mouth, and I started to laugh. "That explains why you're wet."

"I would've been fine if Lilibeth hadn't been trying to 'help'," he finger-quoted. "She tripped me."

Lilibeth gasped. "I did not trip you! You stumbled back, then tripped over a bucket. I didn't have anything to do with it."

Caden glared at her again, which only made her laugh harder.

"But Rhett's definitely okay?" Levi asked.

"He's fine. I'm going back to my side of the ranch now," Caden said before turning on his heels and stomping away.

Lilibeth looked at me and shrugged as another small giggle slipped free.

Levi shook his head at Caden's retreating back, then turned his focus on me. A smile spread on his face, and for a moment, I totally forgot that Lilibeth was even there.

"Thank you, Levi, for joining me on the ride."

"It was my pleasure." He walked up, kissed me on the cheek, then turned to my friend. "See you around, Lilibeth."

We both watched silently as he walked in the same direction as Caden.

When he was out of sight, Lilibeth turned and grabbed my hands. "Okay, what happened between the two of you?"

I gave an innocent shrug. "I don't know what you mean."

Her mouth dropped open, and she blinked a few times. "Don't even try to do that to me, Emeline Wilde! Your cheeks were flushed when you two rode up, and you had a look about you."

I laughed. "A look about me?"

"Yes! And he kissed you on the cheek just now, but I swear he almost went for your mouth."

"He's done that before."

She tilted her head, and I could see the frustration slowly building.

"Okay, fine—we kissed."

Lilibeth blinked again, this time in confusion. "That's all you're going to give me? You kissed? Was it a peck? Did tongues meet? Was it good or was it average? Are you going to kiss again? I need this information, Emeline!"

I laughed and wrapped my arm around hers and headed back through the barn. "Let's go to my office. I don't want anyone to overhear."

Once inside my office, Lilibeth grabbed the bag of Swedish Fish that I always had on my desk and took a few out. She sat down and bit the head off of one. "Go on, I'm listening."

Sitting across from her, I grinned. "The kiss was *beyond* amazing. It was passionate, yet sweet. Levi didn't hold anything back. And his touch...oh my gosh, his touch lit my body on fire."

Lilibeth danced around in her seat like a five-year-old. "Oh my gosh! Are you going to see each other tonight?"

I shook my head. "Not with the camp and everything going on. We're planning to go on a date, though, once this first camp session is over."

Her smile slowly faded. "Why don't you sound more excited?"

Leaning back in my seat, I said, "I don't want to get my hopes up."

"Why not? Emeline, I've seen the way Levi looks at you, and trust me when I say, he isn't thinking about how he wants to be just friends."

I let out a sigh. "The fact that he said he wasn't looking to get into a relationship. What if that kiss didn't mean the same to him as it did to me? What if Rhett isn't ready to see his father date someone? Not to mention Caroline."

Lilibeth leaned forward and pointed a Swedish Fish at me. "Trust me. When I saw the two of you at the perfumery, it was obvious Levi had more than friendship feelings for you. Even Caden said so."

My brows shot up. "He did?"

Nodding, she replied, "He did, indeed. And Rhett only wants to see his father happy. As far as Caroline goes, I don't know her at all. I don't know the story behind why they are divorcing, but it sounds like she doesn't want much to do with Levi or Rhett, sad to say."

"You're right, I know you are. I'm just..." I sighed. "If I'm being honest with you, I'm scared that this is too good to be true, Lilibeth. I mean, I've had feelings for Levi for so long, and I've tried to move on from what I thought was a childhood crush, but there's never been another guy who even comes close. And I'm not talking about just his looks. He's a great father and an amazing friend. Since he came back to town, the more time I spend with him, the more I realized this was far more than a crush."

"You're in love with him," she said softly.

I nodded. "Yes. And I told him I was. I figured the best thing to do was to be honest with him."

Her eyes widened. "What did he say?"

"He was honest back. Told me he wasn't in love with me, but that he felt more than friendship."

Lilibeth smiled. "Then you take it slow and see how things go."

I exhaled and nodded. "I'm just afraid my heart is going to end up being broken."

"No," she said, flashing me that bright smile of hers. "I don't think that's going to happen."

"Can you guarantee that?" I teased.

She laughed. "I cannot. But I have a feeling things aren't going to go as slow as you think."

Frowning, I asked, "Why do you say that?"

"You know how I said I could tell something happened when you rode up?"

"Yeah."

She winked. "Levi had the same expression. I think that kiss affected him just as much as it did you, and don't go saying it's just because he's a man. There's something between the two of you, Emeline, and I cannot wait to see how this goes!"

Reaching over, I took a Swedish Fish. Before I popped it into my mouth, I smiled and said, "You and me both."

The first camp session was always the craziest. If something was going to go wrong, it's usually that first week when we get all the kinks worked out. Things had been going pretty smoothly, though, and I was waiting for the floor to fall out.

Rhett ran up to me with a massive smile on his face. "Ms. Emeline! I got a fish today!"

"You did?" I asked, bending down to look at him. "Did you have fun fishing at the lake?"

He nodded. "So much fun! And we're getting ready to go do archery!"

I glanced past him to see Lynn, one of the volunteer counselors, guiding the rest of Rhett's cabin to the meeting spot. "You'd better go join your cabinmates, so you don't get left behind."

He turned, saw everyone lining up, and took off running. He stopped and looked back at me. "Are you riding with us later?"

"I sure am. It's the River Falls Summer Camp's famous dinner ride, I can't miss it!" I called back.

Rhett fist-pumped then ran over to his group.

The dinner ride was a tradition we'd started a few years back. The last night, we had a dinner ride where the kids either got to ride on horses alone up to the site, or rode with one of the adults on their horse up to a site where we had a chuckwagon cookout. The kids loved it, and everyone on the ranch was involved. *Everyone*, even Caden, who was our designated campfire cook.

I couldn't help but smile as I glanced around the camp. Kids from each cabin were lining up at their meeting points. We had the schedule down to a finely tuned machine, with some kids going to do archery, while others were heading for fishing or candle-making with Lilibeth. Later, Levi would give a presentation on one of our pregnant mares. The kids had been talking about it all day, most of them hoping she'd have the foal during the presentation.

"Emeline?"

Hearing my brother Caden call my name, I turned to smile at him. "Hey, what brings you to the other side of the ranch?" I teased.

He looked like he was in a bad mood, which was pretty common for Caden. He walked up to me, glanced around to make sure little ears weren't about, then said, "I'm going to strangle that friend of yours."

"Which one?"

"The overly peppy one who likes to get into other people's business!"

"Did you forget her name?"

He nearly growled. "Lilibeth."

I tried not to smile. The fact that Lilibeth riled my brother so much was amusing to me. "What happened?"

He crossed his arms over his broad chest. "She asked what we were serving at the chuckwagon cookout. I told her we were having grilled steaks, cowboy beans, cornbread, and coleslaw, plus the veggie chili and baked potatoes. Then she asked about dessert."

"So? Did you tell her the kids will have dessert waiting for them back at the cabins when we return?"

My mother and grandmother, along with other volunteers, always made the kids what they called mud cups. It was chocolate pudding in cups, topped with cookie crumbs for "dirt" and candy worms. They were adorable, and the kids loved them. They'd be brought to the cabins while we were at the cookout.

"Yes."

"You told her about the mud cups?"

He frowned. "*Yes*, Emeline, I told her about the mud cups."

"And...what? She didn't like that idea?"

"She thought it would be fun to make a dessert over the open fire. I informed her it was too late to add anything to the menu."

"What kind of dessert is she thinking?" I asked.

"Peach cobbler!" He practically shouted it at me.

"Why are you yelling?"

Caden closed his eyes and appeared to be counting. When he opened them again, he said, "Peach cobbler, Emeline."

"I heard you the first time when you yelled it out. I don't see what the big deal is. We can make two fires and use a couple of Dutch ovens for the peach cobbler. The kids would probably love that."

"I'm not making peach cobbler. Not tonight, not next month, *never*."

"Oh my gosh, why are you being such a jerk about this?"

"Did you tell her?" he asked.

"Tell who what?"

"The peach cobbler. Did you tell Lilibeth?"

The look of hurt that passed over my brother's face nearly took my breath away. It was then that I realized *why* he was throwing such a fit. It actually had nothing to do with adding the dessert. It was because peach cobbler was Rachel's favorite...and the day he proposed, he'd made it for her.

The day she told him she could never marry him.

My hand slowly came up to my mouth. I shook my head before dropping my hand. "I didn't tell her, Caden. I wouldn't do that to you. And I totally forgot. I'm so sorry."

He pushed a hand through his hair and let out a frustrated sigh. "I thought she was doing it on purpose. I got *so* angry with her. I told her to mind her own damn business, that she probably shouldn't even come tonight."

I put a hand on my hip. "I know Lilibeth, and she'd never purposely cause anyone harm or intentionally try to hurt them. She probably just thought it was a cute idea for the kids, Caden. I'm sorry, but...not *everything* revolves around you. Lilibeth's been having such an amazing time this week, and she's doing me a huge favor by volunteering so much."

He closed his eyes and cursed.

"Why do you hate her so much?"

Snapping his eyes back open, he stared at me in surprise. "I don't hate her."

"Really? Could have fooled me. Every time she comes around, you're glaring at her or saying some smartass remark. And you call her 'sweetheart' when you know she doesn't like it."

"She doesn't seem to give a shit *what* I say, since all she does is smile and go out of her way to try to be so damn... *happy*!"

I laughed. "Because she's a bubbly person."

He rolled his eyes. "Whatever. But I'm not doing peach cobbler."

Before I could say anything else, he stomped off.

"What was that about?"

I spun around to see Levi staring after Caden. He was looking so handsome that I almost let out a moan. His black cowboy hat made his eyes stand out and gave him a boyish appearance. I longed to remove the hat and run my fingers through his thick hair.

"Caden doesn't like Lilibeth because she's too happy."

Levi laughed. "Why am I not surprised by that?"

"How do you not like someone because they're happy?" I asked with a shake of my head.

Levi looked back to my brother. "I think he likes her."

Shocked by that statement, I asked, "You think Caden likes Lilibeth?"

He nodded. "I do. I think she's the polar opposite of Rachel, and something about her clearly drives Caden insane. If he isn't glowering at her, he's staring at her pretty intently."

My brows lifted. "Is he? I hadn't noticed."

"Yep, he sure is." He glanced down at me and smiled. "And how has *your* day been?"

Smiling at him, I replied, "It's been good. Long, but good. The kids are all excited about the dinner ride and the chuckwagon cookout."

"So am I, if I'm being honest."

"You're going to love it."

We started to walk toward the barn. Levi stepped closer, and every part of me wanted him to take my hand. It was silly, I knew. We hadn't even been out on an official date yet. We talked every night, though. If he wasn't here at the camp, we texted back and forth. Today, he helped his father for half the day at the vet clinic.

"How did it go at the clinic today?"

"It was good. I spent most of the morning shadowing my father. I did see a couple of patients right before lunch."

"Really? Did your dad go easy on you?"

He laughed. "He did. It was a kitten due for her first shots, and a golden retriever there for an annual checkup, and a few shots as well. Easy-peasy."

"And how did things go with the staff?"

Levi frowned. "Everyone was great."

"You don't sound like you mean that."

He rolled his eyes as he sighed. "Logan Miller is going to be a challenge."

A tinge of jealousy ripped through my body at the idea of Logan getting to spend hours at a time with Levi. "How so?"

"She's an endless flirt. Either my father's going to have to talk to her, or I'll have to talk to her myself. If she doesn't stop, I don't see her working for me for very long. That is, after I take over for Dad."

Surprised, I asked, "Did she flirt with you *that* much?"

"Let's just say she was a little handsy, as well."

That made my blood boil. "She touched you inappropriately?"

"No, just light squeezes on my arm, a playful tap on my chest. Things like that. But it's not professional, and something I won't put up with at all."

"I don't blame you. How would she like it if you did that to her?"

His brows rose, and I couldn't help but laugh.

"Okay, so she might like it, but any normal person wouldn't."

He chuckled, then grew serious. "I'm going to have to talk to Dad about it. But for now, I don't want to think about any of that. I want to enjoy this evening. How did Rhett do today?"

"From what I could tell, he did great. He's made a lot of new friends and everyone adores him."

Levi smiled. "That makes me happy."

"It's about time you got here," Ensley said as we reached the barn, hands on her hips. "We have a lot of horses to get ready for the ride."

I held up my hands in defense. "I'm sorry!"

"Put me to work," Levi stated.

"Everyone is out in the paddock; follow me."

When Levi looked at me, he winked, and my stomach fluttered. I smiled, followed my sister, and willed my heart to stop acting like a damn teenager.

CHAPTER FOURTEEN

LEVI

I WATCHED AS RHETT rode next to his new best friends, Jimmy and Theo. They were the same age and had been inseparable since they'd arrived at camp. My heart warmed at the sight of my son laughing.

"Rhett seems to be enjoying camp," Caden observed as he rode up next to me.

"He really is. You have no idea how great it is to see him laughing like this. I don't think I've heard that belly laugh since Brooke left us."

"Emeline said he's having the time of his life. He's also been a huge help this past week. I think it's made a difference that he knows you're here most days."

Smiling, I replied, "It's been a lot of fun. It's helped *me* just as much as it has Rhett."

Caden nodded, looking around the landscape. "There's something about this place that's healing. For most people, anyway."

"I've got to say this, Caden. I think you dodged a bullet with Rachel. I know you thought there was a future with her...but you've got to see that you deserved more, right?"

He shrugged. "I didn't see who she truly was for all of those years, Levi. How in the hell can I trust anyone ever again?"

"You'll be able to. *Trust* me."

As we rode up to the large pasture where the cookout would be, excited laughter and conversations quickly filled the air. I hadn't realized how far back we'd fallen as we talked.

"Oh great," Caden mumbled as Lilibeth came riding up on her horse, her two braids flapping in the wind. I glanced over to see him watching her intently, and tried not to smile.

"Why don't you like her?" I asked.

He frowned before looking at me. "She's annoying. Way too bubbly and happy all the damn time. She just drives me insane."

"Because she's a happy person? Have you really turned into that much of a grump?"

Shooting me a deadly expression, he replied, "She's happy *all the time*, Levi. Morning, noon, and night. Bouncy little bundle of pure exasperation."

Lilibeth rode up to us and brought her horse to a stop. "Wasn't the ride up here amazing?"

Caden rolled his eyes. "It was just a trail ride, Lilibeth."

"It's nature, Grump Boy. Everyone should be happy in nature."

I drew back when I heard a growl coming from Caden. "Stop. Calling. Me. That. If you haven't noticed, I'm not a boy."

A wide smile broke out across Lilibeth's face, and she pointed at him. "See, even *you* recognize that you're a grump!" She ran her gaze over him and added, "And you're clearly not a boy, but you act like one."

Turning her horse, she trotted back over to the group, slid off, and did a little jump clap. I busted out laughing as Caden urged his horse over to where Marshall and a few of the other ranch hands were leading all the animals into a makeshift paddock.

Caden went straight to the fire and took control, while I helped the rest of the staff set everything up for the dinner. Rhett was hanging out with Jimmy, Theo, and Katie, and the smile on his face once again told me I'd done the right thing by moving back to River Falls.

"He looks happy."

Emeline walked over and stood next to me. She looked adorable in her pink cowboy hat. She wore jeans and a long-sleeve T-shirt with the ranch logo. Her hair was in a low ponytail, so her light pink cowboy hat would fit. And like always, she wore minimal makeup. Her beauty was all natural, and I was struck by how I hadn't ever really let myself notice just how stunning she was.

I pulled my gaze away from her and looked back at Rhett. "I haven't seen him this happy in a long time. Before Brooke's passing, for sure."

"I'm glad the camp has helped take his mind off things."

I nodded.

"Thank you for helping with all of this."

Turning to face her, I smiled when her soft blue eyes twinkled up at me. "Has anyone ever told you that you have beautiful eyes, Em?"

Her cheeks flushed. "Yes."

My fingers itched to touch her. I balled my hands into fists and let out a gruff laugh. "I should probably walk away from you before I scandalize everyone here."

Her smile turned to a grin.

"The desire to pull you into my arms and kiss you is getting a bit harder to ignore."

"Camp is almost over. This is the last night."

Before I did something I'd regret, I took a step back. "I should go see if Caden needs any help."

We both turned to look in that direction. "Oh dear, Lilibeth is over there."

"What is it with those two?" I asked.

Emeline shrugged. "Lilibeth can't understand why Caden is always in a bad mood, and he can't understand why she's always in a good mood."

I laughed. "I'd better get over there before Caden does or says something he's going to regret."

"I'll go, too, and see if Lilibeth can help me get all the kids rounded back up."

As we set off, we both said, "Good luck!"

I set my plate down in front of me, then sat back in my chair. "I've got to hand it to you, Caden and Gatlin, that was the best steak I think I've ever had. I'm stuffed."

Gatlin grinned, while Caden gave me a barely there smile.

"The kids all seem to enjoy this, as well," I added.

"They do," Gatlin agreed. "The kids talk about it all week. It's a lot of work, but worth it."

Caden put in, "I'll admit, it's worth it to hear how much the kids love the chuckwagon cookout."

"The only thing you need is an actual chuckwagon."

Both brothers laughed.

Gatlin lifted his drink toward his sister. "Emeline tried to talk my parents into getting one, but the trail's too small to get it up here. If she'd been able to find a way, I think she would have talked them into it."

I smiled as my gaze caught on Emeline. Katie, the little girl who'd been playing with Rhett, was now sitting in her lap. It appeared Emeline was telling her a story from the way she was being so animated. Katie was laughing and looking up at Emeline with adoring eyes. A strange sensation washed over me as I watched their interaction. Caroline had never been very affectionate with our own two kids, so I couldn't imagine she'd be that way with a child who *wasn't* hers.

With a shake of my head, I tried to banish all thoughts of my ex. I needed to stop comparing the two of them. They were worlds apart.

"Emeline told me that you two are going on a date," Gatlin said.

Caden's drink stopped at his mouth, and he slowly smiled. I couldn't tell if it was a happy smile, or one of those grins someone gives you right before they tell you to go fuck off. "What's this? You're going out with Emeline?"

My heart dropped. Before I could say anything, Caden continued.

"I think it's great. I hope she took my advice to tell you how she felt."

I nodded. "She did."

"Just remember, she's still my little sister, so if you do anything to hurt her, I'll have to hurt you tenfold."

Gatlin tapped his drink against his brother's. "I second that."

"You're both okay with it? The age difference, and the fact that I'm getting divorced and have a kid?"

"Why wouldn't we be okay with it?" Caden asked. "You're my best friend. I know you better than I know anyone else."

Gatlin cleared his throat exaggeratedly, causing Caden to glance at him.

"Sorry." Turning back to me, Caden stated, "I know you better than you know *yourself*."

His brother smiled. "That's better, thank you."

"Sure thing."

"I will add, though, you should have asked us first before you asked out Emeline," Gatlin said.

I laughed—then quickly stopped when neither one of them joined in. "Wait. Are you serious?"

Caden raised a single brow, while Gatlin just stared at me. I instantly started to sweat. I could ask for forgiveness or defend Emeline. I was going with the latter.

"I didn't know I needed permission to date your *adult* sister, who's very capable of making her own decisions."

Gatlin pointed at me and grinned, while Caden nodded.

"Dude, I knew you'd handle that the right way," Gatlin said with a wink.

"That's because he's older and wiser," Caden added with a nod in my direction. "The guys she's dated in the past have all been little jerks."

I cleared my throat. "Well, I'm glad to hear I pass muster."

Holding up his beer, Gatlin said, "Passed with flying colors."

I wasn't going to lie, knowing that I had both of Emeline's brothers' blessings was a relief. I hadn't realized until now that I even wanted them...or maybe *needed* them was the better word.

Caden stood and let out a long sigh. "Fun times are over. Time to clean up."

Gatlin and I both stood as I said, "Just show me what you need me to do."

The chuckwagon cookout was a well-oiled machine, and I wasn't the least bit surprised by how quickly everything was cleaned up and the kids were put on their horses and brought back to camp. Before long, everyone was settled in their cabins and eating their desserts. It was the last night, so the kids were all having small parties to close out the camp.

I glanced around the main living room area where some of the staff who'd helped with the cookout were having a party of their own. All of the counselors were with their kids in the cabins, so this get-together was adults-only.

Charlotte Hastings, the camp steward, was heading my way. I smiled as she stopped in front of me.

"Rhett certainly had a wonderful time at camp."

Nodding, I replied, "He did. I got to talk to him for a bit up at the cookout. He's met a few kids who are in the same grade as him, so when school starts this fall, he'll have some friends."

"That's wonderful," she said as her smile widened. "There have been long-lasting friendships made over the years through the camp, as well as during the holiday event. This place has meant a lot to the community."

I nodded. "It has. Um, have you seen Emeline? I've been looking for her, but don't see her anywhere."

"Emeline was looking for you earlier, but I think you both kept missing each other. She skips all of this. By the end of the week, she's exhausted and typically heads to her place to get a good night's sleep. Tomorrow will be emotional for her when she says goodbye to the campers. For some, this will be their last time here. The older kids, anyway, unless some get adopted, which is the end goal."

"I was helping get horses back in stalls and out to pastures. I knew the equine side of the ranch had a lot of horses, but seeing them all together is shocking."

She laughed. "It is."

"Thanks so much, Charlotte. I appreciate all you've done this week. I know the kids have enjoyed it."

She squeezed my arm. "It's my pleasure."

Turning on my heel, I headed out the door with every intention of going home.

Instead of turning to the right, toward my truck, I headed left...and walked down the trail that led toward Emeline's cabin.

CHAPTER FIFTEEN

EMELINE

"MEOW."

I glanced down at the five-month-old kitten who was rubbing against my legs. I'd found Luna as a premature kitten in the barn, all alone. I'd taken her in and bottle-fed her. She was white and gray and the cutest thing I'd ever seen. Moose had treated her like his own baby from day one. Cleaning her after each feeding and letting her lie on him while she napped.

"I know you're hungry. If you give me two minutes, I'll have your food ready for you, my queen."

"Meow!"

Her cries of hunger grew louder, and I couldn't help but laugh. I hadn't even had time to get changed before she greeted me at the door to tell me she wasn't happy at all with my absence this week. Moose had somehow made his way home with my mother and father, so I only had one furbaby to tend to this evening. I was okay with that, since I knew Moose would want to go for his usual nighttime walk. I was exhausted and just ready to relax.

"Tomorrow's the last day for a few weeks before I get busy again," I said as I opened my phone and found my Spotify app. "Let's listen to our girl, shall we?"

Pressing play on "Landslide," I smiled when the familiar notes began. Hearing Stevie Nicks always brought up memories of my childhood and my mother having her music on blast. It didn't matter if we were in the car or in the kitchen, Stevie was playing any chance Mom got.

Luna reached up and clawed at my legs.

"Excuse me, I'm not a scratching pole."

Once I got her food, I walked over and set it in her spot. She quickly dove into the wet food. And by dove, I mean she was standing inside the bowl, eating.

"Enjoy yourself while I go get changed."

By the time I got out of the shower, threw on a pair of Caden's sweatpants and Gatlin's oversized Denver Broncos sweatshirt—items that I'd stolen from both of them—Luna was sitting on my bed, bathing herself.

I bent over, grabbed my hair, and threw it up into a haphazard bun. Tonight it was going to be all about me. No one asking me for anything or giving me advice on what to do with the camps. This was my time before the emotions of tomorrow would have me in tears all day. I always spent the last night of camp tucked away in my cabin by myself. It was my way of decompressing after the long week of nonstop activities. My only regret was not finding Levi to tell him I'd be leaving early. I had sent him a text and wondered if he had gotten it. It was strange he hadn't responded back.

Picking up Luna, I held her against my chest while she purred. "How was dinner, my little princess?"

Her answering meow made me laugh. "That good, huh? I think I'm going to make chicken quesadillas as a snack. How does that sound?"

"Meow."

"Okay, quesadillas it is."

Twenty minutes later, I was sitting on my sofa with hot tea on the coffee table, along with a glass of ice water, my dinner, a warm blanket, and the Hallmark channel. Luna was, of course, sitting next to me, waiting so patiently for me to share my dinner with her.

"Okay, you don't have to judge me. I know I used the giant tortillas, but my eyes were bigger than my stomach."

Luna winked, then began to clean herself once again.

Before I could get totally settled in, someone knocked on my door.

I froze, as did Luna.

"Who in the world could that be?" I asked the kitten, who jumped off the sofa and followed me to the door. I picked her up so she wouldn't run out as I opened the door. I was fully expecting to see one of my siblings. Or even my mother standing there, coming to give Moose back because he'd gotten into something.

I wasn't expecting to see Levi.

My heart did a weird swoop of excitement—before it dropped with dread.

"Levi. Is everything okay? Rhett?"

He held up his hands. "Everything's great. I thought I'd stop by really quick to just say…" His voice trailed off.

"To say?" I asked, feeling giddy as I smiled up at his handsome face.

"Well, what I have to say doesn't use any words."

He cupped my face and kissed me.

It started sweet and slow, but when he walked me backward into my house and kicked the door shut, the kiss changed. It turned passionate and hot, and I forgot everything except for how amazing that kiss felt.

I lowered my arm, letting Luna drop the remaining few feet to the floor, then I wrapped my arms around Levi's neck. She, of course, meowed in protest. My fingers laced through his hair, and he moaned deeply into my mouth. My entire body caught fire.

Suddenly, he drew his head back. "Something's climbing up my leg."

I took a step back to see little Luna clawing her way up Levi's jeans. "Luna!"

Levi laughed and pulled the little stinker off his leg, holding her up. She let out another loud meow as she swatted at his face.

"Aren't you full of spit and fire."

Her little paws batted at him relentlessly as he smiled. I wasn't sure what it was about that picture in front of me, but it warmed my heart. He kissed the kitten on the head and set her on the back of the sofa before turning to look at me.

"Hi," I whispered like an idiot.

He chuckled. "Hi."

"Um, I was about to eat a snack. Would you like to join me, or do you need to get home?"

He shook his head. "I'm in no hurry. I also just saw your text when I decided to head this way."

Smiling, I asked, "Do you like quesadillas?"

"As a matter of fact, I do."

"Let me go grab another plate, take a seat on the sofa. I have beer, water, and soft drinks."

"I'll take a beer, please."

My cabin had an open floorplan, with the L-shaped kitchen to the right upon entering and the living room to the left. There was a small table in a nook that overlooked the west, which I never used for eating. Since it was just me, Moose, and Luna, the sofa was my choice for meals.

I quickly made my way to the kitchen, grabbed a plate, silverware, and a beer for Levi. My heart pounded in my chest. I stopped and took a deep breath.

Levi is in my house.

The man I had naughty dreams about for years was currently sitting on my sofa, with my kitten on his lap. And he'd just kissed the ever-loving shit out of me.

"This is a charming cabin, Em."

His voice snapped me out of my thoughts. "Thanks," I replied as I walked back into the living room. I handed him the plate and silverware, then set his beer on the coffee table.

I sat down next to him, ignoring the heat of his body against mine. I cut the quesadilla in half, put his share on his plate, and handed it to him.

"I hope you don't mind sitting on the sofa to eat. I'm not much of a formal person. Most meals are eaten right here."

"Woman after my own heart. If it were up to me, all meals would be eaten this way. My mother insists on eating at the dining room table for every meal except breakfast. That one, we can eat at the breakfast nook." He shook his head and smiled. "I really need to find my own place, and soon."

"Have you started looking?" I asked before taking a bite of food.

"Not really. I wanted to get Rhett settled in the town a bit more before I started looking for a place. He's really enjoying living with my parents at the moment. My mother is spoiling him rotten, doing everything she did for me when I was growing up. She's a far cry from my ex."

Frowning, I said, "I'm sorry to hear that."

He shrugged. "There were times when I wondered if Caroline even had a maternal bone in her body."

"I can honestly say I had the best mother growing up." I smiled. "Now, as well. I know if I needed anything from her or my father, they'd drop everything for me."

Levi nodded. "That's how my parents are. I guess that's why I was so surprised by Caroline's lack of motherly love. Don't get me wrong, I believe she loves our kids; she just doesn't know how to show it. At least, that's what the therapist tells me."

"Rhett did so good this past week. He thrived here at the camp, and it looks like he's made a few friends."

Levi smiled. "He has. You have no idea how much this has helped, Em. He's now looking forward to starting school. Before, he was really worried about not knowing anyone. He's moving from a large school to a much smaller one, and you know how kids can be. Especially in a small town."

I let out a soft laugh. "Yes. I remember a few moments in my own childhood where some kids bullied me."

He turned and stared at me. "Who bullied you?"

With a one-shoulder shrug, I replied, "Just a few kids in elementary. By the time I got to middle school, I'd learned not to take anyone's shit."

Levi let out a bark of laughter. "That sounds more like a Wilde kid."

Smiling, I replied, "Ensley most certainly taught me to stand up for myself, and that hurting people are the ones who hurt others. I really took that to heart. So if someone is rude or mean to me, I try my best to ignore it, since I have no idea what the person is going through."

Levi's eyes searched over my face. The intensity of his gaze made me look down at my food and take another bite.

Pointing his fork at Luna, he asked, "So, who is that little beast, and where's Moose?"

I giggled. "Moose is with Mom and Dad. That is Luna. She's a rescue kitten. I found her in the barn, no mother around at all. She was only about three weeks old at the time, so I took her in and bottle-fed her. Now she's stuck to me like glue. I do think she believes she's a dog, though. She latched onto Moose as well."

"She's cute."

"That's one word to describe her."

We ate in silence, until I couldn't take the suspense any longer.

"Levi...what brought you here tonight?"

He glanced at me. "The kiss wasn't a hint?"

The memory of the kiss caused my cheeks to heat. "I mean, don't get me wrong, I enjoyed it very much."

Wiping the corners of his mouth, he set the napkin down, drew in a long breath, then released it. "I didn't want to be alone tonight."

My heart thumped against my chest as it beat rapidly. I tried not to fidget when the sudden pulsing moved to my lower stomach. "But you're never alone. You're staying with your mother and father."

His eyes darkened. "Not that kind of alone, Em. The

kind of alone when you're lying in bed and your mind won't stop thinking about someone."

My mouth dropped open slightly as I fought to make my brain work. "I know that kind of alone all too well."

Something inside of me clicked. The cautious Emeline Wilde was no longer present. She disappeared the moment I opened the door and saw Levi. This new Emeline was going to take her older brother's advice and do what she wanted.

Setting my plate down on the coffee table, I crawled onto Levi's lap. His hands instantly grabbed my hips. It didn't take long to feel his erection grow.

"We said slow," I whispered.

"Did we? I suddenly can't remember."

I smiled. "But every time I'm near you, my body comes alive, and I've been fighting it for so many years. I'm tired of doing so. I want you, Levi, and—"

My words were cut off when he leaned forward and captured my mouth with his. The kiss was hot and desperate, and I soon found myself squirming on his lap. The feel of his hard erection against my core was heavenly.

Pulling his lips from mine, Levi panted, "If you keep moving like that, I'm going to come in my pants, Em."

With a wicked smile, I moved my hands to his jeans. "We should probably take these off then, don't you think?"

He closed his eyes. "You're fucking killing me."

I bit on my lower lip as I rolled my hips.

Levi dropped his head back and groaned. "Em."

"If you want me to stop, I will. I know you said you want to go slow."

A low growl came from Levi right before he cupped my face and drew my mouth down to his. I moaned as I melted into his body and deepened the kiss. My hips rocked against Levi as he lifted his own to get more contact.

Jerking his mouth from mine, he grabbed my behind and stood, taking me with him like I weighed next to nothing.

"Bedroom," he demanded in a raspy, low voice.

"Down the hall, first door on the left."

Once we were in my room, Levi put me down and quickly started to pull the oversized shirt off, while I stripped away my sweats. Then I stood before him in a red lace bra and matching bikini panties.

"Fucking hell. You're the most beautiful thing I've ever laid eyes on, Em."

I went breathless as I watched his gaze take in every inch of my body. Reaching behind my back, I unclasped my bra and let it fall down my arms and to the floor.

Levi's breath hitched, and he closed his eyes, an almost painful expression appearing on his handsome face.

Waiting for him to open them again, I hooked my thumbs into my panties. Once he was looking at me, I slowly shimmied them down my legs and gave them a little kick across my bedroom floor.

My heart hammered in my chest. I'd never been so brazen as to undress in front of a guy like that before. But this was Levi. The man I'd been dreaming about making love to since I was old enough to know what making love meant.

"Your turn," I whispered as I let one foot slide up and down the side of my other calf, trying not to cover myself.

He shook his head. "I want to taste you."

I swallowed hard. No man had ever done that to me before. It was something I wouldn't *let* them do. It felt too personal...and I'd been saving it for the man I wanted to spend the rest of my life with.

Was that Levi?

If it was up to me, yes, I would spend the rest of my life with this man. But was that something *he* wanted? He wasn't even divorced yet.

The hungry look in his eyes made my entire body tremble. If there was ever a guy I wanted to be so intimate with, it was the one standing before me.

"I've never..."

My voice trailed off as a look of surprise crossed his face. "Em...are you?"

I giggled. "No, I'm not a virgin. I just..." My cheeks heated, and I wished I hadn't said anything.

Levi cupped my face and gently brushed his lips against mine. "We don't have to do that if you don't want to."

I reached up and held on to his forearms, more to keep myself upright than anything. His lips moved down my neck as his hand cupped my breast. I moaned when he lightly pinched my nipple.

Suddenly, I was in his arms, and he was placing me on the bed. He stepped back and reached down to pull his T-shirt over his head. My chest rose and fell quickly as I took in his chiseled chest and abs.

"My God, do you live in the gym?" I asked, my fingers twitched to touch him.

He chuckled as he unbuttoned his jeans and slid them down his hips. My brows rose as I leaned up to recline on my elbows. I took in every inch of him. He was thick and...oh dear...long. "Commando, Mr. Tucker?"

"I need to do laundry."

I laughed and dropped back to the bed as he crawled onto it. He lay next to me and ran his fingers lightly over my body, causing goose bumps to break out everywhere.

"You're so beautiful, Em. I could just lie here and look at you."

"That won't make either of us orgasm, though."

His one brow rose. "Is that a challenge?"

Somehow, I knew he could probably make me come by simply looking at me, but I wanted...*needed* more.

"I want your hands on me, Levi."

He licked his lips and leaned closer, taking my nipple into his mouth while his other hand slowly moved down my body. I spread my legs wide and arched my back when he slipped his fingers inside of me.

"Fuck, you're so wet, Em."

"Levi," I begged as I lifted my hips for more. "Please... *please*."

His mouth was all over my body, causing me to feel like I was on fire.

"Tell me what you want, sweetheart."

I was practically thrashing on the bed as he worked his fingers inside me.

"You. Inside of me. Please."

He went to get up, and I grabbed his arm. "Where are you going?"

Nodding toward the floor, presumably at his jeans, Levi replied, "Condom."

"I'm on the pill. I've only been with two partners, and we always used a condom."

His eyes narrowed. "You don't want *me* to wear one?"

I panicked. "I mean, you don't have to if you..." Squeezing my eyes shut, I wished I could take the last minute back. Opening my eyes, I found Levi studying me. "I'm sorry, I shouldn't have even suggested it."

He moved over me, and I felt his erection pressed against my body. "Are you sure, Em? I mean, I want to feel you bare more than I want my next fucking breath. But I can wear one. I was tested after Caroline and I separated."

I ran my fingertips over his back. "I want all of you, Levi."

He growled right before he pressed his mouth to mine in a kiss that was so devastating, I was almost moved to tears. Then he was there.

I wrapped my legs around him, and when he finally started to enter me, I wanted to cry out in ecstasy. My dreams of this moment were *nothing* compared to the real thing. It had been over a year since I'd been with anyone, and Levi wasn't exactly small in size.

I gasped, and he stopped moving.

"You're so tight. *Fuck*, Em."

Levi buried his face in my neck as he slowly rocked in and out of me until he was entirely inside. My breathing had increased to a pant, and I was willing myself to relax.

"Are you okay, sweetheart?"

Squeezing my eyes shut, I replied, "I just need a minute to adjust to your...size."

He chuckled before he kissed my forehead, then each eye. He licked my lips, and I opened to him. The kiss was sweet and slow, and my body instantly melted around him.

I bucked my hips, and he ended the kiss.

"More, please."

Our eyes met and held as he slowly pulled almost all the way out, then pushed back in.

"God, that feels like Heaven," Levi whispered.

My back arched as he took a nipple again and started to suck. I could feel the buildup beginning already, and I was stunned. Holy crap! I was about to come.

I'd never had an orgasm with a guy inside of me. I'd heard my girlfriends talk about how it felt when *they* had, but I'd always needed something more. My fingers or my partner's on my clit were the only way I could come with a guy inside of me. And now I was about to orgasm, and holy hell, was it going to be a big one.

"Oh God...Levi!" My hips bucked in a silent plea for him to go faster...deeper.

He drew back and met my dazed eyes. "Do you want more, Em?"

All I could do was nod.

Levi knelt, grabbed my hips, and drove into me faster and harder.

"Yes, oh God, yes! I'm going to come, Levi! I'm going to come!"

My entire body shattered in the most intense orgasm I'd ever had. I screamed out his name as he thrust into me again and again. He never took his eyes off me as he moved. When my body finally stopped pulsing, he dropped over me.

"I'm coming, Em," he said before taking my mouth with his and moaning into the kiss. I swore I felt him get harder and bigger as he came. He was the first man to ever come inside me without protection, and something about that felt right. Like he was claiming me as his.

When he finally stopped moving, we lay there, our breathing perfectly matched as we drew in quick, exhausted breaths.

"Holy shit," we both said at the same time.

Levi laughed and pulled out of me, causing me to instantly miss the feeling of him. He rolled over and lay next to me, his hand taking mine.

"That. Was. Amazing," I managed to get out between breaths.

When Levi didn't say anything, I turned my head to look at him, a sudden feeling of dread washing over me. What if he regretted it?

Then he looked at me. Those light brown eyes were filled with pure happiness.

"I've never experienced anything like that before in my life, Em. It was..."

I nodded as I rolled to my side. "I feel the same way."

He rolled over and ran his finger down the side of my face. "Thank you."

With a chuckle, I replied, "I should be thanking *you*. I've never orgasmed with a man inside of me without having to use my fingers on my clit. You have a magical dick."

Laughing, he shook his head. "I don't think that had anything to do with it. That felt...different."

"From?" I asked.

"From every other woman I've ever been with." He palmed the side of my face before kissing me.

I practically melted into the bed as he rolled and got on top of me once again. He caged me in with his arms and kissed me like I was the very air he needed to breathe.

When I felt his erection growing, I wrapped my leg around his, adjusting my hips until he slid back inside. We both moaned as Levi moved inside of me. This time, it was slow and passionate, and when we came together, I squeezed my eyes shut to keep my tears from falling.

CHAPTER SIXTEEN

LEVI

I STARED UP AT the ceiling, listening to Emeline's soft breathing next to me. I closed my eyes and tried for the hundredth time to figure out what in the hell had happened. I'd never experienced sex like that before. Not with anyone, including Caroline.

No, "sex" wasn't the word to describe what had happened between me and Emeline. It was so much more.

And I hadn't worn a fucking condom. Twice.

I scrubbed a hand down my face and exhaled. These feelings were confusing. Not to mention, they scared the shit out of me. I wasn't expecting to feel…so much. Yes, it was Emeline, and there's been something there between us since I moved back to River Falls, but I'd never paid *that* much attention to it, assuming it was just a deep friendship.

"Fuck," I whispered before slowly sitting up. I swung my legs off the bed and looked at my clothes on the floor.

Get up. Get dressed. And leave.

I willed myself to listen to my head, but something was keeping me rooted in the spot. A soft noise came from behind me. Glancing over my shoulder, my heart tripped as

I took in the sight of Emeline sleeping. She had her hand tucked under her cheek. She looked so beautiful.

Can this really be happening? Was I even daring to think of getting into another relationship when the last one had been such an utter disaster? And it wasn't even over.

Even now, I fought the urge to reach out and touch her. My sleeping beauty.

Facing forward, I stood and made my way across Emeline's bedroom and into her bathroom. I quietly shut the door and turned the water on low, then splashed my face a few times. When I looked in the mirror, I saw a version of myself I hadn't seen in a very long time. I didn't look tired. My eyes weren't filled with sadness.

But...was I ready to dive into a serious relationship? My therapist in Denver would most likely tell me to take things slow.

My heart was telling me that Emeline was the best thing that had ever happened to me, and I should just go with it.

Since that very first kiss, she'd been all I could think about. I'd woken up every day since, excited about two things: seeing Rhett and Emeline.

I closed my eyes and cursed to myself. When I opened them again, I shook my head.

"What the fuck do I do?"

Drawing in a deep breath, I slowly let it out and left the bathroom. The sight of Emeline in that bed suddenly made everything crystal clear to me.

Crawling onto the mattress, I softly kissed her on the forehead. She sighed and opened her eyes. When she saw me, a brilliant smile appeared on her face.

"Hey," she whispered.

"Hey."

"Is everything okay?" she asked, sitting up.

My eyes searched her face, and I smiled. "Everything is amazing."

She let out a giggle when I pulled her back down and moved over. Kissing her gently, I whispered against her lips, "Perfectly amazing."

Then I made love to her for the third time.

I woke up to the smell of bacon and coffee. It took me half a second to realize where I was. The memory of last night came flooding back, and I couldn't help but smile. After stretching, I got out of bed and made my way to the bathroom. Emeline was clearly a neat freak because I'd never seen a bathroom so clean and organized. I hadn't noticed it late last night during my mini panic attack.

After using the restroom, I splashed my face with cold water and washed my hands.

"Levi?"

"In here."

I turned to see Emeline leaning against the bathroom doorjamb, looking cute as hell in my T-shirt. It barely covered anything. My dick instantly went hard.

Moaning, I said, "Please tell me you have nothing on underneath that."

She grinned. "Okay, I have nothing on underneath this."

Moving toward her, I put my hands on her hips and drew her to me. "I haven't brushed my teeth, for obvious reasons."

"I have a brand-new toothbrush in the top right drawer. After you're done, breakfast is ready."

"Breakfast?" I asked. "You're spoiling me."

She winked. "Oh, trust me, I want something in return."

"Do you?" I asked. "What would that be?"

Her cheeks turned bright red as she chewed on her lower lip. I reached up and pulled it free. "Don't bruise that beautiful mouth of yours. Tell me what you want."

"For you to…" She closed her eyes and shook her head. With a nervous laugh, she said, "I can't say it."

Cupping her cheeks in my hands, I bent slightly to look her in the eye. "Tell me, Em."

A sigh escaped her mouth. "I love it when you call me Em. I always have."

I swept my thumb over her lip. "Do you want me to taste you…*Em?*"

Her eyes closed, and for a moment, I swore she swayed on her feet before she whispered, "Yes."

"Is something on the stove?"

Her eyes snapped open. "What?"

"Are you cooking something right now?"

She shook her head. "No, not now. I made scrambled eggs and bacon."

I smiled. "Perfect. They can be heated up in the microwave."

A confused expression crossed her face. "I don't think they're cold yet."

I picked her up, eliciting a small screech from her. I took the few steps back to the bed and sat her on the side. She was, indeed, not wearing anything under my shirt.

"Spread your legs open for me, Em."

She swallowed hard and did as I said. I dropped to my knees on the floor, letting out a low groan before I buried my face between her legs.

Emeline's hands flew to my hair, and she started squirming on the bed. Her small moans of pleasure nearly drove me insane. I licked and sucked as I cupped her ass and lifted her to meet my mouth. Her hands went from my hair to the sheets, where she gripped them tight.

When she exploded, her entire body trembled as she screamed out my name. The taste of her against my tongue was the most intense turn-on I'd ever experienced.

She started to crawl backward, away from me, when I didn't stop. "I can't take any more!" she cried out.

I crawled after her, and pushed inside her in one hard thrust.

"Oh my God!"

I could feel her coming again around my cock, and it was all I could do not to follow her immediately. I wanted more. I wanted to see how many times I could make Emeline fall apart. I lifted her leg and put it over my shoulder, moving fast and hard. When I reached between our bodies and found her clit, she exploded again.

"Levi! Oh God. I'm coming again!"

I came so fucking hard, I saw stars for a moment. I slowed my rhythm and soon collapsed on top of Emeline, breathing as if I'd run a fucking marathon.

Slowly, I pulled out of her and fell to her side, still panting.

"Holy mother...that was...oh my gosh!"

I looked at Emeline. Her face was rosy, and she looked exactly like she'd just been thoroughly fucked.

Emeline rolled over and rested her head on her hand. "That was worth the wait."

Laughing, I pulled her on top of me. She rolled her hips against my still-hard dick.

"I can't. I'm exhausted. You have to remember, Em, I'm older than you."

Her face beamed when she smiled. "I'm starving now! Let me go clean up really quickly. I'll bring you a washcloth."

"How about we go take a shower?"

"Together?"

I nodded and sat up, wrapping my arms around her.

"But breakfast—"

"Can be heated up."

She wrapped her arms around my neck. "This will be another first."

"Come on," I said as I tapped her ass. "Let's go shower. I'm hungry myself."

Emeline and I walked back up to the camp together. Parents would be arriving soon to pick up the kids.

"I hate this part."

"The saying goodbye?"

She nodded. "It's always so bittersweet, but this year is different."

"How so?"

Emeline let out a long sigh. "I met with my mother, Caden, and uncles yesterday morning. We're going to reduce the number of camps to one next summer. It's a good thing, really."

"That's a great thing."

Turning to me, she smiled. "I was worried at first when you suggested the clinics, but after talking to Caden and Gatlin, I can see how beneficial that would be for the ranch. I even agreed about the dude ranch idea."

I threw my head back and laughed. "What did Caden think about a bunch of city slickers invading the ranch?"

She laughed. "Caden thinks people would love it, and my parents agree. The one who *wasn't* onboard was Gatlin. He doesn't like the idea of having to teach people to be cowboys."

I nodded. "Yeah, I can see that from him. You'd be getting some free labor, though, if you truly put them to work."

"Which is what *Caden* wants to do."

We stood in silence for a moment before Emeline exhaled once again. "Guess there's no putting this off. Time to make the rounds."

"What can I do to help?"

"You could help load up the vans. Sometimes the staff at River Haven can't send many people over to help. They'll have a few vans, and the kids' items will be stored in the very back. And some of the kids won't have both parents here to pick them up since they can't afford to take time off work. You'll see a lot of carpooling and such."

"I'm on luggage duty then." I leaned down and brushed a kiss against her lips. "I'll try not to think too much about last night. And this morning."

Her cheeks instantly turned a beautiful shade of pink. "I can't make that same promise. It seems to be the *only* thing I can think about."

I winked.

"Daddy! Emeline!"

We both turned to see Rhett running toward us. I bent down and caught him just in time. Standing up, I couldn't help but smile back at my son, and it wasn't because he'd called me daddy for the first time in a week. It was because of his own smile.

"Ms. Lilibeth put me in charge of helping with the kids' bags!"

"Would you look at that. Ms. Emeline did the same with me!"

Rhett giggled, then gave me a once-over. "How come you're dressed the same as yesterday?"

I glanced down, and only then realized I'd never gone home to change. When I looked at Emeline, she was covering her smile.

Before I could say anything, Caden walked up. "Your dad stayed at my place last night and didn't have time to go home and change, bud."

I was positive a look of relief moved across my face as I silently thanked Caden.

"You had a sleepover, Daddy?"

Emeline coughed as Caden smirked, muttering, "Something tells me he didn't sleep much, though."

"Caden!" Emeline hissed.

Taking a step toward his sister, Caden squeezed her shoulder and gave her a once-over, then glanced back to me. "I'm trusting you with someone I love dearly, Levi. Don't let me down."

Then he turned and headed toward the large group of kids gathering in the circular drive.

I looked at Emeline, who watched her brother walk away with a tear sliding down her cheek. She quickly brushed it away.

Taking Emeline's hand in mine, I gave it a squeeze, breaking her trance.

She looked at me and Rhett and schooled her features. "You gentlemen have work to do!"

"Come on, Daddy! We's got to work!"

I set my son down. "Go on ahead, I'll be right there."

After Rhett ran back to his group of cabinmates, I turned to Emeline. She smiled, and her blue eyes sparkled.

"Are you going to be crazy busy tonight?"

"With everyone here today, we'll be able to get the place cleaned up and ready for the next set of campers in no time. And it doesn't start for another three weeks anyway, so there's no rush to get everything in order."

"Would you like to have dinner tonight with me and Rhett?"

Her smile grew even bigger. "I would love that."

"Great, we'll talk later."

Turning, I quickly headed over to Charlotte, who was clearly in charge. Clapping my hands, I said, "Put me to work, Charlotte!"

The rest of the day was spent helping the kids load their belongings, grabbing a quick lunch, then assisting the volunteers in cleaning the cabins. By the time four in the afternoon rolled around, I was exhausted. I swore everyone from the ranch, including the ranch hands, all pitched in to get things done. From what I could tell, the place already looked prepped for the next session.

I found Rhett sitting on Vivianne's lap in the living room area, his eyes half open as she read him a story. I walked up and bent down.

"Hey, buddy, you ready to head home?"

Rhett shook his head. "I want to stay here, with Ms. Vivianne and Ms. Emeline."

Vivianne smiled as she hugged him tightly. "Camp is over, bud. Time to head on back home. I'm sure your grandmother and grandfather have missed you."

Rhett sat up and rubbed his eyes. "I've missed them too."

Vivianne laughed as she helped Rhett down. "You were such a big help this week, Rhett. Thank you."

I swore my son's chest puffed out. "I had so much fun!"

Leaning forward in the chair, she took both of his hands in hers. "I'm glad you had fun! And I'm glad you were able to come to camp and meet new friends."

Vivianne stood and reached out for a hug. "And thank you, Levi, for all the help this week. The kids all loved your talks."

"I had a lot of fun myself. I'll check the vet clinic's schedule for your next session. I'm sure I'll be able to break away at least once or twice and do it again."

She smiled. "That would be lovely. You were the second-favorite camp guest."

I lifted a brow. "Who was the first?"

With a soft laugh, she said, "Lilibeth's candle-making and perfume classes!"

"I'm not surprised. I had a great time when Emeline, Caden, and I went to her shop."

She reached up and kissed my cheek. "You boys drive careful now. Tell your mother and father I said hello."

"Will do."

Vivianne reached for the book she'd been reading to Rhett and started walking toward the kitchen area. Right about then, Emeline walked out of the kitchen, a towel in her hands. She and her mother exchanged a few words before Vivianne slipped into the kitchen. Emeline looked tired. When she caught sight of us, she perked up and made her way over.

"You gentlemen heading home?"

With my hands on Rhett's shoulders, I replied, "We are. This guy was falling asleep on your mom's lap as she read to him."

Emeline crouched and got on Rhett's level. I noticed she did that with every child she spoke to. And she never broke eye contact when she did so. She had a way of making you feel like you were the only person who existed when she talked to you.

"I don't know what we would have done without your help this week, Rhett. Thank you for helping your cabin counselor. He said you were the best helper he's ever had."

Rhett beamed. "I really liked helping!"

She hugged him, and my body jolted at the sight. Not in a bad way, but more in longing. I couldn't help but wish that Rhett's own mother had shown him such love and easy affection.

"Maybe you can help at the second camp?"

Rhett looked at me with hopeful eyes.

Chuckling, I said, "We'll see."

"If you guys are too tired for dinner, I completely understand," Emeline stated as she stood and looked at me.

Rhett perked up. "You're having dinner with us?"

"I was thinking we could go out to dinner. You, me, and Emeline."

I watched as Rhett let those words settle in his head. He started jumping up and down. "Yes! That sounds *awesome*! Where?"

Emeline laughed, then looked at me, a question on her face. I knew she was probably wondering if we would go somewhere outside of River Falls, maybe to Granby. Somewhere people wouldn't start gossiping.

"The new Mexican restaurant that just opened on Main Street. I heard it was excellent."

Now surprise crossed her face. "You want to eat in town?"

"If you're okay with that?"

There went those pink cheeks again. "I'd love it."

Rhett grabbed Emeline's hand, then mine. "This is the *best week ever!*"

Exchanging an amused smile with Emeline, I said, "Do you want us to pick you up?"

She shook her head. "No, I'll meet you both there, that way you don't have to drive in the opposite direction. What time?"

I glanced down at Rhett. "I can promise you he's going to fall asleep on the ride home, so maybe let's say around six?"

"Six is perfect."

A bubble of excitement built up, and I almost laughed. I hadn't felt like this in…a very long time. "We'll see you then."

Rhett hugged Emeline again and repeated my words. "See you then!"

She chuckled and echoed, "See you both then."

I took Rhett's hand and we started for the exit. I could feel Emeline's eyes on us as we retreated. Holding the door for my son, I glanced back and smiled when she lifted her hand in a wave. I waved back, walked through the door, and drew in a deep breath.

Was I ready for this? I wasn't sure my heart was ready to fall in love yet, but it was going to be really fucking hard not to let it.

CHAPTER SEVENTEEN

EMELINE

"I WANT TO KNOW everything!"

I jumped and nearly let out a scream as I turned and saw Lilibeth. She stood there with a shit-eating grin on her face.

"What are you talking about?"

Folding her arms over her chest, she stared at me. "Don't even try that with me, Emeline Wilde. First of all, your face has been beaming all day. I know the look of a woman who's been thoroughly...satisfied. Second, Levi was wearing the same clothes he'd worn the day before. Someone should really alert him to the emergency bag idea."

"Emergency bag idea?"

She looked surprised. "You don't have an emergency bag in your car?"

I shook my head. "Nope."

"Oh gosh. That's rule number one. You always carry a small bag that has a change of clothes, an emergency toothbrush and toothpaste, deodorant—perfume, of course," she added with a wink. "And a fresh set of undergarments."

"Undergarments? What are you, eighty?"

She laughed. "Fine, bra and panties. You never know when you'll need it. For instance, if you decide to hook up with someone. Then you have your emergency bag and you don't have to do the walk of shame the next day."

"You mean an overnight bag?"

She shrugged. "Call it what you want, everyone should have one. But enough about that. What happened?" Hooking her arm through mine, she guided me over to one of the sofas in the common area.

We sat down, and I glanced around. Almost everyone had left. The only people still around were Charlotte, Lilibeth, me, and a couple volunteers who were currently helping Charlotte get the kitchen in order.

"It's just us," Lilibeth said. "Now spill!"

Dropping my head back against the sofa, I sighed. "Oh, Lilibeth. I had the most amazing night and morning with Levi."

She squealed quietly. "Tell me everything! I need to live through your adventures since I'm not having any of my own."

"Well, we'd agreed to go on a date this weekend, when camp was over."

"Right, I know all of that. What I want to know is what happened between when you left last night and arrived this morning."

"I'm getting there!"

We both sat up, turned, and sat crisscross, facing one another.

"Levi showed up last night out of the blue. I invited him in and…I don't know what came over me, Lilibeth, but I just took charge. I wanted him, he was in my house, and I just… I climbed onto his lap."

She gasped. "You brazen little thing!"

I laughed. "God, I have *never* had a man make me feel like Levi did. I orgasmed for the first time with a guy inside of me without having to touch myself, or have him touch me. It was heavenly."

"I've never had that happen to me before, either."

"Orgasm during sex?"

She shook her head ruefully. "Of course, it's kind of hard when I've never slept with anyone."

My mouth dropped open in shock. "Lilibeth...you're a virgin?"

She smiled. "I am."

"*How*? I mean, you're twenty-nine. And you're gorgeous!"

She chuckled and shrugged. "I just haven't met the guy I want to give myself to. I've dated, but nothing serious. No long-term relationships. Once they found out I wasn't going to sleep with them, most of them broke up with me pretty quickly."

"Wow. I admire you for that. Good on you!"

"I mean, I can't say I'm a total *virgin* virgin. I am, after all, only human, and I have desires. I have a BOB. He brings me great pleasure and I don't have to worry about him cheating."

"Have you been cheated on by actual boyfriends?"

She nodded. "A few times. I know it was because I was steadfast in waiting to feel that intimate connection. I have terrible taste in men. But enough about me. Keep telling me about your night."

"Okay, well, things were getting pretty hot and heavy on my sofa, and he said..." I looked around to make sure the others were still in the kitchen. "He said he wanted to taste me."

"Ooh! Oral sex. I've heard it's amazing."

"I'd never done it before."

Her eyes widened. "Really?"

I nodded. "For me, that was just way too personal. I wasn't planning on doing that unless it was with the man I knew I was spending the rest of my life with."

"So what did you do?"

"I told Levi that, and he was such a gentleman about it. We ended up in my bedroom...and let's just say I orgasmed three times in a *very* short amount of time. Levi's the type of lover who makes sure you experience pleasure before he does. It started so lovely, but then got a bit more..."

She leaned in. "Got a bit more *what*! I'm living through you, Emeline, don't hold back!"

I giggled. "Hot. We made love a few times during the night, then I woke up and cooked breakfast for us. When I went to get Levi to eat..."

My voice trailed off, and Lilibeth covered her mouth to contain her excitement. She dropped it and said, "He made love to you again?"

The heat on my face intensified. "He...he, um..." I closed my eyes. "Oh my gosh, this is embarrassing!"

She grabbed my hands and shook me. "Tell me!"

Peeking one eye open, I said, "Oral sex."

Her mouth fell open before she leaned closer. "Was it good?"

I burst out into a nervous giggle.

"Emeline! It was good, wasn't it? I knew it would be!"

Getting over my embarrassment, I nodded. "So good, Lilibeth. Like, leave-your-body-orgasm good. So intense I thought I might die of spontaneous combustion."

We both fell into a fit of giggles. When I finally caught my breath, we smiled at each other.

Lilibeth fell back on the sofa. "Ohhh...I can't wait to find love someday."

"Bless the poor bastard who falls into *that* trap."

Lilibeth quickly sat up, her smile vanishing and a frown taking over her face. I turned to see Caden walking in.

Clearing my throat, I asked, "How much of that did you hear?"

He flashed an evil grin, and I knew then he hadn't heard it all...he wouldn't be grinning if he'd heard details about his best friend going down on his baby sister. I couldn't help the laugh that slipped free.

"Only that flower child here can't wait to find love."

I glared at my brother as he walked closer.

"What are you two talking about?"

"*Real* men," Lilibeth snapped back, but with a sugary-sweet smile on her face. Man, my brother brought out the dark side of her. It was pretty apparent that Caden was getting under her skin.

Deciding not to touch that comment at all, my brother looked at me. "One of the horses is missing."

I quickly stood. "What do you mean by *missing*?"

"Exactly what I'm saying. Missing. Gone. Nowhere to be found."

"Which horse?" I asked.

"Sagan."

Lilibeth stood. "Sagan isn't missing. I saw her earlier when I went into the barn with Marshall to help feed the horses."

"Did you feed her?" he asked.

"Yes."

"Did you go into her stall?"

"No. I hung up her bucket of feed. Marshall was the one who mucked out the stalls. I did food and water."

Caden rubbed at the back of his neck.

"Could someone have taken her out to ride?" I asked.

A look of consideration appeared on his face. "I guess so. Everyone was helping with the campers all day, though, so I'm not sure who would have taken her out."

"Have you asked Gatlin? Ensley?"

"Have they left the camp area?" he asked.

Lilibeth replied, "Gatlin left around one, and Ensley left shortly after he did."

"I told them both we were good on help."

"I'll go see if either of their saddles is in the barn. My only concern is that her stall door was left open. I highly doubt Gatlin or Ensley would do that."

My heart started to quicken. I knew Ensley wouldn't. Gatlin, on the other hand, could be scatterbrained at times.

I followed my brother. "I'll get saddled up and start looking for her."

"I'll come with you," Lilibeth said.

Caden held up a hand. "No need for you to come along, flower child."

Lilibeth let out a frustrated breath but didn't say anything.

"The more people looking, the better, Caden," I argued as I quickly went to the kitchen to let Charlotte know I was leaving.

By the time we got to the barn, Sagan was in her stall eating some oats. Lilibeth and I both turned to look at Caden.

"Are you sure you were at the right stall?" I asked.

He folded his arms over his chest. "Yes, I'm sure, Emeline. This isn't my first time in the horse barn."

Gatlin walked up and smiled. He lived in the apartment above the barn, so he would most likely know if anyone had come in and taken a horse.

"Did anyone ride Sagan today that you know of?" I asked.

"I did. Why?"

Caden suddenly lost his temper. "What the fuck, Gatlin? You left her goddamn stall door open! I thought she got out, or worse, someone had taken her, with all the fucking people here picking up kids!"

"Caden! What in the world has gotten into you?" I asked.

Gatlin looked confused. "Why are you so upset?"

"Because you took a horse out and no one knew."

A look of anger passed over Gatlin's face. "I didn't realize we had to clear it with you first, Caden. Good to know. I rode the north pasture to check on the fence line—like you asked me to."

Caden scrubbed a hand down his face and shook his head. "I'm sorry. I didn't mean to snap at you."

"Is everything okay?" I asked, touching his arm.

His eyes went to Lilibeth, and I was stunned to see anger when he looked at her, too. I mean, Caden was always grumpy, but it seemed he *really* didn't like Lilibeth.

She actually took a step back.

When he looked at me, the anger morphed into something I couldn't read. "Everything's *fine*." He spun and started marching down the aisle. "Shut the fucking stall door next time, Gatlin."

After he'd turned the corner, Gatlin looked at me and frowned. "What in the hell was *that* all about?"

I shrugged. "I have no idea."

At six o'clock on the dot, I walked into El Rey Mexican Restaurant. It was the first of its kind in River Falls, and judging by the crowd, it was already a hit. We didn't have many places to eat because our town was so small. We had River Falls Café, which was more a coffee shop that also sold bakery-type items, Anna's Table formally Anna's Café, which was the town's main café located on Main Street. A sandwich place, a pizza place, and the small café that was located inside River Falls Sporting Goods. It wasn't *really* a café, since there were no tables, but you could grab sandwiches and salads to-go.

It didn't take me long to find Levi and Rhett. Levi stood as I made my way toward them. He wore black jeans, black cowboy boots, a black T-shirt, and, as always, his black cowboy hat. He looked dashing, dressed in all black. And Rhett was a replica of his father.

As I walked deeper into the dining room, I began to notice people from town. When I caught sight of Janet Miller sitting at a table with her granddaughter, Logan, it felt as though someone had dropped a lead weight into my stomach. I nearly turned and walked out. Instead, I focused on Levi. He smiled, and the urge to flee faded away. I reached the table and was stunned when he leaned down and kissed me—not on the cheek, but on the lips. My eyes instantly went to Rhett who was beaming.

"You look beautiful," he said softly, before pulling my chair out for me.

My hands smoothed down the floral-print sundress I'd picked out to wear. I'd paired it with comfortable, short heels. "Thank you." Looking down at Rhett, I grinned. "If I'm not the luckiest girl in River Falls, getting to eat dinner with the two most handsome men in town."

Rhett giggled.

"I hope you don't mind, I ordered some chips and queso. I'm curious about this place," Levi said.

"I hope it's like Flores! That was me and Brooke's favorite," Rhett said before taking a drink of what looked like Sprite.

"I don't mind at all."

The waitress approached and placed chips, salsa, and queso on the table. She took my drink order and slipped away. I glanced around the room and saw nothing but locals. Janet, Logan, Dr. Johnson, and even Billy Marshall—who owned the honky-tonk in town.

My mouth fell open when I saw my parents, sitting with some of their friends.

"My parents are here!" I said with a laugh.

"They walked in with us. We got here a few minutes early."

At that moment, Mom saw me, and her brows rose in surprise before she smiled. I gave her a little wave.

"I took a nap, Ms. Emeline."

Turning my focus to Rhett, I let go of all the anxiety about being in such a public space with Levi. "I bet you needed it."

He nodded before dipping a chip into the cheese and popping it into his mouth. He looked at his dad and gave a thumbs-up.

"Good, huh?"

"So good!" Rhett replied.

"Do you guys know what you want to eat?" I asked, picking up the menu.

"We're getting tacos."

"Crunchy tacos," Rhett added.

"That sounds yummy. I think I'll get fajitas. I haven't had any since the last time I was in Estes Park."

After we placed our orders, Rhett launched into a story about his new best friend from camp, Jimmy. I glanced at Levi, and the sharp focus he gave his son while he spoke was so sweet. I couldn't help but wonder how he was as a girl dad…and I had to push the thought away when I felt tears sting the back of my eyes. I couldn't even imagine what it must be like for him to not have his daughter here. Rhett often mentioned Brooke in his stories, and I loved that they were keeping her memory alive.

Our food came, and it was beyond delicious. Rhett also gave his tacos a thumbs-up and declared El Rey's were better than those at Flores. I found myself laughing a lot throughout dinner, thanks to the stories Rhett and Levi shared.

"Isn't this cozy?"

I looked up to see Logan standing beside our table.

Setting my fork down, I grabbed a napkin and wiped the corners of my mouth before speaking. "Logan, it's good to see you."

She smiled, but it didn't reach her eyes. Moving her attention from me, she smiled wider at Levi. "Is this your son, Jett?"

"Rhett is his name. And yes, he is."

Logan's face turned red. "Right. Rhett."

She reached across the table and held out her hand. "Hello, little guy. I'm Logan Miller, and I work for your father—well, technically, your grandfather too."

Rhett held out his little hand. "Hi, Logan. Do you work with the animals too?"

She smiled. "I do. I love animals."

"Me too, and I'm going to be a vet someday like my daddy and grandpa."

"I bet you'll make the best vet someday."

I was pleasantly surprised that Logan was being so sweet to Rhett. Then again, I was pretty sure it was mostly to impress his father.

She looked at Levi. "Fancy seeing you here, and with," her hand flicked toward me, "*Emeline*."

The way she said my name in disgust wasn't lost on me *or* Levi. Even Rhett frowned.

"Emeline joined me and Rhett for dinner."

"It's a dinner date," Rhett added. "Daddy and Emeline are dating!"

I looked at Levi, who simply grinned.

Logan attempted to smile at Rhett. "Oh, I'm sure it's just a thank-you dinner, since your daddy helped out at the camp all week." She glanced between me and Levi. "I mean... right?"

Before I had a chance to respond, Levi did. "No, Logan. This is a date, and we decided to bring Rhett along."

Okay, I wasn't expecting that.

"A date? Like, as in...a *date* date?" Logan asked, clearly flustered.

"Is there any *other* kind of date?" he asked.

I glanced down at my hands and tried not to laugh.

"Logan, are you bothering Levi and Emeline?" asked Janet, coming to stand next to her granddaughter.

Great. This would no doubt be in *The Daily Dirt*. "No, not at all," I replied.

Logan forced another smile. "Enjoy your dinner."

"Thank you," Levi and I replied at the same time.

Janet added, "Yes, it was delicious, and so nice to have a new place to eat in town. Well, you enjoy your dinner."

Once Janet and Logan walked away, Levi and I exchanged a look.

"Are we getting dessert?" Rhett asked.

"Do you want dessert here or we could go somewhere else?"

Rhett looked at me. "I wish we could have your famous sundaes!"

"What's this about a famous sundae?" Levi asked.

I laughed. "I go to each cabin with all the goodies to make sundaes. It's a fun tradition my mother started."

"If it's a sundae you want, we could make them at home, with Grammy and Grandad."

"Could Emeline come with us?"

I quickly replied, "Oh, no. Not this time."

Levi smiled at me, and my stomach dipped and swayed. "Are you sure you don't want to come over and make sundaes?"

My head was swimming. Was Levi trying to show *everyone* in town that we were a couple?

Leaning forward, I asked, "What happened to slow?"

He winked. "That went out the door last night. Now that," his eyes went to Rhett, then back to me, "that happened, I don't want to waste another minute, Em. I want to spend as much time with you as I can."

"Me too!" Rhett declared.

A wild fluttering started in my chest, and a part of me wanted to pinch myself.

Is this really happening?

Rhett put his hands together and gave me his best pleading face. "Pleeeease, Ms. Emeline."

Laughing, I replied, "Well, how could anyone say no to that face?"

CHAPTER EIGHTEEN

LEVI

I PULLED UP AND parked my truck behind my father's. I sat there for a minute, taking in a few deep breaths.

"What's wrong, Daddy?"

Glancing in the rearview mirror, I smiled at my son. "Your dad is about to take a big step, buddy."

"I can help you."

My heart nearly exploded. "Oh yeah? That would be great."

He smiled and unbuckled his seat belt, crawling into the front of the truck. "What do you need help with?"

"Well, something big is happening in our world, Rhett."

His eyes grew wide. "What?"

"Ms. Emeline."

Rhett stared at me for a few seconds, then asked, "Huh?"

I laughed. "You like Ms. Emeline, right?"

He nodded. "So much. She's really pwetty."

"She is. She's beautiful both inside and out."

Emeline pulled up and parked behind me.

"Come on, bud, let's go make some sundaes."

Emeline walked toward us with a smile that seemed a little forced.

"My parents aren't here." A look of relief washed over her face, and I couldn't help but laugh. "Were you nervous?"

"I was," she replied.

Rhett took her hand in his. "Come on, Ms. Emeline!" He practically dragged her into the house and to the kitchen.

"Do you have everything for sundaes?" she asked, sliding onto a barstool at the kitchen island.

"My mother has everything. I swear the woman is prepared for any occasion."

A few minutes later, the kitchen island was covered with vanilla and chocolate ice cream, sprinkles, whipped cream, hot fudge, walnuts, Reese's Peanut Butter Cups, chocolate chips, and fresh strawberries.

"What 'bout the sour candy?" Rhett asked.

I looked at Emeline, who replied, "There are no rules! You can put whatever you want on your sundae."

"Okay, then. Let me grab the sour candy."

Rhett let out a whoop.

My son put so much on his sundae that we had to put it all in a big bowl. Then he topped it off with chocolate syrup.

"He's going to be up all night," I muttered before taking a bite of my own ice cream.

Emeline closed her eyes and let out a moan that went right to my cock. "Nothing is better than peanut butter cups mixed with chocolate ice cream and an indecent amount of chocolate syrup over all of it."

I laughed. "Not to mention the whipped cream you put on top. How in the world do you stay so thin?"

She winked. "I run every day, and I don't normally eat like this. But when I do, I make it worth my while."

"Daddy, I feel sick," Rhett said just minutes later.

"I wonder why," I replied as I got up and took his empty bowl. "You actually ate it all?"

"It was so good, I had to!"

Emeline coughed to cover a laugh.

"I told you that was too much."

Rhett nodded. "I know. But I wanted it."

I rinsed the bowl out and put it in the dishwasher. "How about we take a bath, then read a story?"

Rhett smiled. "Can you read to me, Emeline?"

"Emeline might be tired, bud. It's been a long day."

"I don't mind reading him a story. You go and bathe him, and I'll clean up down here."

I glanced at the packed island. "Are you sure?"

"I'm positive. If your mother comes home and sees this mess, you're going to be in some trouble."

Leaning down, I kissed her on the cheek. "I'll come get you when he's ready for the story."

Emeline got up and put her bowl in the sink as I took Rhett's hand and led him upstairs and to the bathroom. He was quiet as I filled the bathtub, and for a few minutes after he got in.

"What are you thinking about?" I asked.

Rhett frowned, then looked up at me. "I feel happy."

Smiling, I replied, "That's good."

"But I feel bad about it, Daddy. I miss Brooke."

My heart felt like it shattered. He felt guilty about feeling happy. "Buddy, it's okay to miss Brooke and still be happy. She would want you to be happy and have fun with your friends."

He nodded. "She'd like Ms. Emeline."

"I think she would too."

"Are you going to marry Ms. Emeline?"

I nearly choked. "What? Rhett, we've only just started dating. I think it's a bit too soon to be thinking about that. Besides, we just moved here, and we have to get settled in and start our lives."

"But you gonna keep dating Ms. Emeline, right? I really like her."

"You're going to, not 'you gonna'."

He nodded. "Yeah, that."

I chuckled. "I really like her, too, and I hope so. Come on, let's get you finished up so Emeline can read you that story."

By the time I had gotten Rhett dressed, Emeline appeared at the door to his bedroom. "I followed the voices," she said.

Rhett got up on his knees and held out a book. "This one, Ms. Emeline. It's new!"

She sat down on the bed and looked at the book, reading the title. "*Mr. Maple: A Guide Dog's Journey*, by Paul Castle. Sounds good!"

"Grammy bought it for me, and we haven't read it yet."

"She won't mind if I read it to you?"

Rhett shook his head. "Nope! Daddy was gonna read it, but now you are."

I watched as Rhett got snuggled in next to Emeline. As she read, they talked about the drawings, and Rhett asked questions about what a guide dog does. Happiness welled up in my heart as I watched the two of them.

The sound of the garage door opening caused me to carefully slip away and head downstairs.

Mom was putting a to-go container into the fridge.

"How was dinner?" I asked before leaning down to kiss her on the cheek.

"Lovely. How was the Mexican restaurant?"

"It was great."

My father walked into the kitchen. "Where's Rhett?"

I wasn't entirely sure how my parents would react to the news of me dating Emeline. I had a feeling I would get the it's-too-soon speech, or maybe they'd even think she was too young for me.

Looking up at the ceiling, I replied, "Emeline's reading his new book to him."

Both of my parents stopped what they were doing and turned to look at me. My mother smiled. "Emeline's here?"

Nodding, I said, "Rhett wanted to make sundaes, and he mentioned how Emeline made such great ones. He asked if she could come back to the house, so that's what we did."

My parents exchanged a knowing look before returning their attention to me. "So is this official?" Mom asked.

"Is what official?"

She folded her arms over her chest. "Don't play that game with me, Levi Tucker. Are you two dating? I mean, she went out to dinner with you boys, then came home for sundaes?"

I sighed. "We're dating, yes."

"What happened to not dating anyone and just spending time with Rhett?" my father asked.

A prickly feeling of annoyance danced across my skin. "Are you saying I *shouldn't* be dating?"

Dad held up his hands in defense. "I'm not saying that at all. *You* were the one who said it."

I shrugged. "Things changed."

My mother smiled again. "I've always adored Emeline, you know that. I say you follow your heart."

"It's not like that, Mom. My heart doesn't have anything to do with it."

She raised a brow. "I see. So, it's a purely sexual thing for you then. Does she feel the same?"

I let out a disbelieving laugh. "Did you seriously just ask me that?"

Dad nodded. "I believe she did. Does Emeline know this is purely physical?"

I scrubbed a hand down my face. "I didn't say it was like that at all."

"You said your heart wasn't part of it, so that tells me it's physical. I see how that young lady looks at you, so I think she should know if this is one-sided," Mom stated.

I stared at my parents. "Mom, I don't want to label it anything yet, that's all. We literally went on our first date tonight, and Rhett was with us."

"Where were you last night?" she asked, attempting to hide the smile she was fighting to hold back.

My gaze bounced between them. "Why are you treating me like a sixteen-year-old right now?"

"Because this involves Rhett also, Levi. If this is some kind of itch you want to take care of, you probably should consider *not* involving your son. He's going to get confused," Dad said.

"And I don't want to see Emeline get hurt," Mom added. "It was painfully clear to everyone that she had a crush on you when she was in high school, and it's even more clear now that those feelings still exist."

I rubbed at the back of my neck. "It wasn't clear to me."

"You were too wrapped up in Caroline to notice anything or anyone else," my mother said, turning and opening the freezer. She took out the chocolate ice cream and told my father to get two bowls.

Glancing behind me to make sure Emeline wasn't there, I focused back on my mother and father. "This isn't just physical, Mom. When I'm with Emeline, she makes me feel alive in a way I've never experienced before. When I talk, she pays attention and treats me like I'm the only person in the world at that moment. She isn't worried about something on her phone or what her hair looks like. She's *present*. And seeing her with Rhett..."

My mother smiled softly.

"Something inside of me is sparking, and I thought I didn't want a relationship right now—and hell, I probably shouldn't be in one. My divorce isn't even final yet. But I find myself thinking about her nearly all the time."

Dad cleared his throat. "I hate to tell you this, son, but your heart is *very much* in this."

With a giggle, my mother nodded. "You deserve happiness, Levi. Don't try to keep your heart out of this relationship. Follow it and let it help guide you. With Caroline, you followed your head and did what you thought was right. This time, let your heart be part of the journey."

I walked over and hugged my mother, kissing her on top of her head. "Why are you both so wise?"

She laughed. "It's called experience in our old age."

"Nonsense, you're not old."

Pushing me playfully on the chest, she said, "Go check on poor Emeline. Rhett probably has a row of books lined up for her to read before he'll let her leave."

Hugging her once more, I headed back upstairs, where Rhett did indeed have four more books lined up for Emeline to read.

Emeline leaned against her car and smiled at me. "I had fun tonight."

"I hope my parents talking you into playing dominoes wasn't too much. I told them you were most likely tired after the long day and week."

She waved off my concern. "I loved it. It reminded me of playing with my grandparents when I was younger."

"Shit, don't tell them that. They'll think they're acting old and give up their favorite game."

Emeline giggled, then looked around and exhaled. "I should probably get home."

I took a step toward her and cupped her cheeks. "The last twenty-four hours have been..." My voice trailed off.

Reaching up, Emeline brushed her lips against mine. "I feel the same way."

Running my thumb over her bottom lip, I asked, "When can I see you again?"

She grinned. "Well, after the last week and our adventures last night, I have a feeling I'm going to be sleeping for the next few days."

I laughed. "I'm sorry about that."

Her hands came up to my forearms. "No, don't be sorry. I wouldn't trade the last few days for anything." Looking away briefly, she focused back on me. "What are you and Rhett doing this Sunday for dinner?"

"Nothing that I know of, why?"

"Sunday dinner with the Wildes?" she asked with a shy smile.

I tossed my head back and laughed. "Man, I sure loved Sunday dinners at your place. Rhett and I would love to join you all, if you don't think your mom and dad would mind?"

"Are you kidding me? My mother thinks of you as her other son, and I know she and my father would love to get to know Rhett more."

I brushed a piece of hair behind her ear. "We'd love to join you guys for dinner. What are you doing tomorrow, besides sleeping?"

"Chores in the morning, then doing a tour of the cabins and common areas. I know Charlotte will have everything cleaned up and ready for the next session, but I like to do a once-over. After that, I have a meeting with someone about breeding one of his mares."

"Really? Someone local?"

She shook her head. "No. He's from Montana. He heard about Apollo, one of our stallions. He's from some pretty good lineage, and this breeder is interested. He wanted to buy, and I've told him numerous times he's not for sale. So now he's saying he wants to breed one of his top mares with him."

"You don't sound convinced."

Emeline shook her head. "I'm not. It's been pretty clear he doesn't like dealing with me, even though I've told him more than once that I run the equine side of the ranch. He's asked to talk to my father numerous times, and even reached out to Caden—who told him that *I* was the one to talk to."

"Will your father or brother be there when you meet with this guy?"

"No. They're clearing out the south pastures and moving the last of the cattle up into the mountains this weekend. Gatlin offered to stay behind, but I know they need all the guys they can get. I've got it, though. It's not the first man I've had to deal with who doesn't think women should be in charge."

"I'm free tomorrow. Rhett is going over to his new friend's house for a birthday party. I'm sure my mom or dad can pick him up for me, if need be."

Emeline placed her hand on my chest. "I appreciate that, but I can handle him."

"I don't have a doubt in my mind that you can handle him, but it wouldn't hurt to have some backup."

She chewed on her bottom lip before letting it go. "Only if you're free. And you're sure you don't mind."

My hands went to her hips and drew her body up against mine. "If it means getting to see you again, then I'm all over it."

Even in the moonlight, I could see her cheeks turn red.

"He's getting to the ranch at two."

"I'll come over after I drop Rhett off at the party."

"You're sure?"

Leaning down, I kissed her softly. "I'm sure. You'd better leave before I decide to go home with you."

Emeline turned and opened her car door. I held it open as she slid inside. Once she started the car, I shut the door and she rolled the window down.

"You don't have to come, you know."

Leaning in, I tapped her nose with my finger. "I know. I want to. I have a feeling once my father pulls me into the vet clinic full time, I'm not going to have a whole lot of extra hours, so if we can spend any together now, I'd like to do that."

She smiled, then let out a sigh. "I guess this is goodnight, then."

"Goodnight, Em."

She looked at her steering wheel, then back at me, and laughed. "I feel like a schoolgirl who doesn't want to leave her new boyfriend."

I let out a groan. "Monday I'm going to start looking for a place to move into."

"Even still, I'm not sure how comfortable I'd feel staying at your place with Rhett there."

I frowned. I hadn't even thought about that. "That's true. I don't want to confuse him."

"Is he okay with this?" she asked.

Laughing, I said, "Trust me, he's okay. He asked me when we're going to get married. I had to explain to him that wasn't how it worked."

Emeline covered her mouth with a hand as she laughed. "Poor guy. He's been through a lot, and I don't want to add any stress to his life."

I took her hand and brought it up to my mouth and kissed it. "Thank you for that, Em. You've been something good and positive in his life."

"Okay, I'm really leaving this time."

Leaning into the window, I kissed her once more. "Drive safe, sweetheart."

"I will."

I stepped back and watched her back down the long drive...and tried like hell to ignore the sudden emptiness I felt.

CHAPTER NINETEEN

EMELINE

THERE WAS NOTHING BETTER in this entire world than the smell of hay and horse manure. That was a hill I would die on. I whistled as I mucked out Apollo's stall. Nothing made me happier than being around the horses. As much as I loved the camps, this was my one true passion.

"Need some help?"

I smiled and glanced over my shoulder to see Levi leaning against the door of the stall. He looked so handsome it took my breath away. He was dressed in black cowboy boots, jeans, a light blue T-shirt, and his ever-present black cowboy hat.

"Aren't you a sight for sore eyes," I said with a wink. "Did you come ready for hard labor?"

He held up his hands. "Put me to work."

A deep pull of desire in my lower stomach nearly caused me to drag him into the stall and have my way with him. Instead, I dropped the rake and walked over to him. Lifting his hat some, I stretched onto my toes and kissed him.

The kiss quickly turned passionate; it was all I could do not to crawl up his body. When we broke apart, Levi closed his eyes.

"Fuck, Em. I want you."

I smiled. "The feeling is mutual."

"Has the guy come to look at Apollo yet?"

"He came first thing this morning. And by first thing, I mean by the ass-crack of dawn, he was buzzing the front gate. My father called me and told me I'd better hustle to the barn. When I informed my father he wasn't supposed to be there until 2, he asked who was going to be the one to tell him to come back."

Levi frowned. "You didn't meet him alone, did you?"

"No," I said, running my finger down the side of his handsome face. "Marshall was already here, starting his workday. He met him at the gate and drove him down to the barn."

"How did it go?" Levi asked, moving toward the fork and picking it up. He headed to the wheelbarrow and got a fresh bunch of hay and tossed it into Apollo's stall.

"I think it went well. He was impressed with the horse and his lineage, and also our setup. He's going to ship his mare down here to stay for a few months."

"Here?"

"It was part of my deal. My horses don't leave the ranch. Ever."

Levi laughed. "Guess he wanted the old guy's sperm pretty badly."

"Oh yeah, he did. I told him I would handle it myself, as I always do. He wants the foal as close to the first of the year as possible."

"You don't have many thoroughbreds on the ranch. Why not?"

I shrugged. "I'm not interested in breeding racehorses. My heart belongs with all horses, but it favors the quarter horses."

After getting enough hay in the stall, we both walked out and shut the door.

"When can you take a break?" Levi asked in a lowered voice. His eyes were smoldering, and even if I had a million more things to do, I was immediately free.

"I can take a break now. All my stalls are done, and I just have some paperwork to catch up on."

Levi took hold of my hand and tugged me in the direction of my office. "Is your mom in her office today?"

I couldn't help the giggle that slipped free. "She isn't right now. She and my father ran into town to do some stuff at the store."

Turning the last corner, Levi headed straight to my office. Once we were inside, he shut and locked the door, then pushed me against it and kissed me like it was the last time he would ever get to do so.

"The dreams I had about you last night, Em. I woke up jacking off. I came so fucking hard, I nearly blacked out."

The pulse between my legs grew stronger. "Is that so?" Lifting his hat off his head, I tossed it onto the small loveseat I had in my office, while Levi placed hot kisses up and down my neck. "I had dreams about you, too."

He drew back and looked at me, a twinkle in his brown eyes. "What did you dream about?" My cheeks instantly heated, and Levi grinned. "Something naughty?"

I nodded as he reached down and pulled my shirt over my head. He tossed it to the floor, then cupped my breast with his hand and started sucking the nipple through the fabric.

"Levi," I gasped, dropping my head against the door.

"Tell me what your dream was, Em."

He pulled the cups of my bra down, causing my breasts to lift, fully on display for him. Cupping them both, he sucked on one while fingering the other. My mind was spinning, and I was starting to lose the ability to even think straight.

"What?" I asked in a dreamy voice.

He stopped and looked at me. "What was your dream about? I want exact details."

I stared at him, unable to get my thoughts together in my head as I felt him grinding against my body. Then he started to unbutton my jeans. I did the same to him and slipped my hand into his pants, feeling his warm, hard erection.

"The dream…" I whispered as I licked my lips. "I want to taste you, Levi."

"Was that your dream?" he asked, crouching to pull off my boots, setting them aside so he could take my jeans off.

I shook my head. "No."

He lifted my leg and placed a soft kiss against the inside of my thigh, and I moaned.

"You've got to tell me, sweetheart, so I can make it a reality."

I swallowed and closed my eyes. I couldn't believe what I was about to say.

"Your face was between my legs, making me come."

He let out a low growl. "That's what I was hoping you'd say."

Before I could even process his words, Levi put both my legs over his shoulders, then stood, lifting me against the door.

"Levi!" I cried out as I grabbed onto his head to steady myself.

"You're going to have to be quiet, Em."

He moved my panties to the side and licked up my core, causing me to moan. I slapped a hand over my mouth and let my head drop back against the door.

Then he started to work his magic, and it took everything I had not to scream in pure pleasure. I reached for the door trim to help steady myself and pushed my hips to get closer to Levi's mouth.

He licked, sucked, and bit gently as I fought to keep my senses. This was the most erotic and crazy thing I had ever done. I was in the barn, for fuck's sake! Someone could walk by and hear us—or worse, knock on the door looking for me.

The buildup was starting, and I sent up a prayer that I could keep quiet.

When I dropped my head to look at Levi, the sight of him between my legs catapulted me over the edge. I came so hard, I had to place both hands over my mouth to keep from screaming out his name.

With my eyes squeezed shut, wave after wave of pleasure swept over my body. Sparks of light behind my closed eyelids seemed to burst in rhythm with my orgasm. When I couldn't take any more, I pressed my hand to Levi's forehead and pushed.

"Stop! Oh my God. Please stop!"

He withdrew his mouth from my clit and looked up at me. "Did I live up to the dream?"

My breathing was labored as I stared at him. "That was a thousand times better."

He laughed, then reached for me and lifted me off his shoulders like I weighed nothing. He set me down, then placed his mouth against my ear.

"Want to hear *my* dream?"

I nodded, then reached for his arms when my legs felt weak.

"I was fucking you from behind while you were draped over your desk."

My eyes instantly went to my desk. "It's a good thing we're in my office, then, isn't it?"

He grinned and took my hand, leading me to said desk. "Lie over it and hold on to the other side."

My stomach dropped with anticipation as I did what Levi asked—no, *told* me to do. I loved this side of him and wanted more of it. A hell of a lot more.

Glancing over my shoulder, I watched as he took his dick out of his jeans and slapped it against my ass a few times, which was still covered by my panties. I turned my head and closed my eyes, waiting to feel his hardness entering my body.

"Remember, Em. Quiet."

"Yes!" I gasped out. "I remember." I'd never been so turned on in my entire life. No guy I'd ever been with had suggested anything like this. It was always just get on the bed, crawl on top of me, pump a few times, then roll off. It was definitely about *their* pleasure, not mine.

This was the hottest thing I'd ever done. Well, aside from the whole oral-sex-against-the-door thing moments ago.

Levi pulled my panties down, then he was there, at my entrance. And before I could take my next breath, he thrust inside.

I let out a yelp—and Levi slapped my ass. "Quiet, Em!"

My head fell forward. "Oh, dear God! I'm going to come."

Levi leaned over and kissed my back. "You like that?" His voice was raw and husky.

"Yes," I whimpered as I pushed my ass against him. When he slapped it again, I looked back at him. "More. I need *more*."

He put his finger to his lips before dropping his hands and gripping my hips. Then he gave me what I asked for. He wasn't making love to me. He was fucking me. Hardcore, deep, and fast fucking.

I moaned, and he slapped my ass again.

Fuck. Fuck. Fuck. I was going to come, and it was an even more intense buildup than the last.

"Come on, Em. Come for me, sweetheart."

I pushed back against him as he thrust forward, and he went so deep, I swore my eyes rolled into the back of my head. Clamping my mouth shut, I held on to the desk and dropped my forehead to the surface as my orgasm throbbed around his dick.

"Fuck *yes*. Oh God," he whispered. "I'm coming!"

A few more hard thrusts, and then Levi bent over me, placing soft kisses on my back. I was holding the desk so tightly that my knuckles were white and my fingers felt cramped. After a long moment, he gently pulled out, and my knees almost buckled.

"Are you okay?" he asked, wiping between my legs with a handful of tissues from the box on my desk.

"Never. Better."

I slowly pushed myself up, straightened my bra and panties, then turned to look at him. My legs finally gave out, and I slid down to the floor. Levi quickly followed.

"What's wrong?" he asked, pushing my hair from my face and looking at me with the sweetest, concerned expression. "I'm sorry I lost control. I don't know what the hell is wrong with me when it comes to you." He closed his eyes and shook his head. "I don't normally act that way, I'm so sorry."

I cupped his face in my hands. He opened his eyes, and our gazes met. "Do *not* say you're sorry for that. It was the hottest, most erotic moment of my life, and I want more of it. *Lots* more."

He smiled. "That, I can most certainly do."

A part of me wanted to ask if he'd ever done things like that with Caroline, but I held my tongue. The last thing I wanted to do was bring her into this moment with us, so I pushed all thoughts of her away.

But it was almost like Levi read my mind, because he said, "You know, it was for me, too. My sex life with my ex was very…vanilla."

I leaned closer and kissed him. The taste of my own arousal had my body coming back to life. "Well, I can tell you, I'm already thinking of other places where we can have sex."

Levi laughed.

"But we should probably get off the floor, and I should get dressed."

Levi stood, then helped me to my feet. He picked up the rest of my clothes and helped me get dressed. I grabbed each boot and slipped it on. Right after I finished fixing my ponytail, we heard voices outside my office.

I tiptoed to the door and quietly unlocked it. When I turned around, Levi was sitting in my chair, his feet up on the desk, and my bag of Swedish Fish in his hands.

There was a light knock, then the door opened. I turned to see Caden, and I had to look away so he didn't see my blush. Thank God he hadn't come any earlier.

Caden made his way to my desk and held out his hand to Levi. "Hey, what are you doing here?"

Removing his boots from my desk, he shook my brother's hand. "Came to see if Emeline wanted to go to lunch."

Caden looked between us, a slightly amused look on his face. *Oh God. Oh God. Oh God! He knows we just had sex.*

After bouncing his eyes back and forth a few more times, he finally said, "You haven't seen the paper today, I take it."

I frowned, and Levi stood. We both replied no at the same time.

Gatlin walked in, holding the paper. He smirked as he held it up and read, "'It's been a while since we've had a good piece of gossip in our small town.'"

I groaned and fell back onto the loveseat.

"'Last night, I personally spotted Levi Tucker and Emeline Wilde out to dinner, enjoying some lovely Mexican cuisine from the newly opened restaurant, El Rey. Which, let me add, was amazing, and I highly recommend it. The beef enchiladas were to die for.'"

I slowly shook my head. "Is she seriously doing a food review in the middle of gossiping?"

Caden and Gatlin both chuckled, as Levi winked at me.

"'Back to the other delicious news. After dinner, Emeline went to Levi's parents' house and remained there for several hours, leaving late in the evening. I haven't been able to confirm if Oliver and Sam were home. I was already late submitting this article for today's paper. I'll do an update in the next edition. That's it for your Daily Dirt! We dig up the dirt so you don't have to.'"

"She did not!" I barked, standing up and putting my hands on my hips. "Did she follow us, for fuck's sake?"

Gatlin lowered the paper. "What time did you get home last night?"

"I got home by eleven. Plus, Sam and Oliver *were* home, we weren't alone. We played dominoes."

Caden grinned at Levi. "Oh man, I loved playing that with our grandparents and your parents. Remember how your dad used to get so mad when we stacked the dominoes all up on each other and looked at them that way?"

Levi laughed. "I do remember that."

"What is *wrong* with you two?"

Three sets of eyes flew to me.

"Emeline, it's not that big of a deal. It's not like it's your first time being in the paper," Caden said.

Levi frowned. "I didn't think you'd care if people knew. I'm sorry if I put you in a tough spot."

Shaking my head, I replied, "I'm not upset. I guess I'm just surprised *you're* okay with it."

"Why wouldn't he be?" Gatlin asked.

I looked at Levi again. "You've been gone for so long. I just didn't think you'd want to be the center of attention so soon."

He gave me a gentle smile as he took my hands in his. Kissing the back of each one, he said, "I don't care who knows we're dating, Em. I had to learn a hard lesson. Life is too short to worry about shit like that. The only thing that matters to me is that Rhett is happy and healthy, and that we get to…"

Levi glanced at my brothers, who both raised a single brow.

"Get to what?" Gatlin asked.

"Continue to get to know each other," Levi finally said, still looking at Caden and Gatlin. When he faced me, I saw the twinkle in his eyes.

Smiling, I said, "If you're not bothered by it, then neither am I."

Gatlin cleared his throat. "Um, there's one more thing."

I managed to drag my gaze off of Levi to ask, "What?"

"There's a picture of you."

Gasping, I reached for the paper. "Let me see!"

Gatlin held it up. "Trust me, you don't want to see it."

I blinked rapidly.

"It's worse than the Easter picture," Caden said with a wince.

My hand slapped over my mouth as I mumbled, "No!"

Both nodded.

Levi's brows lowered. "I'm so confused right now."

Gatlin sighed. "If I must be the one to tell the story..."

Levi went to take the paper, and I quickly grabbed it and gasped when I saw it.

"Oh, come on, Em. Now I have to see and hear this," Levi laughed.

Caden leaned against the desk, a smile on his usually grumpy face.

Levi made a quick move and got the paper. I attempted to grab it back, but it was too late. His eyes went wide, and he looked at me. "What happened?"

I lifted my chin. "I fell."

"Into what?" he asked, laughing.

Sighing, I closed my eyes and said, "A pig's feeding trough."

My two brothers burst into laughter, while Levi at least attempted not to. He lost the battle when he looked at the paper again. "The picture makes sense now. Who took this?"

I folded my arms over my chest. "Probably Logan Miller."

Levi's eyes went wide. "Why do you think that?"

"Because she is always there when something like this happens." I growled as I threw my hands in the air and let them slap down at my sides. "She's had a problem with me since...since..."

"Forever," Gatlin added.

Looking at the photo again, I felt my anger building once more. Of course, the picture they used of Levi was one taken at camp this past week.

"Wait, how did they get this picture of you?" I asked, pointing to his perfectly gorgeous photo.

Levi shrugged. "No clue."

I looked at Gatlin and Caden, who both seemed just as confused. Gatlin leaned over and said, "It's a great picture. The slight profile shot is flattering to you."

"Thanks," Levi replied with a grin.

"You guys aren't seeing the bigger picture here. We hire a photographer to take photos each year. They're vetted and have been working for us for the last six years. There is *no way* they would have given Logan, Janet, or whoever wrote this article any pictures from the campgrounds. It's strictly prohibited in their contracts. Someone who was at camp took this photo—*yesterday*."

"Maybe one of the parents took it? It was the last day of camp," Caden suggested.

Worrying my lower lip, I nodded. "Maybe. But how did Janet get it?"

None of us could come up with a reasonable answer to that question, and although the three of them brushed it off, I couldn't shake my uneasy feeling. Someone had taken a photo of Levi, before anyone even knew we were dating, and sent it to *The Daily Dirt*.

Who would have done that? And the bigger question... *why* would they have done it?

CHAPTER TWENTY

LEVI

THE FEEL OF MY mattress shifting woke me. Rhett was literally standing on my bed, looking down at me.

"Daddy! Today's the day! Today's the day!"

I reached up and yanked him to me, causing him to laugh. He snuggled in beside me and we both stared up at the ceiling.

"Do you think we'll find a new house?" I asked him.

"I hope so. Will we be able to get horses like Ms. Emeline has?"

"We'll absolutely be able to get horses, and you know what else I was thinking?"

He turned and looked at me. Those big blue eyes were filled with excitement. "What?"

"A dog, and maybe even a kitten."

Rhett flew back to his feet, a huge smile on his little face. "Daddy! We can get a puppy *and* a kitten?"

"We sure can."

Rhett started to jump for joy, and I laughed, pulling him back down before he fell off the bed. Caroline had never wanted animals. She said she didn't want to deal with all the fur. But this was going to be *our* place, and I'd grown up with a plethora of animals. I wanted Rhett to have the same experience. He loved going out each morning with my mother and feeding the chickens and goats, so maybe that would be in our future too.

"I'm so happy!" Rhett said.

"I can see that," I answered as I swung my legs over the side of the bed and stretched. "Let's go get dressed and head down for breakfast, okay?"

He hugged me, then did a big jump off the bed. Before he walked out of my room, he faced me. "Is Ms. Emeline coming with us to look at houses?"

Things had been going great with Emeline. We'd gone out several times…a little more with Rhett than I'd wanted to, but trying to find alone time was proving difficult. I was picking up more patients at the clinic, and that meant working more, and she'd just finished their second camp session. I did another presentation with the campers, but I hadn't been able to help out as much with the day-to-day as I had during the first session.

My mother had brought Rhett out a couple of days, though, and he was declared the camp's youngest volunteer. I would forever be grateful to my mother and Emeline for letting Rhett help out. He made even more friends, which was a win-win.

Hopefully, once Rhett and I get our own place, I'd be able to see Emeline more often.

I heard my son running down the hall as I pulled a shirt over my head. "I'm going to see Grammy!"

I quickly followed. "Don't run, Rhett. What have I told you before? You're going to end up falling down the steps. Walk, please."

He dropped to his ass and went down the steps that way, causing me to shake my head and smile.

"Grammy! Grammy! We're gonna get a puppy *and* a kitten!"

My mother looked up, brows raised in question.

"When we get our own place," I reassured her before placing a kiss on her cheek. "Morning, Mom."

"Good morning, and that's good to know." She pointed to the table. "Sit down, Rhett, I've got pancakes and bacon for us this morning." She flipped a pancake and then looked my way. "You've got freshly squeezed orange juice in the fridge."

"Wow, what did I do to deserve that?"

"Being the best son a mother could ever want."

I paused at the fridge and turned to look at her. "Why are you buttering me up?"

Sighing, she glanced at the counter, where the newspaper sat. It struck me as odd that most people in this town, including my parents, still had newspapers delivered.

"*The Daily Dirt?*"

She nodded and looked at Rhett, then back to me. I poured the orange juice and grabbed the paper. Opening it, I gaped at what I was seeing.

"What in the hell?" I asked as I glanced at my mother. "Where are they getting all these pictures of me?"

The picture in *The Daily Dirt* was of Emeline and me in the vet clinic parking lot. Emeline was leaning against her car, and I was talking to her. Nothing wrong with the picture, but the headline read, Trouble in Paradise?

"Logan?" my mother asked.

"This was taken yesterday. Logan scheduled a day off to go out of town with a couple of her friends. There's no way she could have taken it."

"Why do they think there's trouble between you? You're just talking."

"What's wrong, Daddy?" Rhett asked, looking up from where he was eating a piece of bacon.

I placed my hand on his little shoulder. "Nothing, buddy. Nothing at all."

My phone buzzed in my back pocket, and I had a feeling I knew who it was going to be. Pulling it out, I met my mother's gaze again.

"Emeline?" she asked.

Nodding, I swiped to answer. "Good morning."

"Did you see the paper today?"

Sitting down at the table, I grabbed a couple pieces of bacon. "I did."

"Who's taking these pictures? And why is Janet putting us in *The Daily Dirt* so much?"

This was the fourth time. The other two were stupid sightings of us out on a date. "I'm not sure, but I promise you that I'll get to the bottom of it."

"No, you have too much going on right now. *I'm* going to get to the bottom of it."

I couldn't help but smile. "Are you free today to go house hunting with me and Rhett?"

"I'm on my way now, just making a pit stop."

With a smile. "Let me guess, to go see Janet?"

"Yep. Do you want to meet at the first house?"

"No, why don't you come here and we can drive together. We're meeting Kendall at the first house."

Kendall was my cousin, and a real estate agent for River Falls and the surrounding area.

"Okay, I'll let you know when I'm close."

I hit end and set my phone down. Mom piled pancakes on our plates, and I pushed away all thoughts of *The Daily Dirt* and stupid town gossip.

"This is it," I said as I stepped out onto the back porch of the house. "This is the house."

"It's not for rent, but I thought if you liked it, we could ask the sellers if they'd be willing to consider it," Kendall said as she came to stand next to me.

Emeline and Rhett were walking toward the barn, hand in hand.

"How many acres?"

"Eighty."

Turning to my cousin, I smiled. "I want to buy it."

Her eyes went wide. "I thought you wanted to rent first?"

With a shake of my head, I looked back out over the land. Pastures were divided by black, four-plank fences. A large barn was directly behind the house, set back about five-hundred yards. And the house itself was amazing. Log cabin, two stories, with a large, updated kitchen and a living room that boasted a massive fireplace. The moment I saw it all, I could picture a Christmas tree in the corner and the mantel decked out in garland and lights.

"I can really see myself in this house, Kendall. Building a new life here with Rhett."

She smiled. "And maybe a certain insanely beautiful woman named Emeline?"

Laughing, I nodded. "Let's not jinx things."

She held up her hands and replied, "You didn't hear anything from me."

"How long has it been on the market?"

"Just came up yesterday."

"The view of the mountain range is insane."

Kendall walked along the back porch. "The wraparound porch is one of my favorite things. You can sit here and watch the sunset over the mountains."

I watched as Emeline and Rhett walked back up from the barn. Rhett took off running toward me.

"Daddy! Daddy! I *love* this place! There's a big barn for our horse!"

Emeline wore a beautiful smile as she approached. "The barn is amazing."

"How many stalls?"

"Ten on each side, with the north side featuring a covered stoop. There's a hay bay, and a shavings bay, as well. A wash and tack-up area. Behind that is a tractor stall, with a tractor already parked in it."

"I can ask about that if you want," Kendall interjected.

Emeline added, "There's also an office, and beside that sits a small kitchen with a table and a Murphy bed."

"It's the perfect place for my horse!" Rhett shouted.

I chuckled and said, "The horse you don't have yet, you mean."

"Ms. Emeline said she has lots of horses and we can buy one of hers."

Our eyes met, and I smiled. It was way too early to think about how perfect this house would be with Emeline in it. But the land and the barn were too good to pass up. This was exactly what I'd dreamed of getting once we moved back to River Falls.

"Did you like the house?" I asked Emeline. I wanted her thoughts on it, especially if I was going to be asking her to spend lots of time here with me and Rhett.

"The house is beautiful. The land is beautiful. I think you guys would be really happy here."

I nodded and looked around before turning to Kendall. "Let's put in a full-price offer."

She laughed. "I haven't even told you how much they want."

Emeline stepped up onto the porch. "Wait, you're going to *buy* it?"

"It's not for rent. Kendall wanted me to see it and thought she might be able to ask about renting, but I think this is the place for us. What do you say, Rhett? Could you see us owning this place and living here?"

Rhett jumped up and down, letting out a whoop as he did so.

We all laughed.

"I think that's a yes," Kendall said as she ruffled Rhett's hair. "Let's get back to the office then and draw up an offer."

Taking Rhett's hand in hers, Kendall walked back into the house. I pulled Emeline to me and kissed her on the forehead. "Do you like it?"

She giggled. "Levi, it's going to be your house. Do *you* like it?"

"I do. I really like it. And I know we've only been together a short amount of time, but I want you to spend as much time with us as you can, so if *you* don't like the house—"

She placed a hand over my mouth. "Stop talking. I adore this house, and that barn is amazing. I don't think they've ever used it. It looks brand new."

Smiling, I leaned down and bridged our mouths with a soft kiss. "You know the best part?"

"What?" she asked back.

"We get to break in every single room in the house...*plus* the barn."

Her cheeks turned red. "The barn, too, huh?"

"Hell yes. That's going to be the most fun to break in."

After one more kiss, we walked hand in hand back into the house. For the first time in years, a peace I'd thought was long gone settled over my body.

Lord, please don't let it all be too good to be true.

"Where do you want this box that's marked 'extra'?" Caden asked as he stood before me.

"Extra?" I asked, walking over and looking at what he was holding. "I don't know what this box is. I don't remember packing it."

"Could your mom have packed it?" he asked, setting it down on a chair.

Taking out the box cutter, I opened the box and looked in. "This is Caroline's stuff. How in the hell did it get mixed with mine?"

Caden let out a long breath. "Should I burn it?"

I shot him a non-humorous look. "No, let's just put it in that corner. I'll text her later and ask her what she wants me to do with it."

Rhett came racing into the living room, his newest friend and our closet neighbor, Timmy, on his heels. I'd already accidentally called Timmy by Jimmy's name, and vice versa. I was hoping his next friend wasn't named anything close to either of those two.

"Don't run, guys!" Emeline called out. "There's stuff everywhere, and you're going to trip."

"Wow," Caden stated with a smirk. "You sound like our mother."

Emeline shot him a dirty look. "I do not."

"Daddy! Daddy! Timmy asked if I could spend the night tonight."

I officially got the keys to the house on August 1st, and Rhett and I set up the tent in the living room that first night. I made a fire, and we ate pizza and roasted marshmallows. It'd been so much fun, especially since it was just the two of us in our new place.

"I'll call Timmy's mom and talk to her about it," I replied as I pulled out my phone. After a quick conversation, Timmy's mother told me she'd be by in thirty minutes to pick up both boys.

"You keep working on bringing things in, I'll help Rhett pack an overnight bag," Emeline said with a smile. Her eyes sparkled, and I knew she was thinking the same thing I was.

Alone time in the new house.

Kissing her on the cheek, I winked. "Thank you, Em."

"No problem. Come on, boys, let's go pack up a bag."

I watched as they headed up the half-log stairs to the three additional bedrooms and bathrooms upstairs. "Don't forget your toothbrush!" I called out.

"I won't, Dad!"

I sighed, and Caden laughed. "Looks like he's back to calling you dad." A swift slap on my back caused me to stumble forward. "Kid's growing up. Come on, let's keep unloading. We're almost done."

"I appreciate the help, Caden. I know your time is valuable and you're busy at the ranch."

He waved me off. "Gatlin's got it covered. It's a nice break, and a different way to use the muscles."

He flexed his biceps, and I rolled my eyes.

Four hours later, everyone was gone, and it was just me and Emeline with take-out Mexican from El Rey's.

"First thing on the list to buy—a kitchen table," I said as I set my to-go container on my lap where I sat on the living room floor.

"I'm also surprised you didn't have any furniture besides Rhett's bedroom stuff."

I chewed and swallowed my bite of chicken fajitas, then wiped my mouth. "I didn't want any of the stuff I had with Caroline. I wanted to start fresh, but it wasn't fair to Rhett not to bring his bedroom set. He got it last Christmas, so it's pretty much still brand new."

"What did you guys do with the rest of the furniture?"

I shrugged. "No clue. I left it all for Caroline. The house sold pretty quick, and the people who bought it didn't want the furniture. I never asked her what she did with it all."

She nodded and set down her Diet Coke. She glanced around the living room. "Once you get some new furniture, and get it all decorated, it's going to be so cute."

"I was hoping you'd help me with that."

"Decorating? Or furniture?" she asked.

"Both. I don't have an eye for that kind of thing. I mean, I know I want leather. I think it stands up better to Rhett and his friends."

"I agree, leather's the way to go. My parents have had the same sofa and loveseat since I can remember, and it's lasted through at least three of their dogs *and* Moose. That last one says a lot."

"Speaking of dogs, I was going to wait until Christmas, but I don't think I'm going to be able to. Do you know anyone who has any puppies?"

She chuckled. "As a matter of fact, I do. Charlotte has a chocolate lab that had puppies about six weeks ago. They won't be ready to go home for a few more weeks, but I think—*I think*—she still has a couple. Her last litter is where I got Moose from."

A jolt of excitement ran through my body. I kept saying the puppy was for Rhett, but I wanted it probably just as much, if not more. "Are the puppies also chocolate?"

She nodded. "Yep. I'll text her now and see if she has any."

I did a fist pump. "That would be amazing. Thanks!" After I stood, I grabbed my to-go container and pointed to Emeline's. "Done?"

She handed it to me. "Yes, thank you."

I walked into the kitchen, which had more boxes than I'd expected, and dumped the containers into the trash. I opened the brand-new refrigerator and stared at nothing but a few bottles of water and three Diet Cokes.

Getting an idea, I headed back to the living room.

"She has one boy left!"

"Seriously? Tell her I want him! I'll send her a deposit right now."

Emeline smiled, then got busy texting. "The puppy's yours. She said you don't need to send her anything. They'll be ready to go to their new homes in three weeks."

"Three? Ugh, I don't think I can wait that long."

Her brow rose. "You can't wait that long, or Rhett won't be able to wait that long?"

Laughing, I pulled her up from where she was still sitting on the floor. She laughed, then quickly let it fall away as I dipped her. With my mouth inches from hers, I asked, "Do you know what I want to do right now?"

She exhaled a breathy sound. "Break-in the living room? I would say yes, but I'm pretty full."

"Too full for ice cream?"

Her brows shot up. "Ice cream, you say?"

Laughing again, I picked her up and tossed her over my shoulder, giving her ass a good slapping. She let out a yelp before she started laughing as well.

In the end, we decided to go to the grocery store, buying ice cream and all the extras to make sundaes back at the house.

"Whose car is that?" Emeline asked as I pulled up to the house after our trip to the store.

"The better question is, how in the hell did they get through the gate without the code?"

Emeline leaned forward. It was dark out, and it was hard to see what kind of car it was.

"Looks like a black Lexus."

My heart nearly dropped to my stomach. "It can't be."

"What?" Emeline asked as I pulled into the garage. The car was parked to the side of the garage. "Do you know who it is?"

Turning off my truck, I looked at Emeline.

"It's Caroline."

CHAPTER TWENTY-ONE

EMELINE

I FELT LIKE I'D just chugged sour milk. My stomach roiled, and I instantly felt sick. What in the world was Caroline doing here, and how did she get through the gate?

"What?" I asked in disbelief. "How? Why?"

My thoughts instantly went to Rhett. Thank God he wasn't here.

Levi exhaled harshly as he pushed a hand through his hair.

This is going to be interesting.

Levi's lawyer had been in contact with Caroline for the last month, demanding that she sign the divorce papers so that Levi and Rhett could finally move on. Levi had started to grow impatient, and said he was prepared to go to Denver to get her to sign them himself.

We both opened the truck doors, and I reached into the back to grab the two bags containing the ice cream and sundae fixings. Levi got out and slammed his truck door shut. I jumped and almost let out a little yelp of surprise.

After getting the food, I debated whether I should go into the house or stay out here. I walked toward the back of the truck to tell Levi I was going to head inside...and that's when I got a better look at Caroline's car.

I'd seen that car before. A few times. First at the camp, then outside of the vet clinic.

Was *Caroline* the person who'd been taking pictures of Levi? But why? And why give them to Janet?

Caroline got out of the car and made her way toward Levi. For a moment, it looked like she was about to hug him, and I felt myself stiffening.

Levi took a few steps back from her, and she stopped.

"How did you get through the gate, Caroline?" he asked. His voice sounded cold and clipped, and for a moment, it completely caught me off guard. I was accustomed to hearing him speak in a calm and welcoming manner. This was completely different.

She let out a laugh. "It wasn't hard to figure out. Our last gate code was Rhett's birthday. You used Brooke's for this one."

"What are you doing here? Do you have the signed divorce papers?"

Caroline's smile faded, and she looked at me. "If you don't mind leaving, Emeline. My husband and I have a few things to talk about."

I was positive my mouth fell open. Before I could even think of a reply, Levi spoke.

"This is *my* house, I'm *not* your husband, and you don't get to tell my girlfriend to leave."

Caroline flinched as a shocked expression appeared then quickly vanished.

A part of me wanted to yell out, HELL YES, at Levi's declaration of our relationship, but I pressed my lips together tightly.

"What do you want, Caroline?"

Her eyes narrowed, and for a moment, I swore she was about to lunge at me and scratch my eyes out. Then she focused on Levi, and a sugary fake smile appeared on her face. "You *are* my husband, Levi. I haven't signed the divorce papers yet. And if you want your little plaything to hear this, then fine—I don't want a divorce. I want to try to work things out."

A loud bark of laughter came from Levi. It was devoid of any emotion whatsoever. "You're out of your damn mind, Caroline. I want nothing to do with you. Rhett and I have moved on, and you need to do the same."

"With *her*?" she asked, pointing a perfectly manicured finger in my direction. "She's what, ten years younger than you? My God, Levi. I remember watching her follow you around like a lost puppy. You can't seriously think you can replace me with...with a *child*!"

"Excuse me?" I said as I took a step forward. "I do have a name, and I've never followed *anyone* around like a lost puppy. That would be you, darling—when you followed Caden, desperate for his attention. And for your information, I'm not ten years younger."

Caroline's lip snarled before she smirked. "The little girl has grown up and grown a pair of balls."

Levi took a step toward Caroline. "I want you to get back into your car and leave."

"We need to talk first," she argued, folding her arms over her chest.

Motioning with his hands toward her, Levi said, "Fine, talk."

"Not outside, Levi."

He sighed. "Yes, *outside*, Caroline."

She looked as if she might panic. Then she blurted, "I want to see Rhett."

"He's not here, and if you want visitation rights, go back to the judge whom you explicitly told you didn't want to be a mother anymore and see if he'll change his mind."

"I was grieving, Levi! My head wasn't in the right place."

He nodded. "Okay," he said, his voice quieter and calmer. "Then do what you're *supposed* to do—go through your lawyer, set up a court date, and get visitation. I told you if you wanted to see him, you could, but only if you did it the right way."

"To see my own son?"

"You can't just decide one day you no longer want to be a mother, then months later decide you do. It doesn't work that way."

She huffed and looked around in the darkness. "I want a second chance with both of you. I want to have another baby."

I blinked several times in surprise. When Levi didn't say anything, clearly shocked, I knew I had to leave. I trusted him, but a small part of me was terrified Caroline would get her claws into him again.

Clearing my throat, I said, "I'm going to bring the ice cream in."

"Yes, you go do that," Caroline spat.

Levi walked over to me. He leaned down and brushed a kiss on my cheek. "I'm sorry. I'll be right in."

I smiled. "It's okay. Take your time."

He wore a pained expression. I was silently thanking God Rhett wasn't home. He would be so confused right now.

Giving Caroline one last look, I turned and headed through the garage and into the house. After putting everything away, I pulled out my phone.

Me: Caroline showed up at Levi's house.

Moreen: SHUT UP!

Kate: Wait, what?

Lilibeth: Who's Caroline?

Ensley: Want me to come and kick her ass and haul her back to the depths of hell?

Lilibeth: Someone tell me who Caroline is? Oh wait... Levi's ex?!

I sighed. "Yep, Levi's not-so-ex."

Me: She reminded him that she's still his wife since she hasn't signed the papers. Also, she told him she wants to get back together and wants another baby. I'm not gonna lie, I'm slightly freaking out.

Ellipses started bouncing.

Ensley: Fuck her. Don't worry, Emeline. There is no way Levi takes her back.

Moreen: I'm with your sister. I've seen the way he looks at you.

Kate: Damn it! I wish I still lived in River Falls. I'm with everyone else. Screw the bitch.

I smiled. I loved my sister and my best friends. I wasn't sure what I would have done if I hadn't been able to text them all.

Me: Thank you, guys. They're outside talking. She wanted to see Rhett, but he's at the neighbors' spending the night.

Ensley: So, she also cock-blocked you. What a bitch!!

God, how I loved my big sister.

Me: Yep, she sure did. I highly doubt Levi will be in the mood for anything once she leaves.

Moreen: Nah, he's a guy. Just strip naked and get on the bed.

Me: There's no bed. Unless you count Rhett's, and gross...hard pass.

Ensley: Yeah, no sex on the kid's bed. Kitchen counter?

Lilibeth: Ohhh yeah! I've always wanted to have sex on a kitchen counter.

Kate: I know we've never met, but the kitchen counter is your go-to, Lilibeth?

Lilibeth: Yep. I know. It's sad. But considering I've never actually had sex with anyone, I'll take what I can get. I'm the almost-thirty-year-old virgin.

Ensley: OMG, what? Why did I not know this! I have a new mission.

Me: Guys! Can we return to my current crisis? The man I've been in love with since middle school is outside talking to his wife! HIS WIFE! I had completely pushed it from my mind that he's actually still married. I'm freaking out here. May I remind you all?

Moreen: Sorry, my mom called. Don't jump to conclusions, Emeline. Lilibeth, Jesus H, how do you drop a bomb like that in a text? We need a girls' night.

Kate: Shit, I need to make a trip home!

I suddenly remembered Caroline's car. I hit FaceTime and made a group call, and waited for each of them to answer. Then I squinted to see if my sister was *actually* in a bath.

"Are you in the bathtub?"

Ensley sighed. "Yes. I got kicked by a horse today, in the ribs, and I think he might have cracked one."

"Oh my God! Ensley, do you need anything?" I asked.

She smiled. "No. It's feeling better now that I'm sitting in a hot Epsom salt bath."

Moreen took a bite of ice cream, and it instantly made me angry. Damn Caroline, for interrupting our night.

I closed my eyes and shook my head to get my thoughts together. "I think I know who took the pictures of Levi."

"What pictures?" Kate asked. Seeing my other best friend from high school nearly brought tears to my eyes. I hated that she'd moved to New York City.

Moreen gasped. "That's right, you don't know!"

I quickly filled Kate in on the pictures and *The Daily Dirt* columns.

"So someone's been taking pictures of you guys together and you didn't know who it was?"

"No, and I asked Janet. She said it wasn't her, but she couldn't tell me who was sending them because they came to her email, and there was no name and a generic email address."

"That's so strange," Kate said.

"Anyway, when Caroline got out of her car, I realized I'd seen it before. Once at pickup day after the first camp session. Then again parked across from the vet clinic."

Ensley leaned forward in the bath, but thankfully she kept her phone up so we couldn't see anything. "Are you saying Caroline's the one taking the photos and sending them to Janet? But why?"

I shook my head. "I don't know. Janet told me when she received the picture of us outside the vet clinic, the person who emailed it said they heard us arguing when they took it. They figured it would be good info for *The Daily Dirt*. I told Janet that wasn't the case, and whoever was doing this was trying to make trouble for us. She promised she'd let me know if she got another picture."

"This is so crazy," Lilibeth said. "How would she even get on the ranch?"

"It was pickup day. Parents and volunteers were everywhere, and Caden had the gate open. I couldn't keep track of *everyone* who was there picking up, and I'm fairly certain no one else was paying close attention, either. Now I need to talk to Mom about better security on pickup days. We can't be having just anyone drive onto the ranch."

"That's scary," Lilibeth said, taking down the towel wrapped around her hair. She began braiding it as she spoke. "Do you think you should ask if it was her?"

I nervously chewed my lip. "I could go back out there. It's been a little while. What could they possibly be talking about?"

My sister sighed. "I've known Caroline since we were kids. Trust me, she always had a way of manipulating things, *especially* with Levi. Caden said that's why Levi married her in the first place. If you think that pregnancy was an accident, think again."

"I always thought she got pregnant on purpose," Moreen added.

Kate nodded her head quickly. "Same."

Lilibeth let out a soft sigh. "I don't know her, so I have no input on this."

"I know for a fact she got pregnant on purpose. I'm going to go out and confront her. If she did take the pictures, Levi needs to know."

"That's my sister! Let the Wilde in you come out!"

"I'm with Ensley, go confront her," Kate said, pumping her fist in the air.

"Good luck!" Lilibeth and Moreen said at the same time.

"Thanks, guys. Love you all!"

"Text us with an update!" Moreen demanded before we said our goodbyes.

After hitting end, I set my phone down on the kitchen island, drew in a deep breath, and exhaled.

"Just go out there and ask her, Emeline," I whispered. Another deep fortifying breath, and I marched back toward the garage and opened the door.

For half a second, I panicked. What if I saw something or heard something I didn't want to hear? I stopped just outside the door. My heart pounded so loudly in my ears that I was sure Levi and Caroline could hear it, too.

"You're not going to sit back and let this woman take him again," I whispered as I balled my fists and started toward the open bay door.

I wasn't sure what I'd expected, but what I ultimately saw was Levi, standing with his arms crossed and a frown on his face, and Caroline pacing back and forth. I stepped back a bit, staying out of sight. I knew it was wrong to eavesdrop, but I couldn't help myself.

"Levi, we were so good together!"

"We were not, Caroline, and you know it. You admitted to me that you got pregnant on purpose, just so we'd stay together. Plus, let's not forget the whole cheating on me situation."

"I had to get pregnant! I was going to lose you!"

"Are we done here? Emeline is waiting for me."

I heard Caroline stop walking. "I always knew you had a thing for her! The way you showered her with attention and gifts made me sick. She was a *baby*!"

"What? She was a friend."

"Are you saying you didn't have feelings for her?"

"Of course I did, she was..."

My brows shot up. *She was what? She was what?*

The silence seemed to last forever.

"I won't deny that if we hadn't stayed together, something could have happened. I didn't have all the feelings for Emeline back then that I do now...but maybe deep down, they were already there. I don't know. We've always had a connection."

"And I *saw it*, Levi. I saw how you looked at her and how she fawned all over you, even if no one else realized."

I frowned. I did not fawn over Levi. Ugh, I couldn't stand this woman.

"Are you saying *Emeline* was the reason you got pregnant?" he asked.

My hand flew up to my mouth as I waited for Caroline to answer.

"Not the entire reason. But yes, she was part of it. Her and Ensley both. I honestly couldn't tell which one you liked."

"Our entire relationship was built on lies and distrust. Can't you see that?"

"You had a nickname for her! You never called *me* by any nickname. Then I find out you're actually dating her. Sure didn't take you long to move on with your new life, did it?"

"Says the person who cheated during our marriage, which has been over for years. I just didn't want to admit it. I'm happier than I've ever been, and being back in River Falls and dating Emeline are the reasons for that happiness. I'm not going to apologize for it."

"So this is it? You're not even going to try?"

"I *did* try! For a hell of a lot longer than I should have. Sign the divorce papers so we can both get on with our lives!"

I heard her heels clicking on the pavement, a car door open, then slam shut. "Here's your precious freedom if you want it so bad!"

It sounded like she tossed papers at him. "They're signed?"

I peeked to see Levi going through the papers.

"Yes! I signed it, okay!" Caroline shouted. "That should make you happy."

He looked up at her. "We can arrange a meeting with a judge about visitation if you want."

"I'm moving."

My head started to spin. What in the hell was *wrong* with her?

With a humorless laugh, he asked, "Now you're suddenly moving?"

I decided I'd done enough snooping. This woman was trying to play games, and I was tired of standing in the shadows. I pushed away from the truck and walked out of the garage.

Caroline saw me first and shot me a dirty look. When Levi spotted me, he held out his hand, and my heart tripped over itself. We laced our fingers together and both turned to look at his ex.

She sneered, then rolled her eyes. "I'm moving to Italy, so I won't be seeking custody of Rhett. Besides, he was always closer to you than to me."

I was positive my mouth dropped to the ground. "You're just going to up and leave your son?" I asked. "Only minutes ago, you wanted to see him."

"This has nothing to do with you, *Em*."

"It has everything to do with her. She's a part of my life; therefore, she's part of Rhett's life."

Caroline rolled her eyes again.

This was my chance. I had to know if she was the one sending the pictures to the paper.

"Why did you send those pictures to Janet?"

Levi's head swiveled, and he gaped at me. Before he could say anything, Caroline spoke.

"How did you know it was me?"

Now he was staring at *Caroline*. "Wait—you sent the pictures?"

I cleared my throat. "I didn't know it was you until I saw your car. I remembered seeing it on two of the occasions the pictures were snapped."

"Fucking hell, Caroline. What is *wrong* with you?" Levi asked.

She shrugged. "I thought if I kept you both in the papers, you'd eventually realize that being with someone so much younger than you wasn't worth it. It would be that much easier for me to come back."

Levi removed his hand from mine and wrapped his arm around my waist. "You need to leave now."

She shrugged again. "I had to at least try before I left."

A part of me felt sorry for the woman standing before me. She'd lied to get Levi to marry her, lost her daughter in an accident, and was now going to cut her only living child out of her life. And for what reason?

Moving her gaze from Levi to me, Caroline lifted her chin. "Have fun with my sloppy seconds."

I didn't even bother acknowledging that comment. Just smiled contentedly.

When Caroline realized I wasn't going to engage, she started her car and drove slowly down the driveway. I'd half expected her to peel out.

I watched until I could no longer see the red taillights.

Levi turned and scrubbed both hands over his face and let out a frustrated growl. "I cannot *believe* she's going to just walk away from Rhett. What the fuck is wrong with her? I thought she just needed some time to work things out in her head."

My heart hurt for both Levi and Rhett.

Looking back down the driveway, he said, "But this is good. It's better that she just leaves and Rhett never sees her again."

I placed my hand on his arm and gave it a light squeeze. "I'm sorry, Levi."

He looked at me, and his somber expression slowly eased, a soft smile appearing. "Thank you."

"For what?" I asked.

"Standing by my side just now. You could have taken one look at Caroline and left, or…I don't know. You didn't. And I appreciate that more than you know."

I reached up and kissed him. "I know you're acting like you're glad she's gone, and I'm sure a part of you is. I also know another part of you is hurting for Rhett…and for Brooke and all that you have lost."

He closed his eyes and nodded. "Thank God Rhett wasn't here tonight."

"I'm glad he wasn't as well. He would have been very confused."

Levi exhaled.

"Let's go inside—we have ice cream sundaes to make."

He took my hand, and we headed through the garage and into the house. He shut both doors and locked up.

He seemed a million miles away, so I quickly got to work making sundaes. We'd bought paper bowls and plastic spoons at the store, since Levi didn't have any dishes.

"I can't believe you figured out it was Caroline taking the photos."

"When I saw her car, I realized I'd seen it before. I simply put two and two together. I'm just surprised she admitted it."

He looked tired. I slid the bowl over to him, and he took it absentmindedly, starting to eat.

I set my spoon down and walked around the kitchen island, putting my finger on Levi's chin and forcing him to look at me.

"You know what I think we should do?"

"Finish our ice cream?"

"No," I whispered as I shook my head. "I think we should blow up that fancy mattress, take a shower, and get some sleep."

He closed his eyes. "That sounds like heaven."

I took his bowl, along with mine, and tossed them in the trash. Levi stood, took my hand, and led us to his bedroom, which was on the other side of the house. While he blew up the mattress, I unpacked some towels and soap that Levi's mother, Sam, bought. By the time I walked back into the bedroom—I stopped when I saw Levi passed out sleeping on the blowup. He'd managed to get a sheet on it, and that was it.

I kicked off my sneakers, pulled off my jeans, and grabbed a blanket. Crawling onto the bed, I snuggled in next to him. He didn't even wake up.

I covered us up and watched Levi's chest rise and fall until my eyes slowly began to close, and I drifted off to sleep.

CHAPTER TWENTY-TWO

LEVI

RHETT OPENED THE DOOR to my truck and climbed up into the back seat, tossing his backpack to the side.

"Well? How was your first day of first grade?"

Giving me the biggest smile I'd ever seen, Rhett replied, "It was the bestest day ever, Daddy!"

"I'm so glad it was. Buckle up, buddy."

He quickly buckled into his booster seat as he talked. "Ms. Kennedy said me and Timmy can sit at the same table! And I had three other friends in my class! Jimmy and Katie, and Luke."

"Timmy and I."

"You? You're too old to be in first grade!"

I laughed. "No, the proper way to say that is 'Timmy and I.'"

When he scrunched up his nose in confusion, I decided to leave it. "Did you learn anything today?"

"The rules of the class. And we got to pick our reading spots. Me and Timmy picked the spot by Ms. Kennedy's desk."

"How fun."

"It was lots of fun!"

"Well, the fun isn't over. I've got a surprise for you."

"Really? What is it?"

"You'll have to wait and see."

"Where's the surprise?"

"It's at home."

Rhett clapped. "Hurry home, Daddy! Hurry home!"

The entire drive from school to home was filled with Rhett talking a mile a minute. He told me what I swore was a play-by-play of his day, from the time he got out of my truck to the moment he got back in.

"Then, Ms. Kennedy told us that we can have guests come eat with us, but they have to go to the office first to make sure they're allowed to come see us. Will you come eat lunch with me?"

Before I had a chance to answer, Rhett added, "I want Ms. Emeline to come to lunch." Then, after a moment, "Is it bad that I want her to pretend to be my mommy?"

I looked at Rhett in the rearview mirror. His little innocent face seemed so hopeful. "But Emeline isn't your mommy, Rhett," I said gently.

He looked down. "I know. I just wish she was."

Caroline had made good on her word. She moved to Italy, and I hadn't heard a single thing from her since. I couldn't have cared less...but I knew Rhett did. He acted as if he didn't, but she was still his mother. I'd *never* forgive her for hurting him the way she had.

I wasn't sure what to say, so I focused on the road. I'd have to ask my parents for some advice in this particular area of parenting.

I clicked the gate remote and waited for it to open.

"I can't wait to see my surprise! Daddy, can you drive faster?"

Laughing, I said, "No, I cannot drive faster."

We finally pulled up to the house, and I parked outside the garage. Emeline was parked inside, so Rhett wouldn't know she was here.

I got out and opened the back door for Rhett. He clambered out as I grabbed his backpack.

When he headed for the side door that led into the mudroom, I said, "We're going to the barn."

"What about Pip and Bull?"

Pip was Rhett's kitten, and Bull was his chocolate lab puppy, who was as crazy as hell. He gave Moose a run for his money. They both shared the same father, and they seemed to understand they were brothers. When they were together, they were two peas in a pod.

"I just need to check one thing in the barn, then we'll go see them."

Rhett frowned. "Is my surprise in the barn?"

I laughed. "That's a silly question. Just this one quick thing, I promise."

Kicking at nothing on the ground, he folded his arms and started walking toward the barn.

"Are you *pouting*, Rhett?"

"No, sir. I'm just mad."

I bit back a laugh and walked next to him. "That's okay if you're mad."

"Grammy would tell me to... I can't think of the word."

"To be patient?"

He looked up at me. "That's the word."

This time, I did chuckle.

We walked into the main entrance of the barn and turned to go down the aisle with the stalls. Once Rhett saw Emeline, he ran toward her.

"Emeline!"

She bent down and caught him right as he launched at her.

"My goodness! You almost knocked me over!"

Rhett laughed.

A warmth spread through my chest as I watched them together. She was so damn good with him, and I knew she'd make a wonderful mother to my son. The thought wasn't something new. As each day went by, I became increasingly sure that Emeline was the one. The woman I wanted to spend the rest of my life with.

"How was your first day of school?"

Rhett jumped for joy when she put him back on the ground. "It was so fun! I got a star for being fast and quiet when Ms. Kennedy told us to get on the rug for story time!"

Emeline gasped and put her hands to her chest. "You already got a star?"

He nodded. "Yep! Sure did!"

She was down on his level, like she always was when she spoke to Rhett. "Well, I think that alone deserves another hug!"

Rhett wrapped his arms around her neck, and she stood, lifting him with her. "My goodness, pretty soon I won't be able to lift you!"

"Grammy said I'm growing big because I eat all my broccoli."

Emeline giggled. "I bet that's one reason for sure."

"Are you ready to see your surprise?" I asked.

Rhett grinned. "Yes! Come on, Emeline, we need to go back to the house!"

"The house?" Emeline asked. "But your surprise is right here."

Walking down to the next stall, she opened the top door—and a stunning white and chestnut paint gelding poked his head out. A soft nicker came from the horse...and Rhett just stared at him.

"This is your surprise, Rhett," Emeline said as I opened the lower stall door and brought the horse out into the aisle.

Emeline put Rhett down, then ran her hand over the gelding's neck as she said, "His name is Orion, but you can change his name if you want."

Rhett looked from the horse to me, and when I saw the tears build in his eyes, I almost fell to my knees.

"He's mine?" he asked, wiping at his tears.

I nodded, unable to speak.

He turned to look back at the horse. Emeline reached down and picked him up, placing him on the back of the gelding as I held the reins.

"Look at you up there." Her voice cracked, and I watched as she wiped her own tears from her face.

"Are you sad, Emeline?" Rhett asked. "Is he *your* horse, and you're letting me have him?"

She let out what sounded like a laugh and a sob. "No, baby, these are happy tears, just like yours. He's your horse, Rhett. Your daddy bought him for you."

Rhett looked at me, and my throat still felt like it was packed with cotton. All I could do was smile and nod. My eyes stung with unshed tears.

"But was he your horse?" Rhett asked again.

She patted the horse's neck and kissed him. "He was one of our horses, yes. But don't tell the other horses—he's one of my favorites. You're going to have to take good care of him and feed him. You know how to clean out his stall, right?"

He nodded. "I sure do! Daddy taught me, and I took care of my other horse. I'll love him always, I promise!"

Emeline smiled up at Rhett. "I know you will, bud. I know you will."

Rhett looked at me, tears still slowly moving down his cheeks. "I love you, Daddy. Thank you for Orion!"

"I love you, too, bud, and you're more than welcome."

Then my son looked down at Emeline. "Thank you, Emeline. I love you!"

Another sob slipped free. "Oh, Rhett, I love you too. So very much." She took the reins from me and said, "Let's see how he feels, shall we?"

"Yes!" Rhett exclaimed.

I watched as Emeline walked Orion out of the barn and to an enclosed paddock, chatting softly to my son. That was the moment the last part of my broken heart healed.

My therapist told me after Brooke's death that she hadn't died for no reason. That her death would change the journey I was on…and she was right. Not that her loss isn't at the forefront of my mind every day, Brooke's death had led me back home and brought Emeline into our lives. I'd never been as happy as I'd been over the last few months. And Rhett was thriving more than ever.

Glancing back over her shoulder, Emeline asked with a smile, "You coming?"

Nodding, I replied, "I wouldn't miss it for the world."

I leaned over the railing as I watched Emeline ride a stunning thoroughbred filly around the pen. A dusting of snow was on the ground, making the black coloring of the horse stand out that much more.

Caden walked up and stood next to me. "Gorgeous, isn't she?"

"She is. The horse is pretty magnificent, as well."

Caden chuckled, then grew serious. "I don't know how she does it. She gets these crazy-ass horses who won't let anyone near them, let alone ride them, and she climbs on and makes it look effortless."

I watched as Emeline slowed the horse down to a walk. "Where did she come from?"

"A trainer friend of Gatlin's was telling him about this horse that he'd saved from the previous owner. The guy wanted to race her, but she couldn't stand to be loaded into the gates. He was going to shoot her until the trainer told the guy he'd take her. He said trying to get her into a trailer was almost impossible. They had to sedate the poor thing."

"From Colorado?" I asked.

"Yeah, he has a horse ranch east of Denver."

Emeline rode up and stopped right at the fence. I held out my hand for the horse to smell. When she let out a soft nicker, I smiled. "Seems like an angel to me."

"That's because she has one sitting on her," Caden teased.

"Want to go for a ride?" Emeline asked.

I pointed to the filly. "Are you going to ride her?"

"I am. I'd like to see how she does with another horse riding alongside her."

Caden clapped my back. "And this is where I leave. Good luck."

I frowned as I watched him walk away. "Thanks a lot."

Waving his hand, Caden said, "You're welcome!"

Turning back to Emeline, I asked, "Which horse did you have in mind?"

"Marshall was saddling up Comet. He was going to ride with me, but since you're here…"

Right then, Marshall appeared with Comet trailing behind him.

"Levi's going to join me if you don't mind, Marshall."

He tipped his cowboy hat. "Don't mind at all."

Marshall and I were the same height, so I knew I wouldn't have to adjust the stirrups. I climbed on, and he handed me the reins.

"Thanks, Marshall."

"Sure thing." He turned and opened the gate for Emeline, who walked out with the thoroughbred.

"What's her name?"

"Starlight. It's like she was meant to be with us with a name like that." She walked up next to Comet and let the two horses smell each other. "It looks like a storm is going to be moving in, so it'll be a short ride."

"Sounds good. Shall you lead the way?"

Emeline started toward a trail, and I followed behind until she motioned for me to come alongside her. Starlight reached over and nipped at Comet, who simply ignored her.

"Smart boy," I said, giving him a soft pat on the neck.

"What are you doing here? I thought you were working all day at the clinic?"

"I was until my father came in and asked if he could see some patients."

She laughed. "So much for retiring."

"It's only been three weeks since he officially retired. He wanted to be done by November first, and he was. Couldn't even make it to Thanksgiving."

Starlight reached over and bullied Comet once again, and he ignored her. Again.

"I'd say you paired up the right horses for this ride."

She chuckled. "Yeah, I figured she was going to have a bit of attitude, and Comet's the most laidback horse we have on the ranch. He has zero fucks to give."

It was my turn to laugh.

"Speaking of Thanksgiving, what are you and Rhett planning on doing, since your parents are going to Las Vegas?"

"We're going to make a turkey."

"You're going to make a turkey?" she asked, clearly surprised.

"Why do you sound like you don't think I can make a turkey?"

"Can you?"

I shrugged. "How hard can it be?"

"A *whole* turkey?"

"Nah," I said as I moved Comet away from Starlight just a bit. She looked like she was ready to take a chunk out of him again. "Maybe just a breast. Some stuffing, green beans, cranberry sauce, and a pumpkin pie."

"You're going to make all of that?"

Looking at her, I flashed my sexiest smile. "I was hoping for some help."

Her head tossed back as she laughed. Fuck, it was the most beautiful sound I'd ever heard.

"Is that a no?"

She looked at me, and the way her eyes sparkled made my heart skip a beat in my chest. "I would love to help you make Thanksgiving dinner. I've never missed one at my parents' before, but I'm sure they wouldn't mind. Unless you and Rhett wanted to come over to my folks' place?"

"I appreciate the invite, but I really want to start some traditions. We always went out to eat on Thanksgiving because Caroline never had the desire to have a traditional family meal at home."

"I'd be honored to join your first Thanksgiving Day meal then. And I have to tell you, I make a mean stuffing."

"Do you?" I asked, my brows lifting.

"Yep!"

"Okay, then you're in charge of the stuffing."

"And the pumpkin pie."

I laughed. "And the pumpkin pie."

We rode in comfortable silence for a bit longer before I looked up at the sky. "Mind if we stop a minute?"

"Not at all," Emeline said as she brought Starlight to a stop.

I slid off of Comet and tossed the reins over his saddle. Emeline did the same. I walked up to her and cupped her face in my hands.

"I love you, Em."

Her eyes grew wide—then immediately filled with tears. "I love you too."

Pulling her to me, I looked into those blue eyes. "I kept trying to find the perfect place and time to tell you, and this suddenly felt like it was the right time. Just the two of us, with one spirited horse and one calm as hell."

She laughed and wrapped her arms around my neck. "You could have told me anywhere, and it would have been special."

I ran my finger down the side of her beautiful face. "You have no idea how much you've healed us. Your love is something I will never take for granted."

A tear slipped free and slowly made a trail down her cheek.

I leaned in and kissed it before pressing my forehead to hers. "God, this feeling, Emeline."

Her hands came up to my face. "I know. I feel the same. You were so worth the wait, Levi."

We drew apart, and thunder rumbled across the meadow. We both laughed.

"We should turn back before this storm moves in."

"I agree."

We climbed back onto the horses and turned them around. Starlight kicked at Comet, but he simply sidestepped. I was beginning to think his indifference pissed Starlight off. She snorted, and Comet answered with a snort of his own.

"Guess he's tired of her shit and is telling her so."

Emeline laughed, then looked at me with a mischievous grin.

"Oh no. I don't think I like that look."

"Let's see how they do in a trot."

Before I could reply, she and Starlight were taking off, leaving me and poor Comet in the dust.

Smiling, I said, "Come on, boy. Let's put her in her place once and for all."

CHAPTER TWENTY-THREE

EMELINE

THE SUNDAY DINNER OF Thanksgiving week was like a prequel, or at least that was what my mother always called it. Instead of turkey, the meal Mom always made was roast with mashed potatoes, roasted carrots, green beans, homemade gravy, and sourdough rolls, and cherry or apple pie for dessert. It was a tradition that my great-grandmother, Lileth, started, and one that my grandmother and mother continued. Joining us was the entire family and a few friends.

"Wow, this is the most food I think I've ever seen outside of a holiday meal," Levi said as he set the basket of rolls on the table.

"It's the traditional pre-Thanksgiving Sunday dinner," Ensley said as she placed the carrots on the table. "It's like a warm-up."

Levi smiled as he asked, "Is there a pre-Christmas warm-up dinner?"

I grinned. "No. The Sunday before Christmas is pizza night."

"Cool! I can't wait until pizza night!" Rhett exclaimed with excitement.

"Same," Gatlin said before picking up Rhett and tossing him into the air, causing a round of giggles from the boy.

"You're going to drop him one of these days, Gatlin Wilde," my mother chastised as she followed my father in, who set the roast down in the middle of the table. Mom motioned for everyone to sit down. "That's it, everyone, take your seats."

The moment everyone was seated, food was passed around.

"May I make your plate for you, Rhett?" I asked.

"Yes, please! Lots of carrots. I love carrots."

"A young man after my own heart," my father said with a wink in his direction.

"I want to grow big and strong like you, Papa!"

My heart warmed as my father beamed at Rhett. He'd started calling my father 'Papa' and my mother 'Minnie' about a month ago, and I knew my parents were over the moon about it. They'd tried to act all nonchalant when it first happened, but I saw my mother's eyes fill with tears. We still weren't sure where Minnie came from, but Mom had declared that was her official grandma name.

"Emeline tells us that you're going to be making your first turkey this week, Levi," Mom said with a smile.

"I am. I've been googling the proper way to thaw and cook it."

"Think you're up to the task?" Caden smirked.

"I do, thank you very much."

Dad had a worried expression. "Please tell me you're baking it and not trying to fry it?"

"You can fry a turkey?" Levi and Gatlin asked at the same time.

"You can, but I wouldn't recommend it," my father said.

Ensley asked, "What sides are you making?"

Levi wiped his mouth and looked around the table, a proud smile on his face. "I'm having stuffing, green bean casserole, fresh cranberry sauce, rolls, and mashed potatoes. Oh, and turkey gravy."

My mother's brows shot up. "That's a pretty hefty menu to handle by yourself."

"I'm gonna be helping, Minnie!" Rhett told her. "And Emeline's gonna make the pumpkin pie and stuffing."

"You're sure you don't mind Emeline spending Thanksgiving with us?" Levi asked my parents.

Mom's grin was answer enough. "We don't mind at all. I love that the three of you will be spending the day together."

"We're still going to a movie afterward, right?" Gatlin asked. "It's our Wilde family tradition."

Rhett looked at Levi and asked, "Are we Wilde family now?"

Before Levi could answer, my father did. "Always have been, always will be a part of this family."

Levi glanced my way and winked. A warm sensation washed over me as our eyes met and held for a few moments.

"Um, *hello*? Can you not stare at my sister like that at the family table?" Caden complained, spoiling the moment.

"Very funny," I said, balling up my napkin to throw at him, but my mother quickly interjected.

"Small eyes at the table, please. Let's not teach him bad things."

I quickly put my napkin on my lap and peeked at Rhett. When I was sure he wasn't looking, I flashed my middle finger at Caden, who laughed.

"Emeline Wilde!"

Lowering my hand, I muttered, "Sorry, Mom."

She shook her head, but I could see the corners of her mouth twitching with a hidden smile.

The rest of dinner was filled with conversations about the ranch, the vet clinic, and Rhett's horse, Orion. After dinner, Gatlin, Caden, and Levi all played a game with Rhett, while my father, mother, Ensley, and I cleaned up.

"It's been so lovely having Rhett and Levi join us for Sunday dinners," Mom said as she hugged me. "They've brought such joy to the house."

"Was the house not joyous before?" Ensley asked.

My mother playfully slapped her on the backside with her hand towel. "Of course it was. I just mean it's been nice to have a little one in the house again."

"I agree. I miss hearing all the yelling and playing in the house," Dad added with a grin.

"We can still do that," Ensley grinned. "We just figured you guys would frown on it."

My father rolled his eyes. "Smart-ass."

Ensley lifted onto her toes and kissed his cheek. "Takes one to know one!"

Mom started to motion for us to leave the kitchen. "You girls go join in the fun, we've got the rest of this."

Ensley clearly didn't need to be told twice; she dashed out of the kitchen without so much as looking back.

"Wow, she really still doesn't like kitchen duty, does she?" I laughed.

When I turned back to look at my parents, they were both staring at me with goofy smiles on their faces.

"Why are you looking at me like that?"

They quickly got back to the last of the dishes, ignoring my question. Once everything was loaded, my mother took my arm in hers and we walked out of the kitchen.

"Are you happy, sweetheart?"

"With?"

She shrugged. "Life? Levi?"

I couldn't help the smile that spread across my face. "I'm beyond happy, Mom. Sometimes I have to pinch myself because this all feels like a dream."

"We're so glad. Levi has always been such a wonderful young man, and Rhett is just the most precious little soul."

"Yes, he is, and Levi...he makes me feel so treasured. That's the only word I can think of. He treats me like I'm his everything, and that's such a beautiful feeling."

"That's how your father makes me feel. How are you doing with Rhett?"

I stopped walking and looked at her. "What do you mean?"

"Well, it's pretty clear your relationship with Levi is serious. So how are things with you and Rhett? Can you see yourself potentially being a mother figure to him?"

Glancing toward the family room, where everyone else was, I focused back on my mom. "I mean, we haven't talked about that, and the last thing I want to do is force Levi into something he's not ready for."

She nodded.

"But I love Rhett more than I can say, and if the time comes, I'd be honored to be his stepmom."

She smiled, wrapped her arm around mine once again, and we walked into the living room, where she dropped her hold on me. Before she could walk away, I grabbed her hand and leaned in. "Why were you asking me all that?"

With a shrug, she replied, "Just curious."

Then she swept away and joined everyone else in the game of charades.

The feel of Levi's soft lips moving up my neck caused my entire body to heat. The smile on my face grew into a full-blown grin as I rolled and looked at him.

I crinkled my nose and asked, "How is it you can just wake up and look hot as hell, but I'm sure I look like a mess?"

He smiled. "You *do* have a bit of dried drool in the corner of your mouth."

I slapped a hand over my mouth as he laughed.

"I'm kidding, Em! By the way, good morning."

As I stretched, I replied, "Good morning."

"Happy Thanksgiving, and thank you for staying last night."

A wave of uncertainty hit me. "I still think I should sneak out before Rhett sees me."

He shook his head as he ran his finger down my cheek. "I love you, Em, and I've already spoken to Rhett about you staying over. Trust me when I say, he wants you here as much as possible."

It still made my entire body tingle to hear Levi tell me he loved me. Those three words were something I knew I would never get tired of hearing.

I felt my cheeks heating. "He just likes my French toast."

Levi chuckled, and I loved how throaty it sounded first thing in the morning. "We *both* love your French toast."

"Should I tell you my secret ingredient?"

He shook his head. "It makes it more special, knowing only you can make the French toast that we love so much."

Moving over my body, he spread my legs apart and teased my entrance.

"Levi...what time is it? Do we have time for this?"

He covered my mouth with his as he worked me with his fingers, causing me to orgasm faster than I ever had before. His mouth captured my moans until my body finally came down from the high.

When he removed his mouth, he smirked. "That was fast."

I giggled. "You're talented."

We both moaned silently as he slowly pushed inside of me. There was nothing I loved more than the feel of Levi deep inside my body. Our lovemaking was slow and tender, which was a far cry from last night, when Levi had bent me over the desk in his home office and taken me from behind. Rhett had already gone to bed, and I'd had a hell of a hard time keeping quiet.

It was the first time we'd had sex here while Rhett was home. I'd been nervous, but Levi quickly took my mind and my body elsewhere.

Framing my head within his hands, Levi met my gaze. "I love you, Emeline."

My legs wrapped tightly around his hips as I whispered back, "I love you, too, Levi."

His rhythm began to increase, and I had to bite down on my lip to keep my moans of pleasure inside.

He buried his face in my neck and panted, "I'm going to come, baby. Come with me."

He slipped his hand between our bodies, and the moment his fingers swept across my clit, I shattered. He groaned into my ear as his own release hit him. When he finally came to a stop, he lifted his head, and we both smiled.

"I want you in my bed every morning from this day forward."

My fingertips moved softly across his back as I relaxed fully into the mattress. "I'd love that. You do know I came with a cat and a dog."

He laughed. "I'm okay with that."

"Daddy?"

Levi pulled out of me quickly, causing me to let out a little yelp.

"I'll be right there, Rhett!"

He grabbed his sweats and slipped them on, almost falling in the process. Reaching for a shirt, he slipped it on and went to reach for the door. He turned and tossed me a wicked grin. All I could do was smile back as I sat up in bed. Levi's gaze ran over my body, hungry even though we'd just made love.

"I'll get breakfast going."

When he slipped out the door, softly shutting it behind him, I let out a soft laugh. Could life get any better than this?

I quickly showered and got dressed in the change of clothes I'd brought in my overnight bag. I put some mascara on, piled my hair up onto my head, and pondered if I should even bother putting any more makeup on. I decided the mascara was enough and made my way to the kitchen.

When I walked in, I came to an abrupt halt.

My eyes scanned the kitchen...and the numerous bouquets of red roses that covered nearly every single surface.

Rhett stood on top of the island, holding one single white rose, as Levi stood behind him.

"What's all this?" I asked as I approached the island. "When did you do this?"

"I got up earlier and snuck down while you were sleeping," Levi replied.

Rhett handed me the flower. "I love you, Em."

My vision instantly blurred with tears as I took the rose. "Oh, Rhett, I love you too!"

He knelt and reached to hug me. Wrapping him in my arms, I started to cry.

I picked him up off the island and held him in my arms. "You have no idea how much I love you, little man."

He drew back and looked at me. "To the moon and back?"

"And more!"

Rhett smiled and hugged me again, tighter this time. My heart melted, and I was overcome with so much love for him. I'd never in a thousand years thought I could love like this. It was the most amazing feeling I'd ever experienced.

When I set him down on a barstool, I shifted my gaze to Levi—and drew in a sharp breath.

He was kneeling on one knee, holding an open jewelry box.

My hands slowly came up to my mouth while I stared at the most beautiful ring I'd ever laid eyes on. When I looked at Levi, I opened my mouth, but nothing came out.

"Emeline, these last months with you have been some of the most amazing moments of my life. I never in a million years dreamed I'd find someone who makes my heart feel whole the way it does with you. Our future is in your eyes. I'm the luckiest man in the world that I get to be yours every single day. This love we share is something you find once in a lifetime."

I felt tears roll down my cheeks and quickly wiped them away.

"Em, your heart is my whole universe. I want to be your last kiss for the rest of our lives. Will you do me the honor of marrying me?"

Dropping to my knees, I cupped his face in my hands and kissed him. Drawing back, a half-laugh, half-sob escaped. "Yes! Yes, I'll marry you!"

Rhett ran over and joined in on the hugging.

"Put the ring on, Daddy! Put the ring on!"

Levi and I both laughed as he took my hand in his and slid the most beautiful ring ever onto my finger. It was a cornflower-blue stone flanked by two white diamonds. The setting looked antique in appearance.

I stared at the ring, then at Levi. "Is this a sapphire?"

He smiled. "You mentioned once that you loved them, and when I saw it, it reminded me of your eyes."

"How did you know I liked princess-cut stones?"

Levi blushed. "I overheard you telling Lilibeth that the princess cut was your favorite. It's a Sri Lankan sapphire set in an antique platinum band. The diamonds are original to the band, but I had them replace the main stone with the sapphire."

I slowly shook my head. "Levi, it's the most beautiful ring I've ever seen."

He smiled and placed his hand on the side of my face. "Now, the next big question. When can we get married?"

"Today!" Rhett shouted.

I laughed and looked at the two most important men in my life. "Should we elope?"

Levi drew back in surprise. "You don't want a big wedding?"

Shaking my head, I said, "Levi, I have been in love with you since I was fourteen. I'd marry you in the county courthouse today if I thought we could get someone to meet us there."

Taking my hand in his, we finally stood up. A wicked smile appeared on Levi's face. "I hear Lake Tahoe is beautiful this time of year."

"What about the Thanksgiving food?" I asked.

"I was never actually going to cook. I just wanted you here so I could ask you. Your mother and father are expecting us over there for Thanksgiving dinner."

My eyes went wide. "That's why you wouldn't let me in the kitchen last night! My parents knew you were going to ask me to marry you?"

"Of course they did," Levi said. "I asked their permission. After I asked Caden first."

A warm sensation flooded my entire body. "You did?"

He drew me to him and kissed my forehead. "I did."

Chewing on my lip, I made the quickest decision I'd ever made in my entire life. Glancing down at Rhett, I asked, "How fast can you pack a bag, Rhett?"

He jumped in excitement! "Super-fast, if you help me!"

Focusing back on Levi, I let out a laugh. "Are we really going to do this?"

He winked. "I'm down if you are!"

"Let's go to Tahoe!"

"Wait! What about turkey and pie?" Rhett asked.

"Let's go to Tahoe after Thanksgiving!" I called out as Rhett jumped and cheered.

EPILOGUE

LEVI

Two Months Later

I KNOCKED ON THE partially open door and peeked my head in. Emeline looked up and smiled as Moose made his way over to say hi. She stood and made her way quickly to me.

"You're early!" she said, lifting onto her toes for a kiss.

"I had the schedule cleared this afternoon."

She looked surprised and happy at the same time before a look of worry crossed her face.

I kissed her again and held her to me for a few moments before letting her go. When she chewed nervously on her lower lip, I reached down and pulled it free. "Don't worry."

"I can't help it. I'm nervous, excited, and scared."

Moose whined, clearly picking up how Emeline was feeling. I reached down and scratched between his ears.

"Did you tell anyone else?"

She shook her head. "I want this to be just for the two of us."

I smiled. "Are you ready to go now?"

Emeline nodded, walked back to her desk, slipped her phone into the back pocket of her jeans, then grabbed her jacket and hat.

"Who are we taking?" I asked.

"I thought Starlight and Comet."

Laughing, I replied, "I think that's a great idea. They were there for the first 'I love you,' after all."

She winked, and my chest filled with warmth.

We worked in silence as we saddled up both horses, then rode to the same spot where I'd first told Emeline I loved her. Moose would wander off the trail for a bit then suddenly appear again. He was never far from Emeline.

Starlight and Comet had become the best of friends since that initial ride. Where one was, the other was never far away.

Getting off the horses, we let them roam as we climbed the rest of the trail and stopped at the top. The view was just as beautiful as the first time I'd seen it. Snow covered the mountains that surrounded us, and you could see the river down below. Parts of it were frozen over. The January day was warmer than usual, which I was glad for.

Emeline faced me. "Okay. I'm ready if you are?"

I nodded. "I'm ready."

"You go wait at the boulder."

I laughed. "You don't want me seeing you do it?"

She shrugged. "I might not be able to do it at all if you're watching."

Holding up my hands, I replied, "Fair enough. You're going to be freezing, though."

Winking, she replied, "Only for a few seconds."

I kissed her before I made my way to the boulder, Moose at my heels. I wiped off the snow and sat down.

About a minute later, Emeline joined me. She sat next to me and slid her gloves back on. We sat in silence, steam coming from both of us as we breathed.

Wrapping my arm around her, I smiled as she lay her head on my shoulder and said, "It's so beautiful up here."

"Yeah, it is."

"Have you ever seen the spot where my mother and father got married?"

I nodded. "Gosh, years ago, when I was much younger. Caden showed me, said that was where he was going to get married."

Emeline sighed. "That's where he asked Rachel to marry him. That bitch."

Chuckling, I kissed her head. "Is it ready?"

Sitting back up, she pulled off her glove and reached into her pocket. Moose stood and we both laughed.

I shook my head and said, "I think he's ready too."

She held the test out in front of us, and we both looked at the same time.

"Oh my God," Emeline whispered.

I jumped off the boulder and pulled her to me. Wrapping her in my arms, I spun her around as she laughed and cried. Moose started barking, joining in on the celebration.

When I stopped, I put her down and cupped her cheeks in my hands. Her big blue eyes stared at me as tears streamed down her face.

"We're having a baby," she said softly with a grin on her beautiful face.

I nodded. "We're having a baby."

She laughed with pure joy. "Levi, we're going to have an instant family. Four kids! A dog and a cat."

I smiled. After talking to our families, Emeline and I had decided to adopt Katie and Jimmy Mills before we even knew this pregnancy was a possibility.

"Don't forget all the horses."

Another bubble of laughter slipped free as she wiped her tears away.

"I love you, Emeline Tucker. So very much."

"I love you too."

Kissing me, she wrapped her arms around my neck. When we inched apart, I grew serious.

"One request."

"Anything," she replied.

"No naming our child after stars."

She tossed her head back and laughed. "Deal!"

Want to enjoy the *Wilde Ride* Spotify playlist?
Scan with your phone by opening the Spotify app, tap the Search icon (magnifying glass), then the camera icon in the search bar; point your camera at the code, and the app will automatically take you to *Wilde Cowboy* playlist.

CONNECT WITH KELLY

Kelly's Facebook Page
www.facebook.com/kellyelliottauthor

Kelly's Amazon Author Page
https://goo.gl/RGVXqv

Follow Kelly on Instagram
www.instagram.com/authorkellyelliott

Follow Kelly on BookBub
www.bookbub.com/profile/kelly-elliott

Kelly's Pinterest Page
www.pinterest.com/authorkellyelliott

Kelly's Author Website
www.kellyelliottauthor.com

ABOUT THE AUTHOR

KELLY ELLIOTT is a *New York Times* and *USA Today* bestselling contemporary romance author. Since finishing her bestselling Wanted series, Kelly has continued to spread her wings while remaining true to her roots with stories of hot men, strong women, and beautiful surroundings. Her bestselling works included *Wanted, Broken, Without You,* and *Lost Love*. Elliott has been passionate about writing since she was fifteen. After years of filling journals with stories, she finally followed her dream and published her first novel, Wanted, in November 2012.

Elliott lives in Central Texas with her husband, daughter, and two pups. When she's not writing, she enjoys reading and spending time with her family. She is down to earth and very in touch with her readers, both on social media and at signings. To learn more about Kelly and her books, you can find her through her website, www.kellyelliottauthor.com.